AS TIME GOES BY

AS TIME GOES BY

W. ROYCE ADAMS

RJK Books Santa Barbara, CA

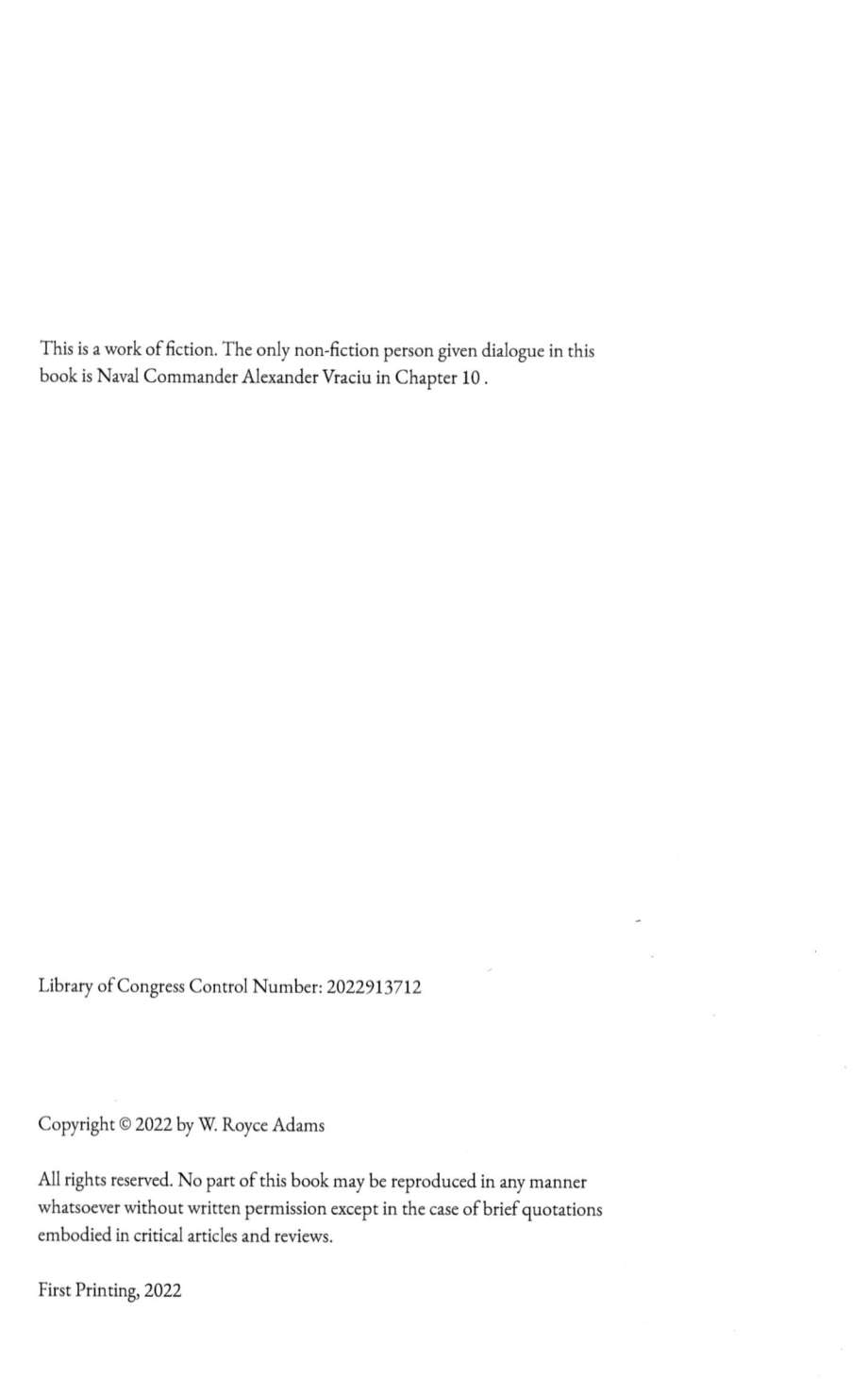

This is a work of fiction. The only non-fiction person given dialogue in this book is Naval Commander Alexander Vraciu in Chapter 10.

Library of Congress Control Number: 2022913712

Copyright © 2022 by W. Royce Adams

All rights reserved. No part of this book may be reproduced in any manner whatsoever without written permission except in the case of brief quotations embodied in critical articles and reviews.

First Printing, 2022

- Special thanks to Jane Brody, Sharon Dirlum and Dawn Raffel for their active roles in helping me write this book. Any errors are the author's.

CONTENTS

Dedication   v

Text Insert   1

1   5
3   12
4   20
5   40
8   84
9   89
10   104
11   121
12   127
13   135
14   142
15   145
16   151
17   163
18   179

19	184
20	192
21	198
22	207
23	214
24	224
25	230
26	237
27	240
28	243
29	251
30	253
notes	257

"We're here for a little window. And to use that time to catch and share shreds of light and laughter and grace seems to me a great story.
   --Brian Doyle

"The question any novel is really trying to answer is,
 Is life worth living?"
   --Nicholson Baker

"We shall not cease from exploration
 And the end of all our exploring
Will be to arrive where we started
And know the place for the first time."
   --T.S. Eliot

Acknowledgements

The following stories reappear in different forms throughout this book:

"Uncle Carl" is an excerpt from "Terror Lynchings," appearing in BLACK FOX LITERARY MAGAZINE, Issue No. 12, 2015

"The Summer Before Lucky Strike Green Went to War" appeared FROM THE DEPTHS, NO. 14, Haunted Waters Press, 2016

"Hands" appeared in CATAMARAN LITERARY READER, Vol. 4, Issue 2, Summer 2016

"Too Late, Naytan" first appeared in CHARITAN REVIEW, Vol. 40, No. 1, Spring/Summer 2017

"The Five-Hundred Word Essay" first appeared in CHAFFEY REVIEW, Vol. XV, 2017

"Down Here on the Ground" first appeared in CATAMARAN LITERARY READER, Vol. 7, Issue 4, Winter 2020

"Blue Pool" first appeared in EVENING STREET REVIEW, Vol. 34, Summer 2022

CHAPTER 1

"Let's Face the Music"

Call me Old.

Some years ago--never mind how long precisely—having nothing to particularly interest me after retirement, I thought I would (Yes, I'm paraphrasing) set about taking a journey through the sea of words to help drive off the damp, drizzly December time of my life. Perhaps at my stage of being the big expedition question for me to ponder should be, "How much longer do I have to sail the seas of life?" But there is no answer to that until the end comes. No one knows when, only that a journey's end does come. More importantly, and more answerable, sits a larger question that has been bothering me of late. I've lived these many years and one would think, since I'm almost finished, that I should know the answer.

I ask, besides just another relic of time, who am I really? I mean-- *Really*.

According to narrative psychologists, our life stories are not just an encyclopedic biography of facts and events of a life, but instead narratives that take those life events apart and integrate them together to make meaning and form an identity that reflects who we are, what our life means, who we've become and what could happen next. What can my own stories tell me about me? Does my life have any significance, or has it all been happenstance?

Silly question, you say.

Not for me. Kafka made it seem simple when he said the meaning of life is that it stops. Joseph Campbell said the meaning of life is whatever you ascribe it to be. Toni Morrison said, "We die. That may be the meaning of life. But we do language. That may be the measure of our lives."

Yet, Roland Barthes says "Who am I?" is a madman's question. The bewildered man's question is "Am I?"

Confusing, isn't it?

I tend more to see it the way Darlene Cohen states it in *Turning Suffering Inside Out*:

> The purpose of our lives may not be to produce something wonderful or to become rich or famous or renowned for wisdom; the purpose may just be to express our own sincerity doing completely whatever it is we do, immersing ourselves in the situation in which we find ourselves.

It's possible you know the meaning of your life, or maybe you don't even care. But isn't it Socrates who proposes that the unexamined life is not worth living? Yes, you could argue, "But look where it got him!" Still, Nietzsche, on the other hand, suggests that in order to know ourselves we must examine the events, passions and thoughts that create our personal theories and moral judgments. But his background is not all that acceptable these days.

Since I am a nobody, you might be asking, "Isn't this quest of yours a bit narcissistic, dropping all these names?" Yes, but I offer a qualifier. Karl Ove Knausgaard, in his novel/memoir, *My Struggles*, offers his views on narcissism:

> Narcissism is a weakness, something unwanted; if it were not, then we would not attempt to hide it, so the fact that narcissism is being exhibited here is an admission of weakness, at the same time as that admission also lifts up the I and distinguishes it, because it is candid, and candid narcissism stands in opposition to hidden

narcissism in that the former aspires to truth, whereas the latter seeks to conceal the truth.

I, too, hereby admit I am exhibiting weakness.

But a candid narcissistic weakness.

Even though I'm just an ordinary male, with no claim to fame, who has lived through the Great Depression, World War II, the Korean War, the Vietnam War, the Iraq War, the following Gulf Wars, the Afghan Wars, the Syrian mess and all those never-ending wars still going on, I'm just now beginning to examine selected windows of my life before it's finished. I'm going to take Nietzsche up on his advice, not clear where what I find will lead me. And as Morrison suggests, I'll "do language." This is my whale story without the whale.

Have I anything relevant to say? I don't know. We'll see.

Little by little as I age, both physically and mentally, I feel bits of myself falling away, evaporating, a derailment of sorts, a sense of detachment to things; so it's important to me that I find answers before all the leaves of my life have fallen off and scattered to the winds, gone for always.

I'm in conversation with someone, and I reach for a word that's right there, a word I know so well, but slip-slides away leaving me struggling, feeling a part of my memory has been plucked, as if an acute piece of my brain wanted to play hide-and-seek in a brain fog. Often, but not when I need it, the word comes back to me, but I've already lost the game. In other moments, when reading, I encounter an unknown word only to realize when I look it up I once knew the word, even used it before.

At times an essential thought or concept I need at the moment escapes unaccounted for, as if my brain wants to taunt me, or doesn't want me to deal with it, leaving me stunned, wondering what's happening to me. I receive an image of a slow phlegm-like mass attempting to smother my thoughts.

It's not just my brain that's not cooperating. Sometimes, when I'm still, I feel images of myself stepping out of my body desperately wanting to flee the cancer I carry, or slip from the constant, painful arthritic joints; the knotted neck and shoulder muscles; the foot, back and hip pain when I walk too far. My old floater-filled eyes play tricks on me. The body parts that used to take my command seem to find pleasure in betraying me, leaving me unaided. Even my waning hearing limits my ability to carry on a conversation without a "Sorry, what?"

In their song, "Why was I born?" Jerome Kern and Oscar Hammerstein II ask:

> Why was I born?
> Why am I living?
> What do I get?
> What am I giving?

To elaborate, does my life ultimately have any importance in any universal scheme? Am I just taking up space? Have I wasted the time given me? What effect have I had on others? Have I unknowingly, worse, knowingly, hurt others in some fashion? What's my worth? Am I supposed to use the time I have left for some purpose? Is someone/something in charge of what's happening? Does anything ultimately matter? These are playful existential questions with no pertinent answers for me. I'll just have to trust Virginia Woolf, who tried to show in her novel *Mrs. Dalloway* that no life is insignificant.

It's time to put down my cane and pick up my pen.

CHAPTER 2

"Stardust"

Where to start?

Let's zoom in on a 1933 black and white photograph showing me, age three I'd guess, sitting on a cheap-looking rocking horse, smiling. My steed may be a Pinto, or maybe an Appaloosa; it's difficult to tell in the grainy picture. The horse looks no wider than an inch thick and perhaps no longer than five feet. It couldn't be very tall, because my feet touch the floor as I hold on with my left hand to one of the small handles where horse ears should be, the other hand resting on my right knee, a pose no doubt suggested by the photographer. My hair is parted on the left side and neatly slicked down. I look happy. I wear what looks to be a crisp, white one-piece outfit-- short pants attached to a shirt with a tight, dark collar, and white ankle-length socks with light colored shoes that could have been taken from a large doll. Do I see buttons fastening the shoe straps? Maybe this attire was fashionable it its day, but seems rather sissy looking today. The sight makes me wonder if I could possibly still be in diapers. I do hope I was past that.

Why am I dressed so? Surely it must have been an occasion; those are no play clothes I wear. Why am I smiling? Was it for the camera, or am I truly happy? Is the rocking horse a new gift? It looks too small for me. At that age, would I have asked for one? Is it even mine, or am I riding an appropriated horse?

I remember nothing of what I see in the photo. What I do remember, whether it was the day of the picture taking or after, and in the most vivid of blue and black, are scores of five-pointed stars in various sizes exactly like the ones cartoonists draw when they want to show someone in pain or being struck on the head.

If we look at that photograph again, we can see in the background an iron grate of some kind, a covering over what looks like a fireplace. I'm guessing I wanted to show off my equestrian ability and forced that rocking horse high enough backwards on its hind legs that I slid off and banged my head on that metal grill.

And when it hit, those five-pointed stars of various sizes exploded in my head, the memory of which still remains. Why did I see blue and black five-pointed stars of different sizes? I wasn't reading comics at that age, so from where did the images come? Did I apply stars to the memory after I heard that people sometimes see stars when they get hurt? No, I insist to this day I saw stars the moment of head impact.

That's my first life memory: five-pointed blue-black stars. And it's all because of the rocking horse, which I don't remember; because of my tilting too far back, which I don't remember; my sliding off the flat, wooden saddle; which I don't remember; and my skull meeting metal, which I don't remember. Too bad there's not a picture of me after I've fallen. That might reveal a more informative after event.

But I do remember the stars. Trauma, no doubt.

I don't remember the pain, though I'm sure I must have cried in hurt. What a noisy fuss I must have made. Or, perhaps my parents made the biggest to-do. Did they discover blood in my hair? Was I held in someone's arms and coddled? Was an ice pack placed on my head? Did a big bump swell where I hit metal? How long did the pain last? Did I lose consciousness, and that's where I met the stars? Did that whack on the head have some effect on me later in life? Those migraines, for instance, I experienced from junior high on into adulthood. Or, did it damage my intellect turning me into a slow learner; or did the blow knock some sense into me, like an introduction to gravity and the knowledge of cause and effect? Or is it going to evolve into a slow brain cancer of some type that could announce itself any day out of the blue-black stars? Why do I imagine the worst? And why, of all that, do I only remember the stars?

And what of the poor rocking horse? Did I whip it or kick it in anger, or slink away in fear? Did I ever mount it again and ride, Sonny, ride? Did they put the horse down, or just turn it out to pasture? I don't remember seeing it again. But how could I? I don't remember seeing it in the first place.

As time marched on, I felt pride when my five-pointed, blue-black stars were borrowed and made physical for others to see in comic books. When older, I saw them as I read and knew full-well what the drawn stars represented. Then Superman and Buck Rogers showed me there are other stars with different shapes from mine with different outcomes as they sent me to those other galaxies far, far away from what was going on in my tiny world.

CHAPTER 3

"Strange Fruit Hanging"

I don't like this memory, but its effect on my life still lingers.

Five years old, I worried the hot June drive from St. Louis to Wiggins, Mississippi, might never end. My dad's heavy, black, 1933 Terraplane Hudson had no air conditioning, no radio, and scratchy grey seat covers, hard on a boy wearing shorts. Mile after mile, it didn't take long to grow bored of singing Old McDonald-type songs. My parents tried to encourage me to be on the lookout for anything unusual or different from home, strange looking buildings, landscapes, or animals that always seemed to be cows or horses. Having me look for the frequent Burma Shave ads along the highway gave my parents some relief. "Past Schoolhouses...take it slow...let the little...shavers grow...Burma Shave."

We entered Wiggins early in the morning. I was semi-asleep in the back seat when I heard my mother say, "Oh, my god!"

My father made some gasping sound.

"What?" I sat up looking around.

"Don't look," my mother said turning to me. "Close your eyes."

But it was too late.

My father hit the accelerator, but I saw out the back window what I was not supposed to see: a black man, clothes torn mostly off, hanging by his neck from a large tree that spread halfway across the street. As the car gained speed, I watched the image fade, but it has never really disappeared.

My mother ordered me to turn around, a harshness in her voice I'd never heard before. "Quit looking!" That tone and look were not like her, so I turned forward in my seat. She looked back at me, making sure I'd turned around, then at my father who kept his eyes on the road, saying nothing. She looked forward again.

Silence became a kind of suffocation.

The sudden tension in the car unsettled me. I didn't understand. Why was that man hanging there? Was it a real person? Was he dead? By my parents' reaction, I sensed a disturbing seriousness. Should I ask questions or stay silent? I wanted so much to look back. I wanted to know the meaning of what I had just seen, make sense of my parents' reaction. But they stayed silent.

At my father's Uncle Carl's home in Wiggins, we were greeted by what some call Southern hospitality. Lots of hand shaking, hugs, introductions, how-was-the-trip questions, and pitchers of cold lemonade. Once the formalities ended and we were shown where we would sleep for the night, my mother and Aunt Lona Mae disappeared into the kitchen. My dad and I joined Uncle Carl on the wide front porch.

"Quite a greeting we had entering town, CW," my dad said, addressing his Uncle Carl. I soon picked up the fact that his southern family relatives called each other by their initials.

"Greeting? Oh, that." He gave a smirk. "Well, let's hope that'll remind 'em of their place." He took a sip of his drink.

"Their place?" my dad asked. The muscles in his cheeks twitched.

"Why, pshaw, B.J. That boy done got what he deserved. Attacked a white girl. When those uppiddies see what we do when they step over the line, they'll remember what's what."

"Son," my dad said, "why don't you go explore, see what you can find."

I knew he wanted to get rid of me, but my curiosity was more than piqued, and I wanted to stay. I wanted to know more about what we'd seen.

"Can't I ..."

"Go on, now," he insisted.

"Sure now, there's a big weeping willow tree out back, sonny. Branches touch the ground. You can hide under it, and we'd never find you." Uncle Carl laughed.

Instead of hiding under the tree, I slipped around the side of the porch where I could hear most of their conversation. The two of them soon got into an argument, their voices rising and falling. I'd never heard my dad raise his voice like that and it bothered me. My dad used words like shame, lawlessness, stupidity. His uncle used words like, well, I won't repeat them; they were foreign to my ears then. I didn't know what that man had done to a girl, but when I realized what other people did to that man, I thought he must have done something pretty sinful.

A pause in their arguing about slavery occurred when Uncle Carl went in the house and came back out on the porch. Apparently, he had gone in to get the Bible, because I heard him say to my dad, "Here. Right here. Leviticus 25:44-46. "... you may purchase male and female slaves from among the nations around you. You may also purchase the children of temporary residents who live among you, including those who have been born in your land. You may treat them as your property, passing them on to your children as a permanent inheritance."

"Shoot, CW. That's history, not an excuse," my dad countered. "Just because it's in the Bible doesn't mean it's right. You can find a quote in the Bible to excuse anything."

"It's in the good book, B. J. They nevea' shoulda' been freed. Gave 'em all the wrong ideas," Uncle Carl insisted.

"You mean the idea they're human?" my Dad's voice rose. "Somewhere in the Bible it also says you can have more than one wife. Do you believe that, too?"

"Not a bad idea," his uncle replied.

The women gave a call for lunch and the conversation ended. Someone hollered for me but I waited a few minutes before going in, not wanting to give away my hiding.

"That's some tree out back, eh?" Uncle Carl asked me at lunch. "Hundreds of years old."

I nodded in a lie. I'd never gotten around to that tree. I still had a different tree on my mind.

What I had heard and seen kept bothering me. Yet, I felt shame because a part of me wanted to go see the hanging body again. What did it mean that the Bible says slavery is okay? What did it have to do with the hanging man?

That evening after dinner and a boring conversation about relatives I didn't know, my dad took me for a walk. "I'm sorry you had to see…what you saw. Are you okay?"

"That was a real man, wasn't it? Why'd they do that?" I blurted out.

My dad didn't respond with a fast answer. He sighed and finally said, "Ignorance. Hatred. For a start."

I still didn't understand. "What did he do that was so bad?"

"They claim he attacked a white girl."

"Wha'd he do to her? Why didn't the police arrest him? Why did they have to hang him?" My murky lack of understanding agitated me. I felt tears coming and didn't know why.

My dad hesitated. "Carl says the young girl accused the man of hitting her. Some people don't want colored folks even talking to a white girl or woman. When word got around town, things got heated. An angry mob formed and they took matters in their own hands."

"Why didn't the police stop 'em?"

"It's hard to stop a mob." Then he muttered, "Chances are the police might have even taken part."

That surprised me. All I could say was, "It's not right, is it?"

"No, it isn't. What they did was horrible…wrong…inhuman. I want you to know that. What's behind this is difficult to explain. I know it's not helpful to say some day you'll understand the history behind this. At least I hope you will. What you've experienced today is a step backwards in time. A step in the wrong direction. Something you shouldn't have had to see or that ever should have happened."

"Why does your uncle say such bad things about colored people?"

"He was taught to think like that. His parents taught him those feelings. His friends feel the same, and they take comfort in that. I'm afraid a lot of southerners feel that way. Today should teach you to not think like he does. I want you to know he is wrong."

"You're from down here. Why don't you think like he does?"

"Well, different backgrounds, I guess. When I was eighteen, I worked in a country store down near Pervis. The owner was a decent man. He had a lot of colored folks who did business with him. Sometimes a client couldn't pay, and they'd trade some crop they grew or a chicken or rabbit for whatever they needed. If they had nothing to trade, he'd give them credit. I saw him treat black folks just like he treated white folks, and he made sure I did, too.

"One night we were doing inventory and a noisy bunch of horsemen rode up to the store front. They yelled for us to come out. Floppy hoods covered their faces, holes cut out for their eyes. Some held guns, some held flaming torches that framed them against the dark. Just the sight of them set me shaking. My boss didn't seem afraid, though."

"What did they want?"

"They wanted him to stop dealing with coloreds, sell only to white customers."

"Why?"

"Well, times were really hard then. Farming was tough. Jobs scarce. A lot of whites blamed the blacks for their troubles. Some thought Negroes had jobs they should have. They needed somebody to blame, and the colored were convenient. When people hurt, they want to blame someone or something. Anyway, my boss stood up to them. Told them to go home. Called some by name even though they wore hoods. He recognized some of them by their horses, or by their shoes or clothes they'd bought in his store."

"What happened?" I asked, surprised by what he was telling me.

"They rode away, but warned him to do as they said or else."

"Or else what?"

"I never found out. They scared me enough that night that I went home, put everything I owned, which wasn't much, in that little trunk you've seen at home, and high-tailed it to St. Louis."

"What happened to the store man?"

"I never found out. I've wondered about it enough, though."

"I hope nothing bad happened to him. I hope they didn't hang him."

"No, I don't think they'd go that far," my dad tried to assure me.

Still lost for any real understanding, I told my father, "Well, I'm glad you're not like your Uncle Carl."

I'll never forget the hug he gave me.

And I'll never forget what I saw.

Over eighty years still have not erased from my eyes that man hanging by his neck. Strange, our family never talked about it again. But after that I became aware of "Coloreds Only" signs at water fountains, restrooms, and restaurants. While in the navy, I even encountered prejudice toward my uniform with signs at some Southern establishments that read "No Dogs, No Sailors, No Coloreds." Outwardly, "Whites Only" signs have disappeared today, but only from view in many cases.

As I grew older I wondered if I had imagined the lynching I kept seeing in my mind, maybe created the incident after hearing and reading and seeing movies about such atrocities over the years. Recently, looking for proof that I had not made up what I remembered, I did some on-line research and discovered a small column on page 21 of the June 23, 1935 *The New York Times*:

> NEGRO IS LYNCHED,
> ANOTHER WHIPPED
> HIDE HIM FROM OFFICERS
> Mob of 300 at Wiggins, Miss.,
> Hangs and Shoots Man as
> Attacker of Young Girl.

> Second Negro is Seized and
> Beaten on Charge He Insulted
> a White Woman
>
> Wiggins, Miss., June 22 (AP) One Negro was lynched and another was spirited into the woods and whipped in the course of twenty-four hours of mob rule by citizens in Wiggins today.
>
> R. D. McGee, 25-year-old Negro, was hanged to a tree and his body pierced with bullets about 9 A.M. for an attack on an 11-year-old daughter of a white dairy farmer. Stone County was in a state of excitement until the mob of about 300 dispersed and Sheriff J.A. Simpson and the Coroner had the body cut down from the tree beside a narrow road. Later the Coroner and peace officers met and held a formal inquest, returning a verdict that the Negro "came to his death at the hands of unknown parties."

So, there it was. I hadn't imagined it.
What a thing for a child to see.
What a thing for men to do.

I continue to wonder what turn of events makes a man like my father and what makes a man like his Uncle Carl. For whatever reason, I don't recall my family venturing into the subject again. Because of segregated schools, neighborhoods, stores, even the one I worked in as a teenager, I seldom saw anyone of color. Or perhaps I was blinded by complacency. It wasn't until my naval service experiences that my childhood trauma in Mississippi resurfaced. Finally confronted with outward signs of prejudice and hate in people I met and worked with,

I awakened to the bigotry and discrimination all around me and realized the sickness behind R. D. McGee's treatment was still alive and ubiquitous.

Over time, with the Civil Rights Act and the Voting Act, much has changed for the better for some, but prejudice and discrimination continues with new forms of lynching taking place. I don't need to elaborate. You've seen it; you're still seeing it after all these years.

CHAPTER 4

"Slip Sliding Away"

The summer before we were asked to "Remember Pearl Harbor," my father lost his job. In St. Louis, at least for him, jobs were scarce and never very permanent, so moving around town became a part of my young life. I found myself in a different school every year until the sixth grade. When we'd relocate, teachers and kids in the class would ask me what my dad did for a living, but I didn't always know. I'd make up some job, and it didn't seem to make any difference. We were never in one place long enough for anyone to find out, or for me to make close friends. I was a loner.

It didn't take much awareness to know we were poor. But the love and affection displayed toward me and between my parents overshadowed all. I never went hungry. I do remember cutting cardboard to put inside my shoes when they got holes in the bottoms and that most of my clothes were hand-me-downs from somewhere. Toys were a rarity, and coming up with a dime for some school event wasn't always easy. But that was my life, and except for being a bit lonely, I didn't know anything else, so I didn't suffer from it.

My dad did, though. At one point early that summer I remember him shouting, which wasn't his style, that things were bad enough to turn a man to drink. Not that he drank. He didn't. In fact, he was pretty religious, always took us to church on Sundays. But his usual answer to problems, "The Lord'll provide somehow," wasn't proving true this time. It wasn't soon after some over-heard talks about bills, "how-are-we-going-to-eat," and "but-what-else-can- we-do," that the three of us collected what little we owned and moved in with my mom's father across the river in Alton. I didn't realize it then, but the move devastated my dad's pride.

Before we were forced to move in, I hadn't seen my grandfather much. I gradually came to understand why later. Of course, I hadn't seen much of any of my grandparents. My mother's mother died before I was born, my paternal grandfather died when I was three, and my dad's mother lived somewhere down south with her other son. So, having a grandparent to deal with was something new.

Even before we arrived, my dad cautioned me in a long, serious talk against getting into things that my grandfather might not want me to touch.

"Remember, son, we're guests in his house, but I hope not for too long.

"Yessir."

"Now, he's not used to being around children, so stay out of his bedroom, and especially stay clear of his office."

I nodded, though I had no idea why he mentioned his office.

"Just try to stay out of his way as much as possible, okay?"

I nodded again, beginning to fear my grandfather.

He hesitated, seeming to have trouble finding what he wanted to say.

"He's got some bad habits, but don't be alarmed or swayed by them." He put his hands on my shoulders. "I'm sorry that things force us to expose you to a hedonistic sinner, but God willing we won't have to live there too long."

A hedonistic sinner? I knew what a sinner was, but not a hedonistic one. It had to be worse. So, for the first few days, fear of the man totally embedded in me, I moved around the house like a burglar.

His place was an old, comfortable two-story clapboard with three bedrooms upstairs. I got the front bedroom with two windows that overlooked the porch roof. In all the moves our family had made, I had never known a room like this one with a fancy double bed, a huge polished-cherry wood dresser and mirror, a chair and table that matched, and a walk-in closet that still looked empty even after I hung my few clothes in it. Best of all, it had a radio that became my night companion.

Downstairs there was a large, but dark, living room with soft mohair furniture draped with fancy flowered cloths and lacy-like things over the arms of the chairs. The dining area could be shut off from the living room by hidden sliding doors that could be pulled from the walls. One huge glass-door cabinet in the dining room displayed more flowered China dishes and long-stemmed glasses than I had ever seen, and a small but elaborate crystal chandelier hovered over the center of the dining table. A walk-in pantry in one corner led to the kitchen. Old gray and brown photos and dark paintings hung on the walls, even along the stairway. To me, it seemed the Lord had over-provided for my grandfather.

On the other side of the dining room, jutting out from the side of the house, was a smaller room with my grandfather's desk in it. I learned later that to make room for the three of us my grandfather had moved his desk and office things downstairs into what once was the sunroom. It was a bright room with three walls of windows covered over by cream-colored venetian blinds that sliced up the view of a huge maple tree outside. Ferns stretched their long green stems out from pots standing around the walls. Other than my bedroom, his office held the greatest attraction.

I'd never seen anything like it. His desk seemed as big as a stage. Solid dark wood with six legs, it had four deep drawers on the right side, a wide, thin drawer in the middle that your legs slid under, and a kind of secret compartment on the left that I was later shown hid his massive, black Underwood typewriter. When closed, it appeared there were four drawers on that side, too.

Thick, black ledgers of various sizes, books and papers, and a long handled adding machine, usually with a trail of narrow paper curling to the floor, covered the top of the desk. There was a wide lamp, too, with a gooseneck you could twist around. And I remember a heavy solid silver cigarette lighter with his initials, ERK, and an ashtray, usually full of stubs and gray ashes that gave off a stale, impermissible odor. While I didn't touch anything, it all held a fascination for me.

About a week after we moved in, still circumspectly exploring the house, I dared to sit in my grandfather's swivel desk chair. I had been eyeing it every day and, thinking my grandfather gone, I swung myself back and forth a little. I just sat there, making the chair go back and forth, my legs barely touching the floor, taking a sort of visual inventory, when I decided to see if I could twirl the chair around in a complete circle. I pushed hard against the floor with one foot, and the chair spun around quickly, almost effortlessly. For some time, I just pushed and twirled, pushed and twirled.

Then I saw him. Panicked, I nearly fell out of the chair in my haste to stop it from whirling.

My grandfather stood at the doorway, watching me, for how long I didn't know. We just looked at each other for a moment while my heart did double time. There was nothing in his look that hinted at what he was thinking, but I remembered my dad's warnings about this man. I was alone, face to face with a "hedonist sinner." I wanted to run, but he was standing in the way.

"So." That's all he said.

I chose reticence, waiting to see what trouble I was in. He wasn't smiling. I felt forced to really look at him for the first time. To me, he seemed tall. His great mane of white hair that contrasted with his dark, heavy eyebrows allowed only his fatty ear lobes to show. A thick mustache the color of his eyebrows covered his upper lip. Fleshy skin hung under his green eyes. His Roman nose reminded me of my mother, but it didn't ease apprehension.

"So," he said again, then came farther into the small room. I moved around him toward the door like a wary, out-matched boxer.

"You like my office?"

I briefly nodded, still not saying anything, waiting for him to do something hedonistic.

"It'll do, I guess." He looked around, as if examining his new environment. "It's brighter in here anyway."

He went to his chair and sat down. "Do you know what all this is for?" he asked, sweeping one arm out over his desk.

I noticed two fingers on his right hand were yellow. I shook my head.

"I'm an accountant -- a bookkeeper -- a CPA." He didn't say it proudly or anything like that. Just matter-of-factly. He seemed to sense my ignorance and went on. "I take care of the books and taxes for some businesses in town. I let them know whether or not they're making any money. I work some at home and sometimes I work on the job."

Then he took a pair of gold-rimmed glasses from a black case, exposed his huge ears as he slipped them on, and began looking through some ledgers. "Right now I have to do some work at home," he said without looking at me. I started to leave, when he swung around in his chair and, looking over the top of his glasses, asked, "Can I trust you won't mess with these important papers?" He gestured again across his desktop.

I nodded again, surprising myself with a dry, "Yessir."

I took his look as a sort of smile, and as he turned back to his desk, said, "Well, you're a polite one, anyway."

Something in his look and the way he said "polite one" put me a little at ease. I still didn't feel comfortable about him, more like confused, but I didn't feel all that afraid either. Still, I quickly and gladly left him to his work.

Because it was summer, there was no school to deal with, but there were no neighbor children for potential friends, either. My father was gone much of the time looking for work or working odd jobs, and my mother was busy getting us settled, cleaning house, and occasionally helping my grandfather with his work. But I was used to spending time alone and didn't really mind.

The old maple tree outside my grandfather's new office became my main haunt, perfect for climbing, hiding and fantasizing. I would disappear into the cool shade of thick, green leaves and straddle a wide branch while I safely spied through the window on my grandfather as he worked. When he'd squint through the smoke from a cigarette that usually dangled from his lips, his eyebrows would run together. His skill on the adding machine amazed me. Without looking, his fingers always tapped the right keys, followed by a quick pull on the handle with a steady rhythm that kept the paper tape rolling. Sometimes he'd rule colored lines on papers, measuring precisely. Papers would get clipped together or stapled, stamped, and piled neatly into stacks. He rolled about easily in his chair, typing something one minute, then swinging back under his desk to complete something else. He and his desk were one.

One day in the tree, I spied my mother typing at his desk while he sat in a chair beside her stuffing and licking envelopes. I felt a surprised pride upon discovering her ability. Later, she told me she had been a secretary, but when the company she worked for discovered she was married they fired her. Something about jobs and the depression and the times.

I enjoyed watching them work and talk together, even though I understood little of what they said. But I never saw them smile or laugh together, and I wondered if my mother was afraid of him, too.

A few weeks after that first encounter with my grandfather, a fierce summer storm struck, keeping me indoors. Except for the frequent brilliant lightning flashes that followed long, endless rolls of thunder, the day stayed dark as dusk. Bored, I explored the house looking for anything new. Knowing my grandfather was out on a job, I nervously dared to peek into his bedroom, forbidden territory. Even though he wasn't home, I halfway expected him to be in there. I quietly stepped inside and switched on a light. His room was smaller than mine with just an unmade single bed, nightstand, and dresser. It smelled of stale cigarette smoke.

Tiptoeing across the room, I glanced into his closet. Nothing but clothes. The clock on the night table seemed to tick loudly, get-out, get-out, get-out, so I quickly satisfied myself there was nothing special about his room and left, forgetting to turn off the light.

After poking around every room in the house and sliding down the banister a few times, I eventually gravitated toward my grandfather's office where I tried to see how fast I could twirl around in his desk chair. I experimented with several positions: sitting down, sitting backwards, squatting, kneeling, even standing. With every turn, the irresistible temptation to look in the desk drawers grew.

I turned on the desk lamp, then slowly and carefully opened the wide middle drawer. Its depth amazed me. I had to push the chair back from the desk three times before I was able to pull the drawer out far enough to see everything. I understood little of the contents, but was fascinated enough to explore all the drawers. They contained a treasure of envelopes and paper of all sizes, shapes and lines; manila file folders; pens and pencils of every color; red, blue and black ink bottles; rolls of adding machine paper; staplers and boxes of staples; wooden handled stamps and colored inked pads; scissors with long points; typewriter erasers; hole punches; rubber bands; rulers, one eighteen inches long; boxes of paper clips; check books; bottles and tubes of glue; and an open carton of Lucky Strike cigarettes. The packs were dark green in those days before advertisements announced, "Lucky Strike green has gone to war." To this day, the slogan stays with me.

I didn't touch anything that time.

Another storm hit that night, this one indoors.

I'd gone to bed and was awakened by the thunder of voices downstairs. I slipped out of bed and opened my bedroom door so I could better hear.

"You're drunk!" I heard mother accuse.

"I've aright," a slurred voice, my grandfather's.

Then a lower voice, my father's, barely audible, "Just don't . . . ever . . . in front ...the boy. . ." Not everything was clear.

"Just wait a goddamn minute, don't choo go tellin' me what I can and can't do in my own house, you goddamn . . ." My grandfather called my dad something I didn't catch, something like "psalm singer."

"Shush," my mother said, "Just please watch your language."

Their words were mumbled, often unintelligible, but the tone of their voices scared me. I just knew it was my fault they were arguing. My grandfather must have found out I'd been looking through his room and his desk. The lights! I'd been told to leave his things alone. I didn't want to hear any more, but a part of me kept trying.

"You just had to marry this . . . this . . ." I didn't get some words, then, ". . . who . . . who can't even keep a job, for crissake."

"It's not his fault and you know it." My mother's defensive voice, a little louder than usual, cracked, broke into sobs.

"Ya broke my heart, ya know that, don't cha?" my grandfather sounded as if he might cry. "... it killed your mother."

"That's enough. I don't like having to be here anymore than you do! But you'll set a bad example if you . . .." I'd never heard my father raise his voice like that.

Other invectives were hurled, many I didn't understand, others I didn't want to hear, all of it frightening me to the point of tears. Not wanting to hear any more, I turned on the radio, buried my head under my pillow, faintly hearing Cecil B. deMille pronounce, "Lux presents Hollywood," but unable to concentrate on the radio portrayal of a movie.

Finally, I heard footsteps, my grandfather's, stumbling up the stairs, occasionally mumbling anger as he tripped or slipped, coughing a deep, dry sound. I shut my bedroom door, pushing my back up against it. I wanted to scream at him for his meanness to my parents, but I was afraid he might come in and yell at me, or tell us all to get out of his house, or maybe worse. But he went to his room, shutting his door more quietly than I expected, muffling his coughing.

I turned off the radio, shivering a little under the sheet even though it was a warm night. I knew my parents were hurt, maybe in trouble because they'd been yelled at, and even worse, we'd have to move again because of me.

Then I heard someone come up the stairs. When my door opened, I pretended sleep. I figured it was my mother, checking to see if I had heard anything. I didn't want her to know that I had; yet I wanted to ask her everything. It seemed that she stood there looking down at me forever, though it was only a few moments. Then I felt a slight kiss on my cheek and heard my father whisper, "I love you, son." The door made a slight click when he left the room. I fell asleep sobbing.

I slept late the next morning. When I went downstairs, I was surprised to find my grandfather cooking in the kitchen. My first reaction was to turn and run, but he held me with his words.

"Your folks aren't here." I immediately felt fear and then anger at them for leaving me alone with him.

My feelings must have shown, because he quickly added, "Your mother's running some errands for me, and your dad's looking for a job." He smiled, and didn't seem at all the vitriolic man I had heard yelling last night.

"Hungry?" he didn't wait for an answer. "Here. Sit down here and I'll fix you some of my special pancakes."

I did as he said in an angry fear, bewildered, wishing my parents weren't gone, waiting for him to yell at me now. I didn't say much, but he chatted away as if nothing had happened last night. It turned out that his pancakes were better than I wanted them to be. After I couldn't finish my third helping, he looked me in the eyes, nodded his head slightly, and said, "Come here, to my office, I want to show you something."

Petrified, I followed the hedonist, remembering last night, trying to recall what I might have done wrong in his bedroom and office. The lights, yes, but I didn't remember touching anything. I hadn't taken anything from his desk. If he yelled at me the way he yelled at my parents last night, I'd shatter on the spot. I hated him for what he'd said last night. I hated my parents for leaving me alone with this man.

"Watch this," he said when we got to his desk. From the tree, I'd seen his Underwood slip in and out of sight, but from a space just above the false drawer front, he pulled out a board that fit neatly under the desktop, making a small workspace.

He opened a drawer, drew out some paper and colored pens and placed them on the desk board. "Here," he pulled up a dining room chair to the board offering it to me, "draw or something."

He said it nicely enough, but I wasn't prepared for this suspicious puzzle. None of the pieces were fitting together. But he stood there, waiting for me to do something on paper, as if I were being subjected to a test I hadn't prepared for. I picked up a pen and started drawing a shaky-looking airplane. Even though he shuffled some papers around while I worked, his presence was intimidating, but I did the best I could.

When I finished, he picked up the drawing. "So, let's have a look." To my surprise, he nodded his head slightly. "Not bad. Not bad at all. Now let me show you how to make that fuselage look round instead of flat."

He spent some time that morning showing me what he called some "shading art tricks." While still not as ease and fighting my hatred, I liked what he showed me, both about drawing and himself. And whether or not he knew I had looked through his desk, he never mentioned it. When I heard my mother come in the back door, I bolted out of the chair to greet her. But my grandfather startled me with a strong, "Hey!"

I froze, certain he was going to tell my mother I'd snooped.

"Don't forget your pictures." He handed me our artwork. "And these pens? You can use them anytime you like," he said softly. "They'll be in this drawer." He smiled slightly.

I nodded and ran with relief to my mother. A few nights later I was awakened by downstairs voices again. This time I didn't go to my door to listen. Instead, I drew deeper under my bedding and tried not to hear. My grandfather had come home drunk again. There were more harsh words, and I think sobs from my mother. But mostly it was my dad and grandfather's muffled misery. Finally, my grandfather managed to make it up the stairs with considerable noise and a lung-ripping cough. Once he closed his door, the house was quiet again. I guess I fell asleep before my parents came up, but it seemed a long time I lay awake.

It was raining the next morning. When I went down to the kitchen, I found my grandfather cooking French toast and bacon. He didn't look my way as I stood in the doorway, but sensed I was there.

"Your dad's going to be gone for a few days. He got a job in Wood River. Your mother drove him over there. She'll be back soon. Have some breakfast." It seemed a command.

Despite my apprehension about him, I couldn't fault his cooking.

After breakfast, we again went to his office. He gave me some paper, the colored pens, a folder, a hole punch and some brads to play with, telling me I should make a notebook of sorts for my drawings. He worked on his books, occasionally looking at my work and offering some suggestions for my notebook. We were a quiet pair, only hearing the rain against the windows and his frequent wheezing cough.

The morning passed quickly. At noon my mother still wasn't back, so he fixed us lunch. Then he really surprised me. "I don't feel like working any more. So, what say we take in a picture show this afternoon? Is there a matinee today?"

It sounded as if he thought I would know, but, of course, I had no idea and just shrugged my shoulders, apprehensive. He splashed through the newspaper until he found the movie timetable. "Good. Good. We can just make that one. I'll call a taxi."

I'd never ridden in a taxi before, and I seldom got to go to the movies. But there I was, in the back of a cab next to my hedonistic grandfather, in the rain, off for an afternoon at the Grand Theater. That day we both laughed as Bugs Bunny made a fool of Elmer Fudd. Then, at least for me, Nelson Eddy and Jeanette MacDonald's singing got in the way of the Royal Canadian Mounted Police action in "Rose Marie," but I caught my grandfather humming along once or twice. Next came Pluto and Mickey Mouse in some silly adventure, followed by a Movietone newsreel showing the Japanese army bombing and shooting Chinese civilians, then thousands of soldiers, each with one stiff raised arm cheering Hitler as he spoke to them. But then Shirley Temple in "The Little Princess" convinced us things always end happily. All that, and popcorn, too.

"Can't go to the pictures without popcorn," my grandfather told me. I noticed he didn't eat any of it himself.

The rain had stopped and it was still light when we got out. I was a little disappointed, because I wanted to take a taxi home and thought now that we'd probably take a bus or walk. We didn't live too far from the movie theater. But my grandfather took a deep breath and said, "Well, now, I need a little bracer, my boy," imitating W.C. Fields when he said "my boy."

Just two doors down from the Grand Theater was the Grand Little Bar. As we approached the doorway, the aroma of beer and whiskey stung my virgin nostrils. Once we entered the semi-darkness, it took my eyes a few seconds to adjust to what I saw. The place was long and narrow. A bar with a foot rail ran for a few feet down the left side of the room fronted by tall, backless stools. A display rack of what I imagined to be every magazine in the world lined the wall on the right. Some tables and chairs were clustered way in the back, but there was no one else in the place.

My grandfather greeted the man behind the bar. "Gene."

"How ya' doin, E. R.?" The bartender looked at me, then my grandfather expecting an explanation.

"My grandson." When he said it, my grandfather didn't look at me. He placed one foot on a brass rail and remained standing. "My usual, if ya' please, sir."

I had no idea what a bracer was, but Gene apparently did. I watched him place a tilted glass under a chrome spigot and pull a lever back. An amber colored liquid and foam quickly filled the glass. Then he took a bottle with four roses on the label and poured a darker liquid into the smallest glass I'd ever seen. He placed them in front of my grandfather.

"How about a Coke for the boy?" my grandfather asked as he tapped a Lucky from his pack and lit it.

"Can't serve him, E. R. 'N fact, shouldn't let him in."

"Ah, well, the boy's all right. If anyone says anything, he's just standin' by the door to keep out of the rain."

It wasn't raining right then, but the way my grandfather said it made the idea seem plausible, made me feel he was defending me, protecting me. And I liked his words, "the boy's all right."

"Give me a Coke, then," my grandfather ordered.

When he was served, my grandfather handed it to me. Neither man made any comment about it.

That was the end of any concern with me. The two of them started on a discussion of the state of the world, my grandfather making references to the war things we had seen in the newsreel and the bartender stating with authority that "ole FDR" would have us "in it" soon, mark his words.

My grandfather and Gene, near the door, seemed unconcerned as I wandered farther along the magazine rack, sipping my Coke. I knew my parents, especially dad, would just kill my grandfather if we were caught here. Still, there was an exciting power about it, a feeling of being detached from my parents' world and stepping into a forbidden one, a world I couldn't be blamed for entering if caught.

Among the various selections, I recognized *Liberty, Collier's, Life and Saturday Evening Post*, but then I saw one that really widened my eyes. Even with the dim light, I could see that the two women and the man on the cover were pitching horseshoes -- naked. I dared walk a little farther into the bar keeping my back to the two talking men so they couldn't see me pick up the magazine. As I stared in disbelief at the cover, I barely saw the bold letters spelling out *Sunshine and Health*. The fear of being caught looking at naked bodies, mostly women, along with unfamiliar stirrings in my groin, warned me that flames from hell were licking at my soul. This was what real wickedness felt like, there in that dark, sinful den with a man who smoked and drank beer and whiskey. I was breathing in un-Christian smells, looking at naked women and men, and even worse, attracted by it, everything my father was against. It was what Sunday school was there to save me from. But at that moment, they'd lost.

Despite the scourge of being caught, I tried with one hand to invisibly turn the pages while holding my drink without spilling it. Each page I turned showed nude bodies happily playing tennis, badminton, shuffleboard, horseback riding, swimming, eating. It was the women's bodies that attacked my eyes. That there could be so many different sized women's breasts and nipples astounded me. And those V's of hair. Some were dark, thick mats of it; some were blond, others had none, as if they'd shaved it all off. Despite the attraction of the pictures, I managed to read enough to learn I'd entered the realm of the nudist colony, a place that offered sunshine and health to those who preferred to go without clothes. The "sin of the flesh" I'd heard about in church captured my eyes.

As absorbed as I was in the pictures, I stayed alert and heard my grandfather tell Gene to keep the change and call us a taxi. I flipped the pages a little faster, not wanting to leave, wanting to steal this magazine and take it home so I could look at the pictures more slowly and carefully. I knew I was having sinful thoughts, now ready to steal even, knew now what it was to experience evil, knew now the power of the dark side of man! My hedonist grandfather had brought me to the gates of hell and I had willingly entered! Lamenting how easy it was to fall into temptation, I felt shame for disappointing my parents.

Despite my remorse, on our way home in the cab, I kept seeing one particular picture frozen in my mind. She was jumping in the air to catch a ball. Both arms were reaching out over her head, her legs were apart just temptingly wide enough that I could have, wanted to, put my hand between her thighs and touch that soft hair. Her large breasts looked firm, with small, taut nipples. The joy in her eyes beckoned me, taunted me. Try as I could to blame her for my hedonistic thoughts, the new sensation of evil I was experiencing and needed to subdue, I couldn't. They were my thoughts and feelings, not hers, confusing thoughts I felt I should hate myself for having but couldn't give up. I hated my grandfather for having brought me there.

He startled me by suddenly singing playfully, "Rose Marie, I love yoooou, I'm always dreamin' of you -oo," one of the songs in the movie. "Makes you want to up and join the Royal Mounties, eh boy?" He winked at me as though he knew every inch of my being. Had he seen me looking at the magazine? I tried to disappear by sinking deeper into the far corner of the taxi seat. But despite the embarrassment and guilt, her picture never left my mind.

When we got home, my grandfather suggested I not mention anything about the Grand Little Bar. I felt torn, thinking I really should tell my parents, but I couldn't admit to what I'd discovered, even hoping, wanting there to be another time he'd want a bracer. I knew I was betraying my father, and it made me uncomfortable, but I knew he would put an end to our little secret if I told him about the sinful place my grandfather took me. I felt I was living on a razor's edge.

Patterns of sorts developed that summer. My mother was given part-time work with one of the companies my grandfather worked for, and my dad found an assortment of jobs in and around Alton, so I didn't see much of them during the day. It fell on my grandfather to keep an eye on me. His desk became a kind of playground, and my drawing notebook began to fill.

He even began taking me to some of his job sites when he knew we wouldn't need to be there long. His accounts were varied, the local brick manufacturer, a mill, automobile dealers, grocery stores, law firms, and a couple of bars.

Every Sunday contained a family ritual. At nine, Sunday school, then eleven o'clock church services, except for my grandfather, who never went. Home for a big one o'clock meal, sometimes cooked by my grandfather. Then long hours with the Sunday newspapers, with ominous discussions about unemployment and the coming war. Then naps for my parents. I was supposed to nap, but I usually listened to the radio instead. A light evening meal and back to evening church services. My dad truly believed it was a day of rest. But for me, Sundays were anathema, a stiff reminder that I was now a willful sinner of the flesh who deserved to suffer and was doomed to hell.

Just as a Sunday ritual developed that summer, another one of sorts developed with my grandfather and me. We went to the movies often, sometimes in the afternoons, sometimes at night. We always took a taxi, and we always stopped for a bracer after the movies. With each new issue of *S & H* that summer, I memorized the bodies of the women I wanted to take home with me, wishing there were some way I could buy or steal the magazine. Instead, I branded the pictures into my brain for later moments of private viewing while I committed another sinful act that came so naturally and pleasurably that it was hard for me to believe God could be so mean as to make it a sin.

The Sunday school teachings and church sermons continued to convince me I was beyond redemption. Smoking, drinking, desires of the flesh -- my mind was occupied too frequently with knowledge of such sinful activities. Thanks to my grandfather, I now knew what a hedonist was. Thinking bad thoughts was as bad as committing them, I was told. But to make matters even worse, he introduced me to another sin: gambling.

One day when we were in his office, he pulled a pack of cards from his desk. I'd never seen them in there before and wondered where they came from.

"So, ever play blackjack?" he asked, knowing full well I hadn't. "Well, I'll show you," he said before I could answer.

He then proceeded to explain the game, which I had no trouble learning, despite the fact that Sundays had warned me of the evils of card playing. When he was certain that I knew how to play reasonably well, he asked me if I had any money, again knowing that I didn't.

"Here," he opened a middle drawer and took several dimes from a small box I also had never seen in his desk before. "Playing for money always makes the game more interesting." I realized at that moment I was about to take another step toward hell at the hands of my grandfather. And I knew I'd enjoy it.

He divided up the dimes between us, and I cut the shuffled deck. We played for several hands, the money going back and forth from his pile to mine. Then I began to win regularly. The excitement of watching my pile of dimes grow helped subdue some of my sinful guilt. When we stopped playing, I had $1.60, more money than I had ever had at one time in my life. Reluctantly, I pushed the money across the pulled-out desk board on which we were playing to give back to him. He pushed it back at me.

"Don't be too cocky, now. I may win the next time we play."

"You mean I can keep it?"

"You didn't cheat, did you?"

"No!" I was hurt at the suggestion.

"Then it's yours. You won it fair and square."

Like other secrets between my grandfather and me, I never told my parents about the money. I couldn't, for I knew that if I did, I would have to tell them about going to bars with my grandfather, his drinking "bracers," and the magazine with pictures of naked people having a good time. He'd made me his silent partner in sin.

Arguments between my grandfather and parents lessened, but when they did occur, they no longer upset me as much. Sometimes I'd listen to their voices arguing; other times I didn't care enough to bother to try and drowned them out with the radio. I began to wonder if the conflicts were always my grandfather's fault. It seemed that my father spoke up more after he started working regularly, defending his religious feelings against what he called my grandfather's "wicked ways," often bringing me into the arguments, saying he wanted me "brought up right."

One time I heard the word "sex" in the argument, so I listened more closely. My grandfather had been drinking, but he was coherent, arguing that Cain must have had sex with his mother Eve, because she was the only other woman around at the time. He quoted the Bible, " 'Cain knew his wife, and she conceived and bore Enoch; and he built a city, and called the name of the city the name of his son, Enoch.' Now, if Adam, Eve and their sons were the only ones living then, why did Cain build a city? Who would live in it?"

My dad argued that the Lord sent Cain away after he killed Abel, to the land of Nod, east of Eden, where he found a wife. My grandfather's retort was well, then, where did Cain's wife come from if Adam and Eve were the first on earth and Cain and Abel were their only children.

"But they weren't his only children, my father argued back, quoting the Bible himself. " 'And Adam knew his wife again, and she bore a son and called his name Seth.' Nothing is said about her having a daughter."

"So, you're telling me that Adam and Eve were the first people on earth, no? Then tell me where Cain's wife came from if it wasn't from Eve? You can't, because the whole story's full of crap."

This sort of talk infuriated my father, who felt the Bible stories were not to be read literally but historically. And my grandfather, the Bible-quoting sinner, got pleasure from pointing out what he called Biblical flaws. "Your god's too goddamn small!" he once yelled at my dad. "Everything in the Bible's a myth. See it for what it is!"

"Yes, some stories are myth, but with interpretation," my father assured him. "You have to know how to interpret. And never let me hear you talk this way around the boy!"

As for me, I was certain that in all probability I, too, would burn in hell as I became closer to my dangerous grandfather. And the closer I got to him, the more my sinner's guilt and betrayal of my father's feelings grew. I knew I should tell my father the secrets between my grandfather and me. But I had turned some corner and was now the devil's apprentice.

By summer's end, my drawing folder was thick with my work, helped by him, and kept in a special file in one of my grandfather's desk drawers. He knew I never told my parents anything about us. Maybe that's why he let me hunt and peck on his Underwood and taught me how to use his adding machine. Of course, I never got as fast. He also showed me how to make pancakes, French toast, and spaghetti. We seldom missed a new movie when it came to town.

Frequently, after taking me with him to some of his accounts, we stopped for a "bracer" somewhere. I was probably the only twelve-year old in town who knew the best bars and bartenders by name and could identify the labels of almost every whiskey on their shelves. Plus, I developed an intimate knowledge of the June, July, and August issues of a nudist magazine.

I knew I'd really reached the bottom of rotten when one day near the end of the summer I dared to be a thief. I stole a pack of Luckies from the carton in grandfather's desk and tried my hand at smoking. I didn't really like it, but I puffed away at two or three cigarettes without knowing enough to inhale. I hid the rest of the pack in a sweater at the bottom of a dresser drawer. Occasionally, when no one was around, I'd sit in the swivel chair, my feet up on the desk, a lit Lucky loose between my lips, and admit to myself I'd become a hedonistic sinner.

By the time I started school in September, I'd won over twelve dollars playing cards with my grandfather, his way of giving me an allowance my parents couldn't afford, I guess. It was a sin-filled summer, the best I'd ever had.

Later that October, I was called home early from school. My mother had found my grandfather sitting slumped at his desk, a burnt-out cigarette between his yellowed fingers.

There weren't too many people at the funeral, just some of his clients that I recognized and a few relatives I'd never met. I remember standing at his casket, looking at his expressionless face framed by his thick white hair, his yellowed, leathery-looking hands folded across his chest. I wanted him to open his eyes and say, "So, time for a bracer." But then I realized my grandfather was going to burn in hell for some of the things he had said and done.

The tears came, and with a sincerity and an earnestness I didn't know I possessed, I prayed. "Dear God, please, please, don't make my grandpa go to hell. If you save him, I promise I'll never smoke, drink, cuss, gamble or look at naked women again if you'll just save him from hell."

Wherever my grandfather may have ended, I'm certain he understands and forgives this well-intentioned sinner who did try, but ultimately was unable to keep his word.

CHAPTER 5

"This Masquerade"

Still living in my grandfather's house, my years containing late grade school and junior high mesh into memories of World War II: "Loose lips sink ships" worries; coupons for food and gas rationing; tin can drives to help build weapons; weaving wool squares to be made into blankets; my dad serving as an air raid warden during blackouts (yes, even that far inland); radio serials, like "I Love a Mystery," "The Green Hornet," and "The Shadow;" chewing gum packaged in cardboard squares with drawings on the back depicting Japanese soldiers bayoneting babies; exchanging Superman, Batman and Wonder Woman comic books (smiling when I noted five-pointed stars when a villain received blows); war movies depicting the evils of our enemies; and, of course, a prominent interest in girls, then sex, particularly the emphatic urge for self-gratification.

And the worry that my dad might be drafted.

It's during this period that I met Bill. I've always wondered what might have happened to Bill had I shared with others what transpired between us. Thinking back, I couldn't have been the only one who knew. He must have harbored some angst, an underlying worry that the wrong people would find out, especially back in those unenlightened days. Apparently, he trusted that I would never tell anyone, though I don't understand why. Maybe he knew more about me than I knew about myself at the time. I see it now as quite a risky gamble on his part.

Bill, then close to two years older than my thirteen years, impressed most everyone by his affability, demeanor and intelligence. Everyone in school who knew Bill saw him as a what's-not-to-like person. Adults labeled him "such a nice young man." His young Henry Fonda sort-of looks didn't hurt his image either. Both his body and mind seemed to have reached adulthood before most boys his age.

I knew him through the church choir and our membership in the same Boy Scout troop. We were just acquaintances until one evening after choir practice, he stopped me and asked me what I thought about the music we sang. Even though I knew him, it was the first time he paid attention to me personally. At first diffident and reticent around him, I became more at ease after a few weeks when it became a pattern to talk after choir. He always found something to say about the music we sang, the composer, or a piece he hoped we would sing. He suggested contemporary music I should listen to. Sometimes he'd ask me what I thought about the Sunday sermons. Inarticulate, I usually didn't know how to respond, wondering why someone like Bill cared what I thought about anything. Compared to him, I felt uninteresting, a dullard.

His friendliness spilled over into other parts of my life. When I needed various rocks for my Boy Scout merit badge, he offered to accompany me on searches up the river road, or he would give me one he found somewhere for my collection. He even offered to help me with math homework when I complained about my mathematic deficiency. So when he started asking me to hang out and do things together, my parents thought it so considerate of him to take me under his wing. Still not surrounded by a wide circle of friends at that age, I shyly accepted his attention and held him in adulation. Secretly, I wanted to be just like him.

But it wasn't all church choir and Boy Scouts. Sometimes we'd hang at his house, sometimes mine. He introduced me to sex flipbooks, those little tomes with cartoon-like drawings on each page set so that when you flip the pages you watched animated sex scenes. Most of the sex scenes were exaggerated, but what did I know? They, along with magazines like *Swank*, *Bizarre*, *Pep* and passages from books like *God's Little Acre* and *Tobacco Road* that Bill provided stirred my loins and opened my eyes to sexual possibilities and improbabilities and stimulated the testosterone surging through young, innocent me.

One summer day, as we often did, Bill and I hiked up the dirt road adjacent to the Mississippi river and climbed up the cliffs to a ledge of a small cave opening. Hot and sweaty, we sat at the entrance and shared water from his canteen. Not much of a talker, I just sat watching a tugboat push a long barge up the muddy water. Scads of birds flocked around whatever the barge contained. The river, wide at this geographical point above the Alton dam, always held some attraction.

"Funny, isn't it?" Bill broke our silence.

"What?" I thought he was talking about the tugboat.

"Don't you think it's strange that girls can walk down the street holding hands and nobody thinks anything about it, but boys can't?"

I had no idea what he was getting at and kept silent.

He wanted an answer. "I mean, what do you think when you see two girls holding hands as they walk down the street?"

"I don't know. Nothing. What if they do?"

"Well, that's just it. Nobody thinks anything about it."

"So why should they?"

"Well, what if you and me, you know, walked down the street holding hands. What do you think people would say?"

"I don't know." I shrugged. I'd never thought about it before. The idea seemed silly, and I had no idea what he wanted me to say.

The barge's gradual movement up river interested me more than whatever point he was trying to make.

"Don't you think people would think it strange?"

"I don't know. I guess so." I felt he wanted me to say something more, so I added, "I've never seen two guys holding hands, except to shake."

"That's just it. So why do you think girls can get away with it?"

"It's just what they do. Maybe they feel safer together."

"What if they're in love?"

"In love? You think that's why girls hold hands?"

"Maybe. Nobody really knows, do they? Friendship? Protection? It's just accepted that girls can walk around holding hands and being chummy, rubbing shoulders and nobody accuses them of being odd or creepy. Guys can punch each other, shove each other around, but if we held hands, you and me, people would think we were queers."

I'd heard the words "queer" and "fag" used in derogatory terms, not fully understanding their meaning. Bill's use and its context cracked a chink in my immaturity. Could two men be in love with each other?

While I was trying to figure out what this perplexing conversation had to do with anything, my understanding grew when Bill leaned over, put his arm around me, turned my head to his and kissed me on my lips.

An explosion of confusion and discomfort stunned me as his whiskers scratched, his dry lips staying on my closed mouth too long, then a flick of an exploring tongue. I jerked for breath, recoiled, and pushed him away in puzzlement and not a little trepidation. If I'd been older then, I might have said, "What the fuck!?" My comfort zone turned into a fear of some kind. I couldn't look at him, so I gazed out at the barge disappearing from view, wishing I were on it.

Neither of us said anything. We just sat there for who knows how long; me, numb, trying to assimilate what had transpired.

Bill broke the quiet. "I didn't mean to upset you. I thought maybe you had the same feelings for me that I have for you."

Feelings for me? Feelings for you? What kind of feelings? I still didn't know what to say with my mind disoriented, struggling to understand, to acknowledge what he was talking about.

"I really care for you. I thought you felt the same about me. My mistake. I can see I was wrong. Sorry."

For a few moments more, we sat in silence; then, to my relief, he suggested we head back home.

I don't remember much of what was said on our way back to town. I knew that the two boys who walked up the river earlier that day were not the same two boys coming back.

"I hope you're not angry," he said dolefully. "Don't be angry, please."

Angry? No. I can't say I felt anger. Surprised, yes; confused, unsettled, uncomfortable, embarrassed, even. In retrospect, maybe I even felt his embarrassment and disappointment.

When we parted, I couldn't look at his face but for an instant.

"I'm sorry I upset you. Didn't mean to. Can you understand?"

I had no idea how to respond other than to say, "Yeah. Okay. I understand...."

No, I didn't understand; not really. Not then.

Unless it was in choir practice or scouts, I didn't see much of him after that and our relationship became turbid. We never talked about it; in fact, no more substantive conversations took place between us, just polite acknowledgments. We just shied away from each other. I no longer knew how I felt about Bill. The phrase about wine turning into vinegar applied. I sensed he sensed it.

As days passed, it began to make sense to me why he had shown me those flipbooks, and why he sometimes gave his views about sex not being "dirty." And while I didn't think about it at the time, I realize now that he left himself very vulnerable. I wondered what went through his mind after I refused him. What had I done that caused him to think I had those kinds of feelings for him? What had he seen in me that lead him to believe I shared his feelings? Did my rejection hurt him? Did he worry I would be disgusted, and tell others? Was he concerned what my parents would do if I told them what he did? Did he trust I'd keep quiet? If so, what made him so confident? Or, did he fear me, worried to death I'd say something?

I never told a soul what happened until now.

I'm not sure what kept me silent. I know I felt an odd sense of embarrassment, even though I had done nothing wrong. And neither had he, as I thought about it. But I also sensed it would not have been right to call him out for his feelings, especially since somehow, though I'm not clear exactly how or why, I was the source of his sensitivities and caring.

While the incident revealed to me that I had no such sexual leanings, it also afforded me an osmosis-like understanding of others who, like

Bill, I would meet and befriend later in life. While I couldn't give back to Bill what he would have liked, he unknowingly gave me a lesson in love and friendship that I began to apprehend as I grew older. I now know what I lost because of the prevailing mindsets of the times, and I think, sexual feelings aside, we could have been friends had I been older and more sentient.

I'm pleased I stayed silent, and I hope Bill safely weathered the prejudice of the times and found love and happiness with someone worthy of him.

CHAPTER 6

"You've Got a Friend"

And then there was Ted.

To most, he was just a weird loner. Brown hair cut short, dark eyes, usually dressed in jeans and T-shirt, Ted appeared to be a normal, average-sized teenager. But that's where it ended. Not the sort to be labeled the most popular boy in the class yearbook, Ted could care less if his picture or name appeared in it. As far as I know, he never attended school events or joined any clubs. But he walked with a bounce in his stride that challenged gravity.

Social skills he had few. Quick to say what he thought, he cared little its effect on others. He thought nothing of interrupting a conversation to tell someone they didn't know what they were talking about. And they often didn't. His sense of humor was somewhere out there in a zone beyond most of us. He enjoyed an annoying Socratic approach to answering teachers' questions with questions of his own, showing a depth in the subject that often surprised and annoyed the teachers. My first read on him lead me to think he got pleasure making himself unpopular. To me, he was an oddball.

Until he became my best friend.

One day in chemistry class, I watched him burn his initials in his forearm with acid. When I asked why, he said to see what it felt like to be branded like an animal.

"Want to try it?" he asked, holding out the bottle of acid.

"You nuts?" I asked in all sincerity. "Doesn't it hurt?"

He looked at the letters T and J swelling up on his arm. "Not as bad as it must be for a steer."

He looked at me. "You think I'm a stupid shit, don't you?"

"It crossed my mind." It came out before I realized I'd said what I was thinking.

He didn't seem offended. "Maybe I am. Who's to say?" He gave a little laugh, and I wondered if he might be trying to impress me with his acid antics.

A few days later, Miss Blackard, our sophomore history teacher, decided to have the class work in pairs on a project dealing with American presidents. When she assigned Ted to work with me on a report on Andrew Jackson, I figured she had it in for me for some reason, and I was being punished. But I resigned myself to the task.

"How do you want to do this?" I asked Ted.

"What do you know about Jackson?"

"Not much. He was president way back and his picture is on the twenty-dollar bill."

"Great start. I see you're going to be an enormous help."

I couldn't think of a smart retort and settled for, "Yeah, well, what do you know about him?"

"He was an asshole, for starters."

That threw me. At that age, I'd never heard any of our presidents referred to as assholes. "What do you mean?"

"Just that. You don't know shit, do you?"

Ted's comments hastened my growing dislike for him and our project. My immediate thought was that maybe if I asked, Miss Blackard would let me switch with someone else. He didn't appear too eager to work with me, either.

"Look," Ted said, "you research John Marshall and Chief John Ross. Take some notes, and I'll dig up stuff on Jackson. When can you meet to start putting it all together?"

With much reluctance and annoyance at Ted's show-off bossiness, I agreed to his plan and to meet a few days later in the library.

I had no idea who Marshall or Ross were or how they were connected to Andrew Jackson. But once I started reading, I soon learned how Jackson betrayed them, as well as the part he played in the brutal treatment of the Native Americans' removal from their homes and their struggles along the Trail of Tears. I began to see Ted's point about Andrew Jackson.

I surprised myself at both my interest in our project and Ted's knowledge of American history. When I asked him how he knew so much, he just shrugged and said he read a lot.

Miss Blackard accepted our final report, praising us for our research, but suggesting our use of language could use some work. I remember our opening line read: "President Andrew Jackson, our seventh president of the United States, was an asshole."

Working together on the Jackson project did not form us into the best-of-friends category. While I had to admire him for his knowledge and accept that he was smarter than I was, I also resented him for those very qualities. Why did he have to act so bizarre? He didn't care what other people thought of him. Me? I did care about my image. Among my friends, to not hang out with him was a given. Yet, I envied him in a way I didn't quite understand. His lack of ordinariness made him interesting to someone like me, a very ordinary teenager.

Not long after our history project was finished, a group of us had gathered at Block's, an ice-cream hangout. Ted was there and we heard him order a Hound Dog without nuts. The server told him a Hound Dog without nuts was just a chocolate ice-cream sundae with chocolate syrup.

"Well, that's what I want. A Hound Dog without nuts," he said.

"Why don't you just ask for a chocolate sundae?" she asked.

"Because a Hound Dog without nuts is the same thing, isn't it?"

"But if I ring up a Hound Dog, I'll have to charge you for the nuts."

"Why? I don't want the nuts."

She gave Ted an arrow piercing stare and told him, "I'm fixing you a chocolate sundae. Take it or leave it!"

Someone in the store yelled out, "Way to go! He's already nutty enough!"

We all laughed, yet I felt sorry for Ted. Was he trying to be funny and make a joke about a hound dog with no balls? Was he trying to show how ludicrous placing nuts on a chocolate sundae turned it into something called a Hound Dog? I don't know. But I didn't like myself for joining in the laughter.

He paid for his order, saw me and nodded as he left. I felt sure I saw a slight smile as he dipped his spoon in his Hound Dog without nuts.

By chance one afternoon, Ted happened to see me at the Grand movie theater. "She Wore a Yellow Ribbon" with John Wayne was playing.

"So, you like Westerns." It wasn't a question.

"Good ones." I tried to sound like I knew the difference.

"Me, too," Ted said. "I like to see how they portray Indians. Half the time, it's some famous white actor with dyed skin speaking in pidgin."

I'd never thought about it before, but I began to notice he was right.

After a newsreel on the progress of the war, a Tom & Jerry cartoon, a travelogue and some previews of coming attractions, the movie started. Wayne plays an army captain named Nathan Brittle who tries to stop an impending Indian uprising by meeting with an old Indian chief. We noticed a real Native American played the part and gave each other a thumbs-up. With tom-toms beating in the background, a fire crackling between them, the Indian elder chief, who seems to have no teeth, struggles to pronounce Nathan's name, declaring in broken English, "Too...late... Nay-tan... too late."

For some reason, Ted cracked up at the Chief's delivery. I'd never seen him laugh before. But the line stuck with him, and it became a phrase he would use whenever he felt it fit the occasion.

After the movie, we stood around discussing what we liked and didn't like about it. We pretty much agreed on everything, which surprised me. It became obvious we both liked many of the movies we'd seen, though he often felt the book a movie was based on was better. I couldn't argue that one. He was better read than I was. I shocked myself by asking if he wanted to go to Block's for a Hound Dog.

He smiled, and imitating the chief's scraggy voice, said. "Too late, Nay-tan, too late," then explained he had to get home.

Little by little we began hanging out together, doing who remembers what. We both liked to hike up the familiar old gravel river road outside town. I can't count the times Ted and I hiked those railroad tracks north of town, the wide, brown river to our left and the scattered growth embedded in the loosed layered limestone bluffs on the right. They called out to us to be climbed. A Native American pictograph of the mysterious colorful winged Piasa Bird stood out on the white, scraggly cliffs just as you left town, supposedly carved originally by the Illini people. Small caves hid themselves in the rugged high bluffs.

"Hey, Naytan, (by then that became my tag) bet I can balance myself on the rails longer than you can," he might challenge, and that would start our hike along the tracks that seemed to merge in the distant shimmering heat waves.

"Can you do this?" might come a dare, as he managed some crazy one-leg leap on the rails.

He'd pull stunts like picking up something at his feet and examining it as if it were a world-shaking geological find or ancient artifact, then try to convince me of its scientific importance.

"You should keep this," he'd say holding out some kind of rock or mud clot.

"Why? What is it?"

"A beautiful specimen."

"A specimen of what? I've got rocks like this in my collection. They're common."

He'd shake his head at me. "Your ignorance appalls me, you know that?" Then he'd throw the item away. Or, for no reason he'd throw it at me, forcing me to retaliate until the rock throwing grew too serious to continue.

About a mile out of town, we'd usually climb the scaly bluffs and sit at the entrance of a deep hole in the cliff we called Dry Cave and look out over the river to the Missouri side. (My episode with Bill always surfaced in my mind, but never stayed long.) The Alton dam forms a huge lake just north of town, so the river is wide and a not inviting milk chocolate color. Sometimes tugs pushing barges would come down river, and we'd make up stories about where it came from and where it was going, what it carried and at what city down the river we'd get off if we were on board, arguing over which offered us the most, Cairo, Memphis, Natchez, Vicksburg, or New Orleans. Our future destinations and plans ran wild, both trying to outdo the other.

Ted relished looking for snakes. He knew the names of every one he caught. If they weren't poisonous, he'd let them go. But the bluffs were full of copperheads. The way he handled them scared me. He would kill copperheads by cutting off their heads with a four-inch knife he always wore in a sheath attached to his belt. The first time I saw him do this he held the squirming four-foot body at my face, proud of his prize. I tried hard to conceal my unease, otherwise who knows how he might play at my fear.

"Let's find out if what they say is true," he said.

"Which is what?" I asked with some apprehension, knowing him.

"Supposedly, a snake's body with its head cut off will keep wiggling until sundown. Let's see if it's true."

He put a rock on top of the severed head, stomped on it, and then carried the body, still squirming, down the bluffs to the railroad. He put the body between the tracks and said, "We'll check on that theory on our way back."

As interesting theory, I never found out its validity. A slow freight train leaving the city headed its way north. We stood back and watched it rattle toward us, its deep horn blaring a warning. The ground shook and the engineer waved. We watched as car after car rolled by us. I'd never been that close to a moving train before.

"Let's catch it," Ted yelled over the noise, his daring grin showing.

I just looked at him, hoping he was kidding.

"Yeah, why not? It's slow. We can jump off when we want to." Without waiting for me to argue, Ted started running alongside the train.

"Are you for real?" I yelled.

I watched as he jumped, grabbed at an iron ladder rung on the side of the boxcar, and pulled himself up. He stepped a couple of rungs up and waved at me.

In a momentary loss of brains, I ran alongside the train. Like Ted, I grabbed an iron ladder rung on the boxcar and lifted my feet up to the bottom rung just over the train wheel. But as I pulled myself up, my feet slipped off the rung. My chest wash-boarded down the iron rungs scraping away skin and my legs dropped down over the wheel. Something like an electric shock hit one foot and it flipped way out from the train. Instinct drew my flailing legs back up, and I finally found a rung to rest my feet on. My eyes blurred with tears as my heart sped faster than the train. I stayed in a squatting position, hugging the ladder like a baby monkey to its mother.

When I looked forward at Ted, he was posed like a trapeze artist, one leg out from the train and one arm outstretched waving to his imaginary crowd. At that moment I hated him.

Keeping my feet firmly on the ladder rung, I slowly pulled myself up hand over hand to a standing position. Nervous sweat made my hands slippery and holding on difficult. I started feeling the pain in my chest and looked down to see some blood on my torn shirt. More painful would be telling my parents when I got home. If I got home.

But that seemed less significant when I realized the train was gaining speed. I wanted no more of Ted's craziness, but that meant I had to jump or stay on a train going who knows where and for how long.

I looked down at the rail dirt and gravel that seemed to be sailing by and jumped as far out from the train as I could. I tried to keep running once I hit the gravel, but that was a fool's errand. That day, I created the term "rock and roll." When I stopped rolling on the rocks and scraggly weeds, I lay there certain I never wanted to move again. I closed my eyes and listened to the steady sound of the train wheels -alump-udet-alump-udet-alump-udet change to you-stupid-boy-you-stupid-boy-you-stupid-boy. But soon all the burning, stinging cuts, scratches and bruises forced me to sit up and check the damage. Nothing felt broken, but my elbows and knees were a mess. My scraped chest carried scars for years after. It was then I looked at my feet and noticed my sock was sticking out the sliced off tip of one of my shoes.

Ted limped toward me, face scratched, checking out a bleeding cut on his arm. He looked at me down on the ground and grinned.

"We almost jumped too late, eh, Naytan?"

Naytan bombarded his wise-ass-best-friend with rocks, even though I knew which one of them was the most asinine.

Speaking of which...

Maybe it was from hanging out with Ted that caused me to go as far as I did that unforgettable day at Blue Pool. No, I can't blame him. For whatever reason, it was one of the most idiotic things I ever did as an insecure teenager. Oh, those teen years...

I looked down at the waiting water, at least forty feet. Some say more, some less. Now that I'd climbed up here, I knew for damn sure it was a whole lot of feet down -- whatever. Blue Pool looked more like Black Pool. A bit scary, yeah. I looked down at them, small now, eager for me to prove the dare. They don't think I'll do it. Think I'll chicken out. Thing is, though, they hope I will. Probably like to see me hit the water and not come up. If I killed myself wouldn't that give them some juicy excitement in their lives. Witnesses to the real thing. My name would be added to all the stories about Blue Pool. I'd become another legend attached to this old Mississippi river road quarry pool where we crazies risked swimming to cool off in the summer despite the fence and those skull and crossbones signs all around the place.

One story has the pool bottomless, so deep that an old train boxcar got dumped in the pool and nobody's ever dived and found it. Probably a bunch of bull, but who really knows? True story I do know, though. Some guy jumped from here a few years back and ended up paralyzed from the neck down. Yeah, lots of stories about Blue Pool. Like, supposedly way back some Indian Chief killed the lover of his daughter because he didn't want the Princess to marry the guy. Broken hearted, she jumped from where I'm now standing and killed herself. Another Indian story had it that she never hit the water. A giant, dragon-like monster known as the Piasa Bird swooped down, caught her in the fall, and flew off with her, never to be seen again. You can still see where the Illini Indians painted the ugly bird creature on the cliff wall near here. Town's people keep it painted. Well, no such bird around this time.

So, here I am. And I'm going to do it. I left my T-shirt and shoes down below and I want her to see when I climb out of the water my bare feet all messed up and bleeding from my climb up the scabby shale cliff. I want her to see me jump, even though she doesn't know I'm doing it for her. Well, for her attention. Yeah, I admit it. That's what I want. And she knows my name now because everybody used it when they called me a nut case for taking the dare. What she doesn't know is how I feel about her. I'm stuck on her. I love her. Dream about her. But now she'll take notice. She'll admire me after this.

I tried to spot her in the group below but couldn't see her. She was there when I left to climb up here. I waved to get their attention, her attention. Hey down there! Look at me! She just has to see me do this. Has to. So…

"Here I go," I yelled down.

I jumped way out, waving my arms like wings to get some distance away from the cliff, then crossed my arms across my chest, pulled my feet together, felt the air force my shorts up my crotch, took a deep breath, and closed my eyes…

The first time I saw her, man, I was pierced by that arrow and understood what people mean by "love at first sight." At Tri City Grocery, where I worked after school and summers in the produce department, she came in with her dad, both wearing sporty tennis duds I'd only seen in the movies. I immediately understood that here were people who mattered to the world. Their white outfits brought out their tans, their classiness, their rich distance from me. No one I knew even owned a tennis racket, let alone played the game. Her dad, tall, a touch of grey in his sideburns, looked strong and confident, like an after-shave ad. But it was her that held me captivated. She was probably sixteenish, my age, and I'd never seen any one more appealing, more, what's the word -- symbolic -- of what I wasn't. Something tight came over me. What was it I was seeing I'd never noticed in people before? Don't know. But she did it.

I had this peculiar urge – for me, any way -- to run my tongue along her bare arms and legs colored light caramel by the sun, so smooth, firm and wholesome sleek. And her long, brown hair, bleached blond in spots from the sun, she'd tied back with a violet-blue ribbon the color of her doe-shaped eyes, every feature of her face perfection, deafening me from understanding the words she spoke. Her light voice, an unfamiliar melody, played counterpoint against her handsome father's deep voice as they examined and discussed the produce. At once, I wanted to be wanted by her, wanted to be what they were, to step into their lives, yeah, to be one of them.

Crazy, huh?

Then she asked me something about the oranges. With no understanding, I sort of froze, feared looking for very long into her clear, violet eyes and stammered some thickheaded sounding answer I don't remember, dropped an orange at her feet, bent down to pick it up, never wanting to rise, only to look forever at her clean, white tennis shoes, her long, firm, smooth bronzed legs. Oh, just to touch them!

My life kinda ripped open in that moment with, I don't know, an inferior feeling. Yeah. Can't tell you why. When I dared look up into her laughing face again, those perfect white teeth, I knew in that moment a life existed to which I didn't belong. She was untouchable, unreachable. She didn't know it, but she had passed sentence on me.

I kept my eye on them as they shopped and then followed them out the door to the parking lot. I pretended I was collecting shopping carts as I watched them get into a brand-new baby blue, 1948 Cadillac Series 62 convertible. Yeah, they were rich alright. The top was down and as they drove away, I felt hollow, empty, a nothing, a "no" thing.

But her image? It stayed to haunt me. I kept hoping, even praying, they would come back to the store, but if they did, it was never when I was working.

I began to look for her everywhere I went, aching to see her once more. I couldn't help myself; she'd made me her prisoner. How did that old Russ Columbo song go? The one my mom liked? "I'm just a prisoner of love..." I know, I know. Foolish me.

Then, in the Fall, the first day of school, I was leaning against my locker talking to my best friend, Ted, when I saw her walking down the hall. I let my knees buckle, and I slid toward the floor. It was a silly dramatic act on my part, but I wanted Ted to see how flipped out over her I was.

"Hey, you okay?" He grabbed my arm and helped pull me back up.

"It's her. There she is," I barely got the words out.

Ted didn't need to ask me who I was talking about. I'd bored him to death talking about her so much, he'd often start to whistle a tune to drown me out, or just plain tell me to shut up about her. He turned to look.

"The one coming this way?"

"Un-huh." Oh, my god, there she was.

Ted gave her a good look. "Yeah. Okay. Well, what makes her so special?"

I couldn't believe him. "You don't see it?"

"She's okay, I guess." He didn't seem impressed, and it made me want to punch him for lack of good taste. He had to be kidding me.

As she walked down the hall straight toward us. I froze. She was wearing – I don't remember, but it doesn't matter. There she was, my wish come true.

Then she was right there. Say something, say something. Quick.

"Hi," I dared.

She smiled. "Hi."

Her velvet eyes. I, me, was in them for a moment.

But then, I watched her walk on."That's it?" Ted asked. "You've been mooning over her all summer and all you can say is a mousey 'Hi'?"

Speechless me.

"I can't believe you." Ted sounded really pissed. "She said 'hi' back. Go. Catch her."

But I just stood there, an immoveable force, watching her disappear around the corner. "You're unbelievable, you know that? You missed your chance, you idiot. Perfect timing. Missed." He shook his head and gave me a-you're-an-idiot-smirk.

Normally, I would have said something nasty back, but he was right. I blew it.

Well, come on. What did I expect? She didn't know me. Why would she remember me from the store?

She said "hi" back. And I think she smiled a little. Yeah.

I held on tight to that while Ted kept telling me what a bonehead I was and that I was never to mention her to him again, or he would personally kill me or do something worse.

Of course, I knew Ted was right. I could've kicked myself for being too afraid to talk her up. Why hadn't I introduced myself, reminded her we'd met. I'd been wishing for this moment and I bombed. Ted's right. I'm a moron, a blockhead, a halfwit, a nincompoop—all the names Ted called me -- and more of my own.

I got in a little bit of trouble that first day of school. That's because I was late for every one of my classes. See, in order to find out what classes she was taking, I had to follow her to each of her classes.

Unfortunately, she was in none of mine. So, by the time I followed her, I was late for my own classes. But it didn't matter. I knew where she was every class period, so now I could meet up with her after school one day, maybe even get up the nerve to talk to her.

All I could think about was how I might approach her. Should I remind her that we had met at Tri City Grocery's? That was a possible entry, but I was so gaga around her that day, stammering and dropping an orange, she probably thought I was a jerk. More likely, didn't even remember the incident. I needed a plan.

The next day, when the lunch bell rang, I tore out of my classroom and headed for hers, which I knew was upstairs, but by the time I got there she was gone. I searched the halls looking, but didn't see her. I finally gave up and went down to my locker to get my lunch. Ted was there, waiting. We always ate lunch together.

"You're late, dim wit."

"You're so observant, oh wise one."

I took my lunch from my locker, and we headed outside where we usually sat on the lawn to eat.

"Need I ask why you're late?"

"Do you have such a need?"

"Not really. I'm guessing you didn't find her, or you'd be fine dining with her instead of me."

"God, you're brilliant. How do you stand yourself?"

"What's her name, by the way? I can't keep calling her *her*."

I didn't answer right away.

"Don't know." I hated to admit it, knowing him.

He stopped walking and gave me this you're-in-love-with-this-girl-and-you-don't-even- know-her-name-or-anything-about-her look.

"Don't gimme that. I'll find out."

"Yeah? When? Not at the rate you're moving."

We found our usual eating spot and sat on the grass. We checked out each other's lunches and found nothing to swap.

Right then, I decided what to do.

"I'll follow her around, learn more about her. Find out where she lives. Where she plays tennis. Who her friends are. What her interests are. Stuff like that."

Ted shook his head. "That's your plan? Follow her around? Listen to yourself, Numb- nuts. You don't even know her name and you're talking about stalking the poor girl."

"No. Not stalking. Just keeping an eye out for her. You know, getting to know more about her."

"Come on, ace. Call it what it is: spying."

I just shrugged my shoulders. He didn't understand. "It's detective work."

"So, what's your first step? Get a disguise? Become her shadow?"

"Shut up, will ya."

"Wait! That's it. Like the radio announcer says: 'Who knows what evil lurks in the hearts of men? The Shadow do!' Ah-ha-ha-ha." He tried to imitate the mocking radio laugh.

I punched him on the shoulder a little harder than I meant and he dropped his peanut butter and jelly sandwich in the dirt. Before I knew it, he grabbed my sandwich and started wolfing it down.

I didn't care. I'd had enough teasing.

"Naytan, you crack me up." His words munched together as he chewed.

"Go ahead and laugh. You'll see."

"See what, exactly?"

I didn't answer. I didn't know.

The rest of the school day was torture. I knew I had to get to her last class after the bell rang before she got away again. Before the final bell stopped ringing, I was out in the hall and halfway down the stairs. I got to her classroom just as she was leaving with another girl. Lucky for me I saw Mary Ann, a girl I'd had classes with in the past. I felt pretty sure she'd remember me so I got up the nerve to stop her. It wasn't like we were great friends or anything. We just knew each other from around. She wasn't my type or anything, and I didn't want her to get any wrong ideas. So, I tried to be casual and all.

"Hey, Mary Ann. How are... things?"

She looked surprised I'd stopped her. "Hi. Okay. You?"

"Guess we don't have any classes together this semester."

"Didn't see you in any." She gave a little laugh at the obvious.

"Yeah." I didn't know what else to say, so after a hard swallow I just came out with it.

"Say, do you happen to know the name of that girl over there in the plaid skirt talking with Maureen?" I was pretty sure the girl's name was Maureen.

Mary Ann looked at them. "You mean Grace?" Grace. The name sang in my brain.

"Uh, yeah. She's new here, huh."

"Yeah. She moved here last summer. Why?"

"Just wonderin'."

"Ah, I get it. Wanna meet her?"

Only more than anything. But what came was, "Ah, no. Just, you know, wondered who she was."

I was so glad Ted wasn't around to hear me.

Mary Ann laughed. "And why are you wondering who she is?"

I didn't like the way Mary Ann was making a big deal out of my interest in Grace. And I was worried Grace and Maureen would stop talking and leave. I needed to follow Grace to see where she lived if that's where she was going.

"Nothin' really," I said, digging a deeper hole. "Friend of mine wanted to know who she was, maybe ask her out. Told him I'd see what I could find out."

"Who's the shy friend?"

"Best I don't say. Don't think he'd like it if I told anyone. Anyway, thanks for telling me her name. I'll pass it along."

I turned and started walking away when she yelled, "Bye. I'll let Grace know she has a secret admirer." Then she laughed and I knew she knew the truth. I turned back, hoping Grace hadn't heard Mary Ann yell. But she must have heard her name because she looked our way.

Embarrassed, I turned the corner and once out of Mary Ann's sight, I ran all the way down the hall and out another side exit. Then I made my way back to the door I knew Grace would come out when she stopped talking with Maureen. I hung back out of sight hoping I hadn't missed her. I didn't have to wait too long before Grace came out – and alone. Perfect.

The after-school crowd started to thin out and I had to be careful Grace didn't see me following her. I stayed back, following her to the bus stop. I don't take the bus. I can walk to school. But it looked like I might have to take it today. She started talking with someone in the waiting crowd. She looked so – I don't know – above them all. Yeah. She kept shuffling the load of books in her arms and I wanted to rush up to her and say, "Here, let me carry those for you."

That's when I realized I'd been in such a hurry to find Grace I'd left my own books on the desk of my last class. Oh, well.

The yellow bus arrived and everybody started piling on. For a moment I wondered if I really wanted to do this. I held back, but when Grace boarded, I dashed and made it on just before the doors closed. I knew she was on the bus so I didn't bother to look for her. I didn't want to be noticeable. I slipped into a seat up front and kept looking straight ahead, waiting for Grace to get off. After about four stops and the bus started emptying, Grace got up to get off. She stood so close to me I wanted so bad to reach out and touch her. That's when I wasn't sure what to do. Was I going to get off with her? That could be awkward. If I didn't, then how would I know where she lived, the whole point of my following her?

While I tried to figure out what to do, the bus stopped. Grace was the only one to get off, and the bus started up again.

I thought fast.

I stood next to the driver and gave him my pitch. "Sir, I'm sorry, but I missed my stop. I wasn't paying attention. Could you please stop here?"

"Sorry. Too late. Against the rules. I can only stop at designated stops."

Crap, crap, crap.

"Where's the next stop?"

"Five blocks."

I just stood there, looking at the door handle lever. No. Don't even think it.

"You'll have to sit down," the bus driver ordered.

I did as told; sure in my heart I'd never make it back to Grace's stop in time to see where she lived.

When the bus finally stopped, I was the first one to get off. As soon as I hit the sidewalk, I started jogging, then running, back from where we just came. Oh, please, please, please, let me find her before she gets home. I knew my chances of seeing her were poor, but I couldn't give up. When I made it to her bus stop, I stopped running hot and sweaty. I looked around, but no one was on the streets.

I walked around the tree-lined neighborhood aware I'd never been in this part of the city before. These were some fancy houses I was noticing. Some two and three stories tall. Mostly brick. Some with tall, white columns in front like plantations I'd seen in the movies. Curved driveways leading from the street to the house curved back down to the street. Gardeners working on at least two of the yards I passed.

I was about to give up when luck stepped up to the plate. That baby blue, 1946 Cadillac Series 62 convertible pulled up the long driveway of one of the houses. The top was down so I got a good look at the driver. Grace's dad.

He didn't get out of the car. He just sat there for a few minutes. I hid behind a thick Sycamore tree and watched. He gave a toot on his horn. The front door opened. And there she was. She was still wearing her plaid skirt and said something to her dad I couldn't make out. She got in the car with him, gave him a kiss on the cheek that I wished belong to me. Then he backed out the driveway and headed in my direction. I inched my way around the tree trunk as they passed so they couldn't see me.

But now I knew where she lived and my heart filled.

Once they left, I took a good look at the house. A two-story brick house with two, I think you call them gables, on either side of the second floor. Five windows faced the front, all trimmed in white wood. The front door was framed white like the windows. Actually, two carved wooden doors, or at least it looked like it. Big old maple trees stood guard on each side of the house. You could play croquet on the lawn; it was so big and smooth. Couldn't tell for sure, but I'd bet there was a pool in the backyard. Sure different from my place.

I stood there a while, just taking in her house, imagining her walking around in the different rooms, going up and down the stairs, sitting cross-legged on her bed listening to Frank Sinatra, Jo Stafford, Doris Day, or maybe Nat King Cole or Ella. I hope she does, 'cause they're my favorites. I'd bet her family even has a piano. Yeah, a big one.

Some woman, I guess Grace's mother, opened the front door and looked at me kinda funny, so I started walking away. After a few steps I realized I didn't know where I was. I forgot to pay attention on the bus. I walked a few blocks checking street signs but nothing sounded familiar.

I began walking, hoping I'd see somebody or a store and could ask directions to my neighborhood. And that's what happened. I stopped some guy walking his dog, and he gave me directions to a street I knew would take me toward home. Even though it was miles back, I mostly walked on air with my thoughts of Grace in her ritzy house. My thoughts of Grace caused me to not pay attention to where I was going. I should have turned at the second corner, but I didn't and got a little mixed up. I wasn't really lost, but it took me a while to get my bearings.

I tensed inside when I realized where I was. Half a block away, I saw him cutting the lawn.

Bill.

I wanted to turn around before he saw me. Then I told myself not to be stupid, but I did cross to the other side of the street. I wanted to just walk by, but he saw me and waved. I didn't know what to do, so I waved back and kept on walking. It didn't feel right. Stupid. Stupid.

After I recovered, my thoughts went back to Grace. Now that I knew where she lived, I needed to find out where her dad drove her. Piano lessons? Dance class? Tennis? No, she wasn't dressed for that. Doctor's? Jeez, no. She didn't look sick. More to find out.

I called Ted later that evening. "Hey. I know where Grace lives."

"Grace who?"

"Very funny. I told you I'd find out."

"How swell, how witty. What now? Gonna pitch a tent on her lawn?"

"Screw you, a-hole. It's a really nice place. Over near the country club."

"That's a far piece from where you live. How you gonna keep tabs on her?"

"Thinkin' about a bike."

"You don't own a bike."

"No, but you do.""Oh, no. You're not borrowing mine. I don't believe in spying on young girls…or old ones, either."

"Quit calling it spying. I'm just…you know…."

"Naytan, it's spy--ing."

"No, dammit. I just want to know more about her. Hope to get to know her. Come on, Ted, I really like her. A lot."

"Then why not walk up to her and say, "Hi. I like you a lot. I want to get to know you better. What's your favorite hobby?"

"Lay off, will ya. Don't be a smart ass."

"I'm not. Why go through all this mystery stuff? Just introduce yourself. What's she gonna do? Bite you?"

"No, It's just … I'm too shy, that's all. I wouldn't know what to say to her. That's why I want to know what she likes, so I can talk to her about stuff she's interested in."

"I'm tellin' ya. You're goin' about this all-wrong. She'd probably be all flutter-bugged at your interest in her, think you're cute or something. I mean, I know you're not, but you can't tell what girls think."

"But what do I say? See, I need to know more so I can talk about things."

"You're the one who's gone ape over this girl. What do you want to say to her? What 'things' are you talking about?"

"Just... things! Everything! I don't know! That's my problem!"

"You're your problem."

"And you're no help."

"You're not listening to my wisdom, Naytan."

"Are you gonna loan me your bike tomorrow or not?"

"Not. Definitely not."By Saturday, he gave in and loaned me his old, rusty-red Schwinn with dirty white fat tires. It was hard to pump, the brakes squeaked and there was no chain guard, so I had to be careful not to get my pants caught in the chain. But it beat walking to Grace's since I had trouble remembering exactly how to get there. It didn't do me a lot of good though, because almost the minute I got there, I saw her drive away with her dad in that baby-blue Caddy. I tried to follow them, but I couldn't keep up, plus I didn't want them to see me so I fell behind and lost them. I pedaled around her block about ten thousand times waiting for her to come back, but I gave up and decided to head home.

That's when the right leg of my Levis got caught in the bike chain, and bam, I met concrete. I couldn't get up with my leg stuck under the bike and lay there for a minute, pissed, watching the front tire spin round and round while I went nowhere. To get up, I had to struggle with the bike and ripped my pant cuff trying to get it loose from the chain. Of course, the chain came off the bike's pedal gear and, after too much struggling with the greasy thing, I couldn't get it back on and limp-walked the bike home.

Sunday, after fixing the bike, I wheeled over to Grace's place again, wheeling around her neighborhood, hoping she'd come out. Nothing. When I felt like her neighbors might be getting suspicious of me hanging out and maybe call the cops, I left and returned Ted's bike.

"So, what did the spy master discover about his lady love today?"

"Go ahead. Think I'm a dork. I don't care."

"Like the song on the radio says, 'Falling in love with love is playing the fool'."

"Funny."

"I just feel sorry for you in your self-made misery."

The school week dragged by but nothing much happened. I managed to catch Grace walking the halls, or talking with friends. No boys, just girls. That kept me encouraged.

One day, I did catch the bus again just to be around her. Instead of waiting for her stop, I got off before she did. I ran most of the way and got to her house just as she walked in her front door. I walked up and down her block a few times, but she never came back out, so I high-tailed it home.

But Friday at school, I hit it lucky. I happened to overhear some girls asking Grace if she wanted to go with them Saturday up the river road to Blue Pool. They told her it was where a lot of us hung out, picnicked, went swimming. When I heard her say yes, my body felt juiced. This could be my chance.

Saturday, I talked Ted into hiking up to Blue Pool with me in the morning. It was something we did pretty often anyway. I didn't mention that Grace and friends would be coming sometime. I didn't want to get into his stalking-frame-of-mind accusations.

Like I said, Blue Pool is part of an abandoned quarry hidden behind some wild shrubbery set back in the cliffs. Once you make your way through the growth and under some rusty barbed-wire fence, you come across a nice sized circular pool of water cleaner than the river. With not much room around the edge of the water, you had to suffer togetherness with whoever was there.

I saw one or two familiar faces, guys, but not Grace and her group. I started to worry they might have changed their minds. But I didn't need to worry. Soon their girl talk could be heard before they came through the bush. Then one by one they popped out like the brush was giving birth to young girls. One, two, three, then Grace, and then Mary Ann. When they got closer to me and Ted, Mary Ann waved and yelled a "hi, guys."

Ted let out, "Ladies! Howdy-do."

I was myself and just waved. All the girls looked at us to see who Mary Ann was greeting. My eyes wouldn't let go of Grace. She wore a man's white dress shirt, hanging loose, sleeves rolled up. The shirttail almost covered her dark blue shorts. I remembered those smooth, tanned legs from that tennis outfit she wore in the store. She had on brown penny loafers, and I wondered why someone hadn't told her to wear better hiking shoes. A couple of the other girls wore men's dress shirts, too. A fad, I guessed.

The moment of truth. What do I do now? How is music going to help me in this situation? Then Ted jumped the gun. "Hey, Mary Ann. Introduce your friends."

We sort of gathered around and Mary Ann went through the niceties. I half-heard and sort of knew the names of the other girls, a Peggy and a Joyce, don't remember the other one. Just Grace. She looked right at me and I knew she had no idea we'd met at the store or in the hall that first day of school. But she smiled those perfect Pepsident-white teeth and said, "Hi," velvet eyes giving me the once over.

Then, Ted, never one lost for words, asks Grace, knowing full well the answer, if this is her first time coming to Blue Pool.

She gives the answer we all know while I'm pissed because I didn't think of asking.

But it broke the ice, and she explained just about everything I wanted to know: her family had moved here from Chicago in June; her dad was a lawyer-politician type (her father knew the governor); she was an only child; her mother was still getting their house organized after the move; her family just joined the country club and she wanted to learn how to play golf; she loved tennis; took ballet lessons; so far, she liked the school; hoped to go to Harvard like her dad; played the piano and oboe; liked some popular music, but mostly she played classical stuff.

I began to feel very far away from her even though I was now practically sitting next to her.

When she asked what the big deal was about Blue Pool, Ted started to talk, but from somewhere I found myself cutting him off and my usually moth-filled mouth started moving and I blurted out everything I knew about the weird bird myths and the dangers of jumping off the cliff into the pool.

I guess I finished abruptly, because it got quiet for a minute.

Then Mary Ann chimed in. "He's right. It's really dangerous. You could get killed. Nobody wants to jump from up there."

I saw Grace look up at the top of the cliff.

Her words still stick in my ears. "That would take a lot of guts."

"I'd do it."

I'm not sure where my words came from, but out they came. Some laughing followed.

"Yeah, sure you would" kind of things.

Grace put an end to the talk. "I dare you. Do it. Right now."

Not really what I wanted to hear from her.

Thinking back, it seemed a long time before I hit the water. Maybe my memory is off, maybe I'm making this up, but while I was falling...all the lyrics to the song Ted mentioned stuck in my head...I think I sang them...falling...falling in love with love...juvenile fancy...playing the fool....

Here's what they tell me 'cause I don't remember it all. When I popped out of the water, there was blood all over my face and I was what they call semi-conscious. Ted and someone else helped me out of the water. Lots of talk about the blood on me. Must have hit and scraped my face on a rock under water, they said. Then more about the blood and maybe get me to a doctor. They tried to stop the blood over my forehead gash with my tee shirt but it was now all red wet. Mary Ann, surprise, had driven the girls to Blue Pool in her dad's car and volunteered to drive me wherever Ted suggested. Ted said the hospital. I said home. They took me home. Parents took me to the doctor. Stitches. Bad, but not as bad as it looked. Probably a slight concussion. Lots of scrapes on my legs. Bed a couple of days. Parental what-were-you-thinking lecture.

Mom wouldn't let me go to school for a week. Ted called a couple of times to see how I was, filled me in on what I didn't remember. Said I'd made a name for myself. Told him I didn't want to know what it was. I thanked him for his help, told him to thank Mary Ann for the ride. That reminded him she said to tell me I owe her a new towel. Seems my blood ruined hers. No talk of Grace.

And here's the thing. And I can't explain it. I left or lost my feelings about Grace back in Blue Pool. Strange. As fast as my interest in her hit me, it left just as fast. It's like that deep water baptized me and washed away my...what?

Don't know.

I just know I came out of Blue Pool on the other side of elsewhere and still have the scar to prove it.

CHAPTER 7

"Hard to Say I'm Sorry"

I was about seventeen at the time, and other than horsing around, I'd never hit anyone before, not in the face with my fist. As I watched blood run down over his mouth, his chin, onto his white T- shirt, his cupped hands trying to catch the bleeding, recurring mixtures of panic, regret, fear, shame, disbelief and a touch of unfamiliar boldness swirled through me.

I did warn him, though.

Sort of.

But he didn't listen.

I told him, "Call me that one more time, Tyler, and you'll be sorry," not sure myself what I meant.

"Oooh, and what's Four Eyes going to do about...."

I didn't let him finish his sentence.

To be honest, I didn't know at that moment that I would do what I'd wanted to do all week. For days, this smart-ass Tyler, about my age, had been calling my friend Kenny and me "Four Eyes," because we were nearsighted and had to wear glasses when we did certain camp activities, like archery or wildlife identification. I'd only had eye glasses for about a month, and I admit wearing them did embarrass me, and made me feel a little wimpy.

I can't say I cared much for Boy Scout camp, but my parents gave more credence to the organization than I did, so off they sent me for three weeks of sunburn and poison ivy. I managed to tolerate it, though. It helped that I knew guys from school that had been assigned to my cabin: Kenny, Dan and Ralph. I don't know why they call it a cabin. It's just one of those raised wooden floors with tent covering.

Trouble was, Tyler and some of his friends were not helping to make camp fun. Little stuff became big stuff. Like, if Kenny or I had trouble recognizing a bird in a tree being pointed out by the counselor, or couldn't recognize something in the distance, Tyler would snicker and make a crack like, "Put your glasses on, Four Eyes. That's a bird up there, not a plane or Superman." Once, seeing me drop my glasses out of the case, he said, "Four Eyes need a little help?" and when I bent over to get them, he knocked me off balance pretending he was trying to help me. And if we weren't wearing our glasses, he'd make a quip like, "Where's your guide dog?" Once he referred to us as "the blind leading the blind."

Why he had it in for Kenny and me, I don't know. Just one of that kind, I guess. Picture the standard movie street-gang bully who gets his kicks picking on people and you'll see Tyler, the clichéd bully. He enjoyed his role. He no doubt figured Kenny and me for a couple of pushovers, that we'd take whatever he dished out. Even more irritating, his tent pals laughed along with him, giving him an encouraging ringleader status.

I only slipped on my glasses when I had to. So, one day I tried doing archery without them and missed the target altogether. Tyler didn't skip a beat.

"Put your glasses on, Four Eyes, or you'll kill one of us."

So, that's when I warned him. He didn't stop, and now there he stood, bleeding.

What really surprised me was an unfamiliar surge of dominance that overcame me as I stood before my bloodied tormentor. Fists closed, my body feeling more excitement than my brain, I warned him further. "If you ever call Kenny or me Four Eyes again, you'll get more than a bloody nose."

How easy those words slid out of my mouth, like I'd prepared all my life for this one powerful moment. Me, a skinny hundred-ten-pound model for those before pictures in Charles Atlas body building advertisements, now threatening even more bodily harm to someone who physically had it over me. What alien world had I punched myself into?

No words came from Tyler. Just blood. His friends gathered around him to look at the damage and in disbelief at me. Still riding high, I gave them my best "Okay, who's next?" look.

Rick, one of the counselors, saw us gathered, came over and asked what happened. That's when my ballooned macho-boy feelings deflated, opening room for fear and apprehension. I was in deep shit now. The powers that be would call my parents to come get me. I'd get kicked out of camp, maybe even the Boy Scouts. Maybe I'd done more physical damage to him than a bloody nose. Tyler's parents would no doubt sue mine. One stupid microsecond loss of emotional control and now I had to pay for it, maybe for the rest of my life.

No one said anything for a moment. Then one of Tyler's buddies told Rick the obvious, "Tyler has a bloody nose."

"Let me see." Rick took a look, holding Tyler's head back. "You get nose bleeds often?"

Tyler nodded.

"You okay, Tyler?" Rick asked. Tyler nodded again, still silent.

Shit. Here's where he tells Rick. Taking a scout scarf from around his neck, Rick told Tyler to hold it against his nose and keep his head back. "One of you help him up to the first-aid tent. The rest of you get back to your cabins and get your walking sticks. Meet at the lodge in fifteen minutes. We've scheduled a nature hike for this afternoon."

The group broke up, but not before Tyler gave me a narrow-eyed look. But he didn't talk. The idea of confessing to Rick and not waiting for the inevitable crossed my mind. Be sensible and get it over with. Just claim an unplanned spur of the moment loss of control got the better of me. Declare it an example of a scout's honorable defense against bullying. Or, just say you're sorry and apologize to Tyler.

But I wasn't sorry, not really.

Waiting won out. Back in our cabin to get our walking sticks, I got another surprise. Before I could say anything about regrets, the guys started congratulating me.

"Hey, we got a regular Raging Bull in our midst," Kenny said, feigning a punch at my shoulder.

"Yeah, that was unbelievable," Dan said. "Nice work, man."

"That asshole deserved it," Kenny said. "Wish I'd had the guts to punch him. You've got my thanks."

Ralph, who never spoke much in our group, said, "Did you see all that blood. Wow! For sure, he won't call you guys Four Eyes anymore."

"Hey, how's your hand?" Kenny asked. "Does it hurt?"

I noticed for the first time my blood-skinned knuckles bore slight teeth scrapes and began to throb.

"Naw, it's nothing," I lied.

Their surprise admiration for what I'd done polished my ego more than a bit. I wasn't used to being the center of attention. But it didn't bury my concern over why Tyler hadn't told on me. Neither had his friends. I couldn't get the why of it, and that worried me. I couldn't believe that Tyler would let this go.

All through our nature hike, minus Tyler, of course, my mind kept repeating my hitting Tyler and surprise he hadn't tattled. And it bothered me all through dinner, where I kept slyly eyeing Tyler sitting among his followers. He didn't seem any the worse for wear that I could see. Cotton in one nostril. At least he'd stopped bleeding. That's also when I realized he had a good fifteen pounds on me. And maybe a little taller. Watching them convinced me that he and his friends were planning something. And I wasn't going to like it. Too late now. I couldn't take back what I'd done.

After dinner, Rick requested our attention for an announcement.

Oh, oh, I thought, here's where I get my comeuppance in front of the entire camp, an example of undisciplined, bad scouting behavior.

"Listen up," Rick said. "Tonight is a special night for you Boy Scouts. One of you from each tent unit will be elected by secret ballot for the prestigious honor of indoctrination into the Order of the Arrow."

We all quieted down.

As most of you know, the Order of the Arrow is a service organization of the Boy Scouts dedicated to four purposes. Those of you selected will be chosen by your peers as one who best exemplifies the scout oath and law, for camp spirit, for habits of helpfulness, and for leadership in the best scouting tradition. Those of you selected tonight will be subject to an ordeal. You'll be 'tapped out,' taken to an isolated place to sleep alone, then brought back in the morning to work all day on a designated camp project."

He was interrupted by several voices.

"What does tapped out mean?"

"What's so great about sleeping in the woods alone?"

"Yeah. That's an honor?"

Some guys laughed.

"Okay, knock it off now and let me finish. In the morning, the ones selected will not be allowed to talk until sunset or until the designated project is finished. They will be given only one meal during that time."

"Doesn't sound like an honor to me," someone offered. "More like a punishment," another said.

More laughs.

"Wrong!" Rick interrupted the mumbles. "This is serious scouting. It's an ordeal meant to see if the one selected is worthy of being a member of the Order. It's an honor to be selected. Remember that. Your job is to select someone who can survive the ordeal and will do the organization honor, one who shows the best of the Boy Scout tradition. Now go back to your cabins and take a secret ballot on your choice to be tapped out. The secret voting forms are by the door. When it's dark, a bonfire will be lit on the main field. In order of your cabin numbers, you will line up single file facing the fire. And you will remain silent. You'll learn more later. Now, dismissed."

I heard someone say as we left, "Vote for me, guys."

"That'll be the day!"

Back in our cabin, we discussed the "ordeal." None of us liked the idea of being taken out in the woods some place and left alone for the night. Our field trips had shown us some of the wild life, like snakes that might get in your sleeping bag, all kinds of lizards, mice, creepy bugs that could crawl over you face while sleeping, and deer droppings which meant there were probably wild cats hunting at night.

"Yeah, but it's a badge of honor," Ralph said. "My brother got selected last year. He says it's a big deal and a mark of distinction to be in the Order."

"Wasn't he scared…you know…sleeping alone in the woods?" Kenny asked.

"At first. But he figured the counselors weren't going to put him in any real danger. It was just part of the initiation." Then Ralph added. "He felt proud to be selected. He's part of a special national group."

We learned from Ralph that being "tapped out" meant that if you were selected by your tent mates one of the counselors, running back and forth along the line of scouts, suddenly stopped in front of you and tapped you on the shoulder. The "tap," however, was hard enough to knock you backwards off balance where someone behind would catch you and take you away, not to be seen again until the next night at dinner.

It sounded to me like Ralph would like to be selected, so I voted for him.

I wasn't worried they'd vote for me. My punching Tyler did not show exemplary Order of the Arrow behavior.

That night, when the bonfire lit up the sky, the whole camp turned in our votes to Rick and then lined up facing the fire. No moon and scattered clouds helped give the huge fire an eerie feel to the night. All the electricity in the camp turned off, the bonfire supplied our only light. We were made to stand in solemn silence, ordered never to turn away from facing the fire no matter what might happen. If you spoke, snickered or sneezed, you would be sent to your cabin in the dark, alone.

At first, the only sounds came from the snap of the flying sparks or an occasional fall of a burning log. After too long a time just standing there, a cry, like from a coyote, pierced the silence. Another louder wail came in response, followed by another long moment of silence.

Then, the shrill of jungle bird-like sounds shattered the air and became mixed with human evil laughter, growing louder and louder. Abruptly the noises stopped and soft drumming began, like Native American tom-toms in the movies, gradually building in pace and pitch.

Boom-boomboom...Boom-boomboom...BOOM-BOOMBOOM...

At one end of the line, a figure holding a burning torch and dressed like a Plains Indian, feathered war bonnet and all, let out a piercing yell. We couldn't help but turn or heads. He started running from one end of the line to the other, back and forth, back and forth until he stopped dead in front of someone I couldn't see and tapped him.

Then he started running back and forth again, up and down the line, all of us wondering where he would stop again. I could hear the sound of the flaming torch trying to keep up with the runner as he passed by me. A moment later, he ran past me again.

When he came running back from the other end of the line, the runner stopped right in front of me, his torch emphasizing his face covered in streaks of red and black colored paint.

Wait! No! Not me!

Shoved backwards into the arms of someone behind me, I got pulled away from the line by two others dressed as Indians with painted faces. I kept thinking they'd made a mistake.

Before I knew it, they blindfolded me and warned me not to speak. Even with my eyes covered I could tell one of them had a flashlight, and they were leading me into the deep, dark unknown where I most definitely did not want to go.

Branches from bushes brushed and snapped against me. I stumbled over rocks and roots I couldn't see, but my captors kept me from falling. I don't know how long we walked or in what direction, but when we reached our destination, they took off my blindfold. When my eyes adjusted to the flashlight beam, I saw we'd stopped in a small clearing, waist-high shrubs all around. The light shone on my sleeping bag on the ground.

"Stay here until we get you in the morning." Then they and the bobbing light disappeared into the night.

The "brave boy" who attacked Tyler had a strong fear of being alone, barely able to see anything but some scattered stars breaking through the dark grey sky. I had no options but to stay put until they rescued me in the morning. Afraid to move, I sat on my sleeping bag, then immediately jumped up and shook it out as best I could. I didn't know if they had brought it with us or had placed it here earlier. My body tensed even more as I imagined copperheads and bull snakes already in my sleeping bag, waiting to coil themselves around my legs; or maybe field mice, blue-racer lizards scurrying over my face and through my hair; ticks, chiggers and mosquitoes feasting on my helpless body. And what about wild cats? Were they really in these woods?

I stood in a frozen stupor holding my sleeping bag off the ground, turning in circles, peering into the blackness, wondering if those were wild eyes over there staring back at me. My glasses were back in the tent. Didn't matter; Four Eyes couldn't see very far in the dark anyway.

I jumped as the crickets surrounding me started their incessant serenade. Then frogs did their thing, with no concern for harmony. Together, both groups would sound off in the dark silence, then stop. Why? What did the crickets and frogs know that I didn't? That rustling noise in the bushes behind me. What could it be? Crickets started again, then the frogs, one group trying to out noise the other. No doubt they were communicating, telling every living wild creature out there my vulnerable location.

Rattled, I had to decide. Stand all night holding my bag, or get in it. Not much of a choice. I shook it out one more time, and then placed it on the ground. Shoes and all, I crawled in, failed to find a soft ground spot and pulled the zipper up to my neck, leaving as little space as possible for any critter wanting to join me. That lasted for less than five minutes. Too hot wrapped up like a mummy, I had to unzip my bag, leaving me exposed and defenseless to whatever lurked out there in the wild.

I lay there swatting mosquitoes doing their best to infiltrate my eyes, ears and nose, wondering why the guys elected me for OA. I had a few merit badges, but I was no hot-to-trot Boy Scout. My fellow tent mates knew that. I'm a city boy, not a nature boy. They betrayed me, that's what. They did this to me so they wouldn't have to suffer the ordeal. Traitors. Chickens, too afraid to go through this ordeal, they voted for me. And after what I did for Kenny. This is how he thanks me?

Wait. Maybe Tyler's behind this. He and his buddies voted for me to get revenge.

Or maybe Kenny and the guys voted for me because I stood up to Tyler' bullying. Am I the only one who voted for Kenny? He'd want to be here. This isn't right. I don't deserve the honor.

But then, on a cosmic karma scale, I could look at this as payback punishment for punching Tyler. I suppose I should be sorry I hit him, but then again why should I be? He'd quit bleeding, seemed fine at dinner, and he'd be sleeping on a bed in his safe tent with human beings, not out in the shadowy whazoo with wild life and troublesome thoughts.

Along with the hard ground, my fear of the wild, and my anxiety that Tyler would get even somehow, kept me uncomfortably awake late into the night.

I did fall asleep at some restless point, because just at daybreak, a rustling noise scared me awake. Rick appeared from the bush and stood over me.

"Bring your bag and follow me."

I started to say something, but remembered, no talking allowed. I rolled up my bag and followed him through the bush. In less than three minutes, we were back at the camp's main building. My captors last night must have walked me in circles making me think I was being taken far into the boonies.

Still barely light, the only ones up were the cooks and the counselors. Rick took my sleeping bag. "Sit over there on the steps. When the other two get here, we'll explain the project for the day. Remember, no talking."

I'd forgotten others got tapped out last night. I sat down as directed and wondered what the project would be and who I'd be working with. Groggy and bushed from fear and lack of sleep, I felt relieved I'd made it through the night. All I had to do was get through the day. I started feeling my hunger and thirst. And still sore at Kenny and the guys for electing me, I couldn't believe they were really honoring me. Since when do you get honors for giving someone a bloody nose?

Another tapped camper soon arrived with orders to sit next to me. His curly red hair and freckled face looked familiar, but I didn't know his name. His nickname had to be Red. He nodded. I nodded back and moved over a bit on the step for him. I wondered how three of us could work through the day on a project without talking.

Then the third person we were waiting for arrived. Every muscle in my tired body became rigid.

Tyler didn't look happy to see me either. Our stares shared our surprise, then, as directed, he sat down on the step next to Red.

"Listen up," Rick said. "You'll each get a canteen of water to last you the day, so go easy on drinking. At noon, we'll bring you some lunch. That'll be it until dinner, unless you haven't finished your project by then. In that case, you won't eat again until you do finish. Understood?"

We all nodded. I wondered if he was trying to trip us up and get us to speak, because I almost did. My mind snapped, crackled and popped as he spoke. Spend the day working with Tyler, anticipating his revenge at any moment? And if Tyler had been picked for the

OA, what did that say about me being picked? Neither one of us belonged in the OA.

"Now, for your project," Rick went on. "We want a flagpole erected in front of the dining hall. The exact spot has been marked. Over there," he pointed to the side of the building, "you'll find everything you need – instructions, tools, shovels, wheel barrow, cement mix, the pole pieces and the sleeves, cleats and pulleys for running the flag up and down." He paused and smiled. "Any questions?"

Install a flagpole? I didn't know about the other two, but I had no idea how to run a flag up a pole let alone erect one.

I tried to ignore looking at Tyler as Red took the lead and headed toward the tools. We stood around looking at what we had to work with. Red noticed printed instructions in the wheelbarrow. He read silently, showed them to us, and pointed to number one on the list. Our first task: dig a circled hole sixteen inches round and thirty-six inches deep where someone had already marked it out on the ground.

Maybe because I didn't want the shovel in Tyler's hands as a potential weapon, I grabbed it and started digging the hole. Maybe I just wanted to get going on the project. Maybe it was an excuse for not having to look at Tyler. Maybe I didn't want Tyler to take the lead on the project. Or, maybe I didn't want Tyler's nose to start bleeding. Whatever the real reason, I started to dig.

With a lot of finger pointing as to who would do what, we worked well together once we realized Red seemed to know what he was doing. Somehow, Tyler and I managed to avoid any angry confrontation as the three of us took on the task. In fact, he acted like he didn't know me. And that bothered me.

At noon, they brought us each an egg sandwich and a glass of milk. We rested a bit after eating, then went back to work. There was no shade where they wanted the pole and the July sun didn't make the task any easier. By evening, our canteens empty, we finished our project. All that was left was inserting the pole, now crowned with an ornamental eagle, into the pole sleeve in the cemented hole. The directions stated the sleeve should dry in the cement overnight before inserting the pole.

Pleased and proud to be finished, we moved off into some shade, stretched out on the ground and waited for the counselors to release us from our vows of silence. As much as possible, I tried not to let Tyler see me watching him. I kept wondering what payback plans he had and when I'd get my due. I wanted to be ready. The whole time we worked together Tyler could have found ways to physically hurt me. He could have "accidentally slipped" and driven the screwdriver through my finger when I held the cleats to the pole. Or, he could have run the wheelbarrow over my foot. Or, hit me when he swung pieces of the eighteen-foot aluminum pole around. I spent the whole day on guard, waiting for him to strike.

Rick noticed us doing nothing and started chewing us out.

"What do you three think you're doing? You're not finished. I don't see a flagpole reaching for the sky. You're not through here until that pole is up and ready for the flag."

Apparently, the counselors didn't know the concrete sleeve needed to dry overnight before inserting the pole. Since we couldn't talk, none of us spoke up. Still, I felt we should let them know somehow. Maybe I should point to the written directions they gave us. Do something.

Rick stood there, waiting for us to move. Red motioned for us to pick up the pole. So, looking like the statue of those soldiers raising the flag on Iwo Jima, we followed orders and stuck the pole in the sleeve.

The counselors congratulated us on a job well done, released us from our ordeal, told us there would be an Order of the Arrow award ceremony after dinner, then left us.

Before we split up, I asked, "Should we tell 'em? I mean about the cement drying?" Tyler shrugged and smiled. "Hey, it's on them. They told us to put the pole in."

I started to disagree, but Red came back with, "Boy, I can't wait to see their faces."

"They're not going to like it," I said, trying not to sound like a four-eyed wimp.

"Hey, they told us not to talk. Besides, they should've read the directions themselves," Red said, grinning and wiggling his eyebrows impishly. He took my silence as an agreement with the conspiracy.

"Nice working with your guys," he said, and took off. Tyler laughed and left me standing there not certain of one damn thing.

Not true. I was certain the three of us were not worthy of being in the Order of the Arrow.

On my way back to my tent, my unsettled mind wouldn't leave me alone. I knew we should not have put the pole in the sleeve. I should've said something. I could say something now, but Red and Tyler would think I was a fink. Plus, I had spent last night afraid of the dark and worried all today about Tyler's next move that never came. I shifted blame back on my tent buddies. I thought of several scenarios I might create to let them know how pissed I was. I could say nothing when they asked questions, just act sullen and angry. Maybe I should yell and cuss at them for voting for me. I could call Kenny a four-eyed traitor, or call them all sissies, cowards for being afraid of going through the ordeal themselves.

When I walked in, I didn't get a chance for any of that.

"Hey, look! Our hero's home from the war," Kenny yelled. "Congratulations!" Slaps on the back. A sense of more guilt ran through me knowing Kenny really wanted the honor and deserved it more than I did.

"We knew you could handle the ordeal," Ralph said, giving me a look of admiration. "You should have known we'd pick you."

I looked at Ralph and thought, "It should have been you."

"We had faith in you," Dan said. "Here, have a Milky Way. You earned it."

My anger diminished with their smiles and respect.

"How was it out there in the dark last night?" Kenny asked.

"Dark," I said, flippantly. Then I offered a bit of subterfuge. "No big deal, really. I slept great until they woke me up this morning."

(What prompted me to lie?)

"We saw you working with Tyler today. How'd that go?" Dan asked.

I shrugged as if I deserved their admiration; then my swollen head took over. "No problem. I think he's too afraid of me to try anything."

(Listen to me!)

"Yeah, he learned his lesson," Ralph assured me.

"Maybe." I took a bite of the Milky Way, but the taste was lost as I tried to chew on my lies.

Later, on the way up to the lodge for my Order of the Arrow award, I noticed, even without my glasses, the tilt in the flagpole.

CHAPTER 8

"Cuts Like a Knife"

Through most of high school, I never had a steady girlfriend. My painful, upsetting adventures with Grace put me on guard. I also saw eye glasses as an embarrassment. If, as the saying goes, men seldom make passes at girls who wear glasses, wouldn't girls feel the same way about boys? I did my best to only wear them when I couldn't see very far.

Then in my senior year, I met Suzanne.

To tell the truth, I don't remember much about Suzanne's face. I know she was almost as tall as I was then, a dishwater blond, thin, but not skinny, strong-headed, a dancing partner, and that's about it. Strange after spending so much time with her that I can't picture her now, but it's probably psychological, and I really don't care at this point. Despite all that, she had a profound effect on my life.

I met her at the Dungeon, a teenage hangout sponsored by an Episcopal church, a safe place where you could just hang out, meet friends and dance to recorded music. I dropped by the Dungeon whenever I had nothing else to do and sometimes met Ted.

On this particular night, I didn't see anyone I knew and was about to leave when some girl I'd never met approached me.

"Hi."

I said "hi" back, trying to figure out if we knew each other. I only needed my glasses for long distance, so I had slipped mine off and put them I my jacket pocket.

"Do you like to dance?" she asked.

"Yeah. Sure."

"Well, see that girl over there by the Coke machine?"

I looked. I'd never seen her before from what I could tell. "Yeah."

"She'd like to dance with you."

Basically, I'm shy and this whole scene felt unfamiliar. It took me a minute.

"Why doesn't she ask me herself?"

"She's too shy."

"What's her name?"

"Suzanne. She thinks you're cute, but don't tell her I said that."

I must have liked her looks and felt a bit flattered by the attention. So, yes.

And that was the beginning of a steady dating period.

We had an attraction for each other, and I considered her "my girl." I could easily have been jealous if I'd thought she dated anyone else, but as far as I knew she didn't. Most of our dating consisted of movies, dances, sitting in my dad's '48 Plymouth sedan listening and singing to radio music and what then was called "heavy necking." It got comically awkward sometimes, since my driver's license required glasses for driving and I tried to discreetly remove them at the appropriate time, if you know what I mean. I had to hold myself back from going too far. I always went home horribly horny after a date with her.

Back then, I found my testosterone troublesome and complex, mostly because I placed girls I liked on a pedestal created through movie portrayals, and my shyness or lack of confidence. (All of that!) On the one hand, I would have loved nothing better than to "go all the way" with Suzanne. I realize now that I had placed all my naïve Christian and romantic feelings about the opposite sex in her. We never really talked about anything of much substance, just floated along in a sort of dreamy existence. At least, I did.

Then the night before I left for college, Suzanne and I were parked in my dad's car in a lonely spot up the river road making out when Suzanne surprised me.

"Let's get in the back," she said.

Her words detonated an explosion in my imagination.

She didn't wait for me to say anything. She climbed over into the back seat. I just sat, holding on to the steering wheel. Had my time come?

"Don't you want to?" She tugged on my arm.

Want to? It's all my young blood dreamed about, thought about, desired. Yes, I wanted to. I climbed over and felt my body resting on hers in awkward anticipation and anxiety. It wasn't clear to me what I should do next. Keep kissing? Feel her breasts? I was embarrassed at my hardness. Yet she seemed to know, surprising me all the more. She guided my hand up her dress and between her thighs until I had my fingers where they'd never been before. I tensed with excitement at the strange, unfamiliar moist feeling. Suzanne was pulling on my zipper. I was on my way to the moon. I was living the impossible dream, about to enter that prohibited yet always beckoning unknown territory.

Then...

"I can't," I said, pulling myself away from potential ecstasy.

"What?" I felt Suzanne tense beneath me. "Why? I thought you wanted to."

Yes, why, why, why? I did want to. Why'd I stop?

I searched for something to say. "I don't have a ... you know ... thing ... you might get pregnant." True, but not the reason. I hated myself for stopping, feeling like an unknown force had control of me.

"It's okay. You don't need to worry. I want to," she assured me.

Words, not really mine, babbled out, "I ... I think we should save ourselves for the person we marry."

What was I saying? Did I really believe that? Some religious Sunday School brainwashing embedded in me more deeply than I knew came alive at the wrong moment, and it sounded weak and pathetic and foolish. And I felt all of it.

She pushed me away, straightened her clothes and climbed back in the front seat. She sat there, saying nothing, while I tried to discern if she was embarrassed for suggesting it or mad at me for declining.

I drove her home in hard silence, trying to unscramble some sense into what I'd just done. Should I apologize? Could I change my mind? Had I hurt her feelings? What was she thinking? Was I right or wrong in giving up a chance at what every male friend I knew wished for, talked about, including me?

I look back on a boy-man filled with church teachings that pounded in the notion that you should save sex for marriage, be pure for your wife. I grew up sitting on a church pew. Hundreds of sermons, Sunday school lessons, youth league, summer church camp, all did their number on me. At one adolescent point I thought I might want to become a minister. Then there was the problem of getting the girl pregnant. That could be a sin, or end up in one of those shot-gun weddings I'd heard about. I thought about my friend Roger who had to get married to a girl he didn't even like. Were these good reasons? All that, mixed up with a shy fear of actually doing it, held me back, and bothered me like a scab on a never-healing sore. At any rate, I'd permitted the disease of religion to relieve the burden of decision, and it failed me in my hour of desire. Jesus did not love me.

The moment I stopped at her house, Suzanne got out of the car, slammed the door, and leaned in the window. "I'm not a virgin, you know," and made it to her front door before I could absorb what she'd said.

Her words splintered in my head and then burst into flames of questions all the way home and all through the night. Did I believe her? Had she been seeing someone else besides me? When did she lose her virginity? Did I know him? If it were true, then what was my relationship with her all about? What must she think of me? I wasn't sure what to think about myself. Why was I holding back but she wasn't? Had all those religious teachings begrudged me of pleasure? Was I just a religious fool? Was I a sexual coward and using what I'd been taught as an excuse? Did it really matter if you weren't a virgin when you got married? I felt I'd stepped into a foreign country and didn't understand the language. What was I? (Yes. All those questions.)

Sometime late in the night, as the burning questions became embers, the only answer I had was a scorched awareness that I was a bona fide brainwashed simpleton, a halfwit, a blockhead, a nincompoop. The ship had sailed without me, and I was probably the only virgin in my senior class.

I didn't know if I should call Suzanne or just slink into my after-school job at the grocery store. I fought a lingering desire, on and off, to contact her.

Then, one day while working at the store, there she stood with a friend. Odd thing, she looked familiar but unfamiliar to me.

She didn't say hello or introduce her friend, just stared at me and said as if I weren't there, "He's the one I told you about, the one who wants to save himself for marriage."

Her friend cupped her hand at Suzanne's ear and whispered something. They stared at me for a moment, then, with hurtful little smirks, left me standing there holding a bunch of bananas.

CHAPTER 9

"I'm Beginning to See the Light"

Okay, I got over it, as well as accepting that I was the only virgin in my college freshman class.

Anyway...

Picture this: a young man, eighteen years old, sits in the back row of a university remedial Freshman English composition class. His legs are drawn up underneath his student desk chair; he has no awareness of the rapid jiggling of his crossed feet. Both elbows rest on the desktop supporting his drooped head pressed between his sweating hands. His slouched body tenses. His stomach wants to give back his breakfast. His eyes close and his whole being craves entrance to a safer dimension as the instructor begins to read to the class the young student's first essay.

To refer to this young man as a student is overly generous, because I, yes, that very person just described, was that proverbial naked babe lost in the woods of academia.

Unprepared for college, I blamed my poor high school education on World War II. During the early and mid '40s, all the best teachers, surely the ones who might have inspired me, had been drafted into the service or taken on jobs of war that paid more than a teacher's salary. That left only ancient spinsters and one-armed men like my PE teacher to expose me to their priggish brand of wisdom and knowledge. What, after all, did these depressing dregs have to teach a young teenager who feared he would soon be living the military life he witnessed in newsreels and Hollywood propaganda war movies.

There is, of course, another side to my educational narrative; no teacher or subject provoked my learning stimulation. So, I drifted and day-dreamed through those years, far more interested in my growing puzzlement of the opposite sex, or hanging with my friends, or disappearing into the movie fantasies and radio shows. My brilliance lay outside academia. With great pride, I impressed my friends by telling them the name of almost every song and singer or musical group on the radio after hearing the first few bars.

By the time I was sixteen, my work at the grocery store allowed me to leave school early in the afternoon. I was making a little money, I had a girlfriend (Suzie), and most importantly, the use of my dad's car at night. I couldn't wait to graduate so I could go to work full time.

Enter my dad, who had other plans for me.

A few weeks after graduation, he handed some papers to me and told me to fill them out.

"What's all this?" I asked.

"Your college scholarship application."

"Scholarship? What scholarship?"

Now, granted I wasn't a swift student, but I knew enough to know you need good grades or some athletic prowess to get a scholarship to any college.

"I went to see your principal, Mr. Lemon. I wanted to know if there was any way you could get into college somewhere."

"You what?"

In my head, I screamed in a very loud voice, "Where the hell do you get off doing this without saying anything to me? I have my own plans, and they do not include more meaningless schoolwork!"

Instead, since I was talking to my father, I tried to use reason. "But, Dad, my grades aren't that good. No school's going to let me in. And what about money?"

"I checked," he said. "Your grades aren't bad. Being in the Order of the Arrow is a plus, along with a recommendation from your employer. You qualify for what's called a 'normal' scholarship at

Southern Illinois University in Carbondale. Mr. Lemon said he could get a couple of your teachers to write recommendations for you."

Really, I wondered. Who might they be?

I brought up the money angle again. "Even with a scholarship, it would be too expensive. Room and board, books and stuff."

"I'll worry about that," he answered.

Too bewildered to say much, I looked at the papers without really seeing them. Then I looked at my dad wondering what in the world had gotten in to him. We'd never talked before about my attending college.

"Look, I knew you wouldn't look into this on your own, so I did. You may think you're all set working right now, but there are better things than spending your life putting other people's groceries in a bag. I never finished high school, and yes, I have a job. But it just pays the bills. I don't want you to end up working in that store the rest of your life. College will open doors you don't even know exist. You have a chance to do better than I did."

My protests against opening doors I had absolutely no desire to open didn't come to much in the end. This hotshot grocery clerk got his heels cooled and my sagacious father got his way.

And so, I went, a stranger in a strange land of ivory towers. My first two weeks of classes proved to me that I did not have much in the way of an educational background. My classmates seemed comfortable and able to relate to the materials and class discussions no matter what the course. I felt tangled in cobwebs of the unfamiliar and immersed myself in envy. Why hadn't my teachers taught me about these people, the places, the theories, the philosophies other students knew about? Maybe they did try while my head was busy hearing the likes of June Christy exploring "How High the Moon" or Glenn Miller down here on the ground with "Moonlight Serenade." Or thinking about girls like Grace. Those were things I understood. I didn't count on lasting more than one semester before returning to the grocery store where I felt I belonged.

Among all this uneasiness was my English composition class, a subject never dear to my heart. Naturally, I was placed in a Subject A class, meaning I didn't pass the placement test for a regular Freshman Comp course. My regard for the subject took an even deeper dip when the instructor gave us the first assignment: a five-hundred-word essay on hickory-nut hunting. I didn't know the difference between a hickory nut and a garbanzo bean. Does one even go hunting for hickory nuts?

Staring at a blank sheet of paper, an inarticulate, unprepared freshman waited for the Great God of Writing to zap my pen into action. Nothing happened, of course. Come on, I told myself. Where might I have seen hickory nuts growing? I found myself thinking about where I was the summer before the semester had started, wishing I were still there. As in many previous summers and weekends, I had hiked and climbed the bluffs along the Mississippi River near Alton. But I didn't remember seeing any hickory nut trees. But I had to write about something, so I began jotting down some of the things I did remember seeing on my many hikes: the wide, muddy river itself, backed up by the Alton dam with its frequent, slow-drifting barges; the train tracks on which my friends and I practiced balancing acts; the exploring of damp, cool caves in the bluffs; the snapping insect noises in the summer stillness; the copperheads sunning on the boulders; the big, colorful Piasa bird said to have originally been painted on a cliff wall by Indians over a hundred years ago.

Desperate for something to turn in to my English instructor, I began my essay by saying I started out to go hickory-nut hunting, describing my hikes as best I could. I think I even had rocks telling me hidden river history or some such and ended with a line similar to "I gathered no hickory nuts that day."

I could already see my paper given back with a note in red saying, "Please see me!" Or worse, "Who let you into college?"

And so it was that I found myself mortified and ready for humiliation when my instructor read my essay to the class. For a few moments the class was quiet when he finished reading. Then one of the students spoke up and said what was obviously wrong with it, "The essay's not even about the subject."

To which the instructor replied, "Yes, and that's what makes it so interesting."

Now, let your imagination run wild here with words describing the young man's palpable mixed feelings of shock, surprise, incredulity, astonishment, relief, even a bit of new-found, unknown pride as he uncrossed his legs, sat up in his chair giving the instructor his full attention.

When my essay was handed back, it had noticeable red marks, and it did say, "Please see me," but not for the reason I originally thought.

When I went to his office, I couldn't find a place to sit down. Books and folders were stacked high everywhere, some scattered on the floor. He moved a stack of them from a chair so I could sit.

"Sorry for the mess, I'm trying to re-organize things between home and office."

He was in his fifties, I guessed, but couldn't be sure. He looked tired. Bags under his eyes, like he'd been reading all night.

"You said on my paper you wanted to see me?" my voice showing timidity as I handed it to him.

He gave it a quick glance through glasses perched on his nose. "Right. Yes. I wanted to suggest you transfer to my regular Freshman English class."

Wait! What?

I thought it best to remind him.

"I, ah, I failed the English placement test."

He went on, unconcerned. "I think your writing shows some imagination. Your descriptions were quite vivid, and I think your writing could be better developed in my 10 o'clock class. I'd like to help you develop your writing skills. What do you say?"

A brilliant "Huh?" echoed in my head.

"What kind of writing would I have to do?" I couldn't think of anything else to say.

"Some imaginative pieces and some critiques of other writers." He picked out the textbook he used for the course, opened it to the table of contents and handed it to me.

It only added to my depressed feeling that I didn't belong in college.

He went on. "I want my students to read works by well-known writers, then discuss their works in class. You'll learn a lot about writing just reading their different approaches to subjects. Sometimes I'll have you write your views of their work. Sometimes I'll have you write your reactions to their views."

"I've never read most of these writers," I admitted. "I'm not very well read."

"Good time to learn, don't you think? That's why you're here, isn't it?"

I didn't know what to say.

He sensed my concerns. "Look, it's up to you, of course, and I don't want to force you into anything, but I wouldn't suggest you transfer if I didn't think you could handle it. I'll give you all the help I can."

His words of encouragement and confidence gave me the nervous courage to follow his lead. I transferred.

Every essay I wrote for him became a challenge for me to do even better. His office door was never closed to me, and I took advantage. I began to admire and respect him for what seemed to me a colossal erudition he so willingly shared. He helped me discover how to read beyond the words. This emphasis on writing and literature expanded as I began to realize their connections with my classes in psychology, history and philosophy.

I developed an unexpected joy in learning. My mentor found something in me I didn't know I possessed in the morass of my muddied mind—imagination and curiosity. He opened and restructured my mind, helped give it shape, and sent me on an enjoyable quest that hasn't yet ended. Sadly, and ashamedly, I don't remember my professor's name. I want to say Paul something. I've researched to no avail. Would that I could let him know how he changed my life.

In the midst of this, the Korean War interrupted my growing comfort with academia. I may have forgotten algebraic and science formulas, certain historical names and dates, psychological patterns, but those can be found through research. What I haven't forgotten, and never forget, is that the most important things I brought away from my educational beginning came from reading fiction. Reading novels, short stories, and poetry has shown me the truths of this complicated, mixed-up, imaginative human world.

This is not to say that reading literature is the answer to the world's problems. But it opened my eyes and heart to the diverse world outside my own. Understanding someone's feelings and beliefs could go a long way in bringing us together rather than driving us apart.

Now picture this: a man with grey hair sits comfortably and content in his favorite chair, feet up on a footstool. He places the novel he has just finished on the table beside him, his mind working to digest what he just read, and feeling thankful once again for that five-hundred-word essay on hickory nut hunting.

He takes another sip of Bailey's Irish Cream over ice.

"Good Golly, Miss Molly"

In 1949, Ted and I had gone our separate ways to college. Ted, with far better grades than mine, obtained a scholarship to Northwestern University. Back home during a sophomore semester break, we got together for our last hike up the river. Mostly, we bragged about girls we'd met, talked about how different college was from high school, the influence of the books we were reading. At that time, we both felt a connection to Sartre and existentialism. Was God dead? Was God ever alive? Was God male or female? What was consciousness? Were the bluffs we sat on, the river below us, real? Were the two of us seeing everything as identical images? How adult I felt discussing ideas college had planted in our heads.

But then we broached the Korean war mess and the country's fight against communism, which we really didn't understand and later learned was mostly lies anyway. What we did understand was the fact that we would be drafted soon. Neither of us liked the idea of going in the army, not from what we saw in newsreels and war movies. For a while, we sat in silence wondering what our futures held. I watched the quiet, drifting, grey-brown water below, aware that this might be the last time we would share our river adventures.

Ted raised a thorny issue.

"Do you think you could kill someone – I mean, like in a war?"

"I guess if I had to. Before they killed me, I'd hope." I'd never asked myself that question before.

"Imagine yourself in Korea. A Korean or Chinese soldier is coming at you, firing away. Does preservation take over? Is it automatic to shoot back? Would you freeze in fear? Do you think about the fact you're killing someone?"

"We'd get training for that, wouldn't we?"

"Yeah. Training to kill. Think about that. We're taught that 'Thou shalt not kill' here at home. Yet, we do kill. We give the death penalty to people who murder. We go in the army and they teach us how to kill. Why isn't that called murder?"

"I don't think you can call it murder when you kill someone who is trying to kill you."

"Okay, let's just call it 'taking a life.' When is it okay to take someone's life?"

"In war. Our enemies want to kill us, so we try to kill them first." I was beginning to doubt the simplicity of my words.

"War's really stupid, you know. Our so-called enemies are trained to kill us; we're trained to kill them. They probably don't want to fight any more than we do. But our politicians and generals, who never have to do the dirty work, tell guys like us to line up, be patriotic and kill some enemy who has been told by their politicians and generals to kill us. Whichever side has the most guys standing after the shooting wins. And we don't get a choice. Not really. You're labeled a coward or unpatriotic if you don't fight. But what have all the poor dead guys on either side won when it's all over?"

"I think it's more complicated than that." I didn't really know what I was talking about, but it had to be more complex than Ted's description. Yet, his simplistic explanation made some worry-sense to me.

"When they teach thou shalt not kill, they should put an asterisk at the end."

That sent us both into silence for a time.

Ted broke the quiet, shouting at the river. "Screw the army, Naytan! Korea's a land war. I'm joining the navy before the army makes us gun fodder."

I knew my draft number made me potential gun-fodder, too. Just as I'd jumped on that freight train with him, I jumped on Ted's idea and rather than go back to college, I joined the navy. I told my parents my decision, which they accepted reluctantly. I could see their worry for my safety, but I also sensed they felt proud, if that's the right word, of my volunteering.

Within weeks, I found myself at the Great Lakes Naval Training Center. It appeared many others felt as Ted and I did about not wanting to be drafted into the army. The navy had more recruits than they could handle. Hundreds of us had to sleep on cots in a gymnasium until they could clear enough barracks to accommodate us. If I remember correctly, it was three days before we received our uniforms and received placement in a company barracks.

Then I was confronted with my first naval engagement.

I had just made up my newly appointed bunk bed and stowed my uniform and gear. My mood had slipped from excitement at joining the navy to disappointment at being separated from Ted who was placed in a different company. I now felt alone, a growing apprehension regarding boot training, and homesickness starting to set in.

I couldn't help but notice three fellow recruits were eyeing me and conferring together. My body stiffened as they approached and blocked any movement on my part. Their looks gave me pause, and I had no idea who they were or what they wanted. And the demeanor of these particular three did not convey, "welcome sailor." Two of them had "Fogerty" stenciled on their shirts; the other name I don't remember.

The two Fogertys could have been twins. Their eyes were set deep in their faces and seemed colorless under dark, thick eyebrows. Over six feet, they crossed their arms in unison exposing their taut biceps stressing against their regulation blue denim shirts, a move with seeming intimidation. Already weathered looking at a young age, their recruit haircut left the sides of their heads and necks pale compared to the rest of their sunburned faces, a bit comical looking in a way, like that Bogart haircut in the movie "Treasure of Sierra Madre." But these two no one would ever want to laugh at.

One of the Fogertys spoke up.

"What's your name?" A demand more than a question.

I told him my name, though plain to see stenciled right there over my shirt pocket.

"Yeah. We thought so," the other Fogerty said. "You look like him."

He grew even larger as he spoke, while I shrank from my five-foot-ten inches and 125 pounds. Where their uniforms were filled in tight, mine hung loose, my drooping belt pulled as tight as it would go, making me feel even more vulnerable to whatever was about to transpire. I looked at the third member of the trio, almost a look-a-like to the brothers. Every nerve in my body seemed to know more than I did and sent out a flood of warning signals.

I cleared my throat and somehow managed to speak up. "I don't remember meeting you guys before." I knew if we had there'd be no memory lapse on my part. Despite my growing unease, I couldn't help but think of them as Eeeny, Meeny and Miny, thanking god there was no Moe.

"Yeah, well, we haven't exactly met, but me and my brother, we know who you are," Eeeny said. Clearly an accusation, of what I had no idea.

"Yeah, lots a times," Meeny, the other brother, said. He reached to scratch his ear and I flinched. What did they want?

"Oh? Where? I don't remember." I kept looking from one to the other.

"We seen ya' whenever you brought our sister home from a date."

The one I now labeled Eeeny said this as if he had just made everything clear.

"Your sister?" Ah, relief. They think I'm someone else.

"Yeah. You know. Molly. Molly Fogerty."

"Molly?" Then I realized who they were talking about. "Molly. Sure. Of course. Yeah." I'm not sure I ever knew or paid attention to her last name.

"Well, she's our little sister," Eeeny emphasized.

"Oh, so you guys are from Carbondale. Yeah, sure. That's where I met her. I was going to SIU when I dropped out and joined up." I scrambled for words worrying about what she had told them. Sounding natural with no saliva in my mouth wasn't easy. If she was pregnant, it wasn't me.

If these two were Molly's brothers, they had to be from a different father. I remembered her as a petite, slight five-two at best with fair skin and short, light hair.

Meeny spoke up. "Yeah, we know where you're from. But we been discussin' somethin' she wondered about. Got us thinkin' about it, too."

I felt a drip of perspiration leave my armpit and slide down my side. Any manly qualities I might have thought I had wafted into vapor puffs. I had never tried anything inappropriate with Molly. What might she have told them?

Miny, the friend, spoke up. "Yeah. She says you're a really good dancer." The emphasis he placed on "dancer," along with a smirk, gave away his opinion on the subject.

"Molly's the good dancer." A feeble retort as another drop of perspiration took its time following the first one down. Where was this going? Wanting to get to the point I asked, "Is there a problem? What did she say?"

"Ya' hurt her feelings," Eeeny said.

"Yeah," Miny said.

"I did?" My shocked memory went on a swift search and rescue mission trying to think how I might have hurt her feelings. Nothing surfaced and I felt myself sinking. She's told them something. They want revenge for something I didn't do.

I noticed other recruits in the barracks started gathering around, sensing something interesting was developing.

"Yeah. She says you'd walk her home but would never kiss her." Meeny cocked his head at me. "That's kinda strange, innit? All those times made her feel bad, like somethin' was wrong with her."

Miny, the friend, was quick to insert, "Or somethin' wrong with you, maybe?"

Oh, oh. Are they thinking what I think they're thinking? Like an unexpected bullet train whooshing out of a dark tunnel, it hit me. How do I tap dance out of this one?

True, I never had kissed her, but did that make something wrong with her or me? I remember Molly was cute, but I never had that kind of feeling for her. I saw her maybe five or six times at local dances. She was just fun to dance with. Sometimes I'd walk her home afterwards. But nothing happened. We never officially dated. She apparently took our relationship more seriously than I did. I guess I could have kissed her, but I was shy in that way.

Was that what all this was about? I should have kissed their sister?

Almost in syncopation, the three of them folded their arms across their chests as if they were trying with difficulty to keep their hands off me. They looked at me expectantly.

What was I supposed to say?

"You like girls or not?" asked Miny, face flushing.

"Whoa, wait. Look. Yeah, I like girls. And I like your sister. If I insulted her I didn't mean..."

"You got a girlfriend?" Miny again.

"Well, yeah. Sure." The only answer possible at this juncture.

Actually, not any more I didn't, but this was not the time to explain.

"What's her name? Got a picture?" Miny stayed relentless. He didn't want to believe me.

I learned a body could freeze and sweat at the same time. Now they wanted proof of my phantom girlfriend. Why did I listen to Ted and join the navy? Another absence of good sense on my part.

In desperation, and beginning to feel the pain of the damage they could do to me, my mind shifted into overdrive, and I prayed the photo was still there. Just maybe. Grabbing my wallet, I fingered my way through its contents. With welcomed relief, I pulled out a black and white photograph of a young, blond woman in that classic bathing suit pose by a pool and showed it to them. Was this why I'd kept it?

At first, they seemed almost disappointed I could produce one. As they passed the picture around, I told them her name, Suzanne.

Then Eeeny, to my relief, nodded approval. "Yeah. Not bad, not bad. Nice."

"Yeah. Real nice. A looker. You wanna hang on to that one," Meeny said, his tone now complimentary.

Miny seemed a bit let down, took another look, then handed the photo back.

"Look, guys, I like Molly." I tried to wet my lips and took a deep breath. "She's really nice. I never meant to insult her. But Suzanne and I, well, I didn't want to lead your sister to think…." I shrugged my shoulders as I tried to conceal shaky fingers putting the photo back in my wallet. "You understand." I hoped they grasped what I was implying.

The brothers looked at each other as if silently conferring.

"Sure, we get it. You was just bein' faithful to your girlfriend," offered Eeeny, smiling as if he'd just discovered his brain really worked.

The gathered crowd, showing disappointment, began to disperse.

"Hey, okay. It's cool. We appreciate you not leadin' our sister on like," said Meeny. "We'll let her know the story. She'll understand." He slapped me on the back of my now damp shirt and looked at the other two for agreement with his interpretation. They nodded in unison and, now my best buddies, introduced themselves whose first names I've long forgotten.

To cinch my acquittal, I added to the charade, "Believe me, if it hadn't been for Suzanne, I, well, you know…. I really liked…like … your sister."

"Yeah. Otherwise, who knows, maybe you'd been our brother-in-law someday." Eeeny's playful punch on my shoulder knocked me off balance.

The brothers thought this hilarious. The thwarted Miny frowned and looked like he'd lost a piece of a puzzle. I figured he had a thing for Molly, hence his involvement. I wanted to say, "She's all yours, you idiot, but you'd better learn to dance."

Satisfied I was worthy to serve in their navy, my interrogators made some small talk, began shrinking in size, then moved off, no doubt to make sure the company barracks remained uncontaminated.

With the three sentinels of proprietary behavior gone, my bottled-up fear and tension melded into a nauseous irritation with them and the whole ludicrous episode. Kiss my sister or you're gay? Such logic overwhelmed me! None of my college courses had prepared me for such reasoning. Eeeny, Meeny, Miny, Moe, catch a homo by his toe. Is this why they call it "boot camp?" I couldn't help but think about Bill. How would he have fared in a situation like this? What would they have done to him?

Had it not been for that picture of Suzanne, they would have made me their Moe. Accepted now as a worthy fellow recruit, I wasn't about to tell them the real story behind Suzanne's picture.

I kept the photograph of Suzanne during boot camp, just in case. But later, I hoped Suzanne, wherever she was, felt each... slow... rip...rip and drop into the waste can.

Are you there, Suz?

CHAPTER 10

"Nice Work If You Can Get It"

When I joined the navy (don't expect any heroic war story here), the recruiter neglected to tell me that you could sign up as a Seaman or an Airman. I had no idea there was a choice and was signed up as a Seaman. I soon discovered in boot camp that most of my new buddies had enlisted as Airman, meaning they would be assigned duty involving aircraft. That appealed to me, so before my training was finished, I switched to an Airman status.

At the completion of my training at Great Lakes Naval Training Center, nearly everyone in my company received orders to serve on the aircraft carrier, the USS Boxer, except me. I was told that because I had switched from Seaman to Airman, I now had to wait for orders for Airman service, too late now to join the others. Depressed, lonely, and angry, I fell into a funk wishing I'd never joined the navy.

While waiting to receive my orders, I had to remain at the training center to do what is termed as "shit details," cleaning toilets, sweeping the floors, polishing brass, emptying trash, anything menial to keep a sailor busy. Waiting for orders felt like a prison sentence.

When my orders came, I was assigned duty at Los Alamitos Navy Air Station near Long Beach, California. Things began to look bright. I'd always dreamed of going to California, and now – California here I come.

Upon arrival at the naval station, the personnel office had no idea where to place me, as boot camp had not prepared me for any special task as a Seaman or an Airman. Plus, the base served naval reservists, yet I was regular navy. What was the navy's reasoning? To make it even more puzzling, someone with a perverted sense of humor decided my low-test scores in mechanics qualified me for work with airplanes and had me report to the Chief Petty Officer out on "the line."

The line referred to a row of a few shiny silver SNJ and SNB training planes and about a dozen dungy-grey World War II F6F Hellcats and F6 Wildcats, fighter airplanes designed to serve on aircraft carriers. Some had their engines exposed as mechanics worked on them. One of the mechanics directed me to Chief Bradley in a small office inside the main airplane hangar. I introduced myself, and while he looked over my orders, I looked him over. I guessed he was about fifty or so, fit physically, tall, tan and reminded me a bit of the actor Sterling Hayden.

"Ever work on plane engines before?' he asked.

"No, sir."

He sighed and nodded his head as if he knew he hadn't needed to ask the question.

"Know anything about engines?" his voice full of hope.

"No, sir. Not really. I mean, I sorta' know how a car engine works." I tried to give him hope, but I dashed any he might have held when I added, "My lowest test scores are in mechanics."

He nodded his head again. "Figures. That's par for navy." He scoffed, looked at me with doubt on his face. "Can you read at least?"

Oh, that hurt.

"Yes, I can read." I said with my best offensiveness.

He smirked. "Follow me."

He took a clipboard hanging on the wall and led me to one of the F6 Hellcats.

"Get in," he ordered.

Taken aback, I just stood there looking at the plane, then at him. "In the plane?"

"Yes, in the plane. Preferably the one you're standing beside."

Now his words went from insult to injury, as my Dad used to say. But when I looked at the plane again, I realized it was much bigger than it looked in the war movies. And now he wanted me to get in one.

Feeling as low and as incompetent as possible, I looked for a way to climb into the cockpit and found what I guessed were places to put my feet. Once seated, I felt a surprised sense of excitement. I was sitting in a WW II fighter plane. It had no doubt seen action in the Pacific, flying on and off aircraft carriers, hunting down, maybe shooting down, Japanese planes and ships. I'd seen pictures of these planes in action in newsreels. Now, here I was sitting in one.

Chief Bradley interrupted my historical reverie when he popped up on the wing next to the cockpit. Handing me the clipboard, he explained the printed form it held. My job, once the plane engine started, consisted of filling in items on the check list, such as the rpm counts, oil pressure, battery function, fuel level, and flap movements. Excited with the assignment, I felt a tinge of luck my orders had been delayed. Cleaning toilets at Great Lakes had been worth it.

For my first few weeks, after a plane had been serviced, I would climb in the cockpit and watch for a ground crew member to give me an all-clear sign to begin. Then I would start the engine, feeling the powerful strain of its slow, whining, sputtering start, watch the propeller's erratic spin gradually gain momentum as I added more throttle, creating more noise, sending steady vibrations through my body, deaf to the outside world. Once the engine ran clear, I'd sit there checking off the list of stats and, like a kid, fantasized myself a big-shot pilot. If everything checked out, I shut down the engine and signed the form verifying the airplane fit for flying. Sometimes, I took longer than I needed just to enjoy the fantasy of flying.

A few weeks after I had signed clearance for several airplanes, I learned that if anything mechanical went wrong when a plane was in the air, the one who signed the checklist was held responsible. I didn't think too much about it. By that time, I had been taught basic mechanical repair and replacement of parts and began to feel as if I knew what I was doing.

Until...

I had just finished an engine run check and began climbing down from the cockpit when a siren went from a low whine to an ear-blasting shrill. I saw crew members running in several directions and watched a fire engine come from nowhere. A truck load of sailors raced behind it onto the outskirts of the runway.

"What's happening?" I yelled at someone near.

"I don't think this is a drill," he shouted.

I had no idea what he meant. What kind of drill?

Then excitedly he yelled over the blaring siren, "It's no drill. See?" He pointed to one of our Hellcats, coming in low, smoke coming from the engine. I noticed the wheels were still up. How could he land? Did he forget to lower the landing gear?

The siren stopped. The only noise was the sputtering sound of the plane's engine. Smoke flew back at the cockpit. Could the pilot even see to land?

The plane lost more altitude and seemed to be coming in too fast. Then the plane hit the runway on its belly and slid its way until there was no more runway, just a grove of trees. One wing was ripped off, then the plane stopped abruptly and appeared to split in half.

When the firetruck and crew reached the plane, the pilot was still strapped in his seat, his feet dangling in the air, the engine torn away from the rest of the plane.

To everyone's amazement, the pilot was unhurt. The plane was destroyed.

When the excitement waned, I had a chilling thought. Had I signed off on that plane? Was I going to get the heat for the accident? Had I done something wrong?

After a few days of the accident investigation, the Chief called me in.

It was my fault.

I'm going to be court martialed.

I must have looked as pale as a snowbird when I entered his office.

"You signed off on that Hellcat," he said bluntly.

My knees almost buckled.

He took a deep breath. "But they're calling the accident "pilot error."

For a moment, it didn't sink in.

"Yeah. That engine was fine, when the pilot took off. He tried to hotdog it, and screwed up a perfectly good plane."

"You mean I didn't do anything wrong?"

"You're in the clear. Nothing the inspection showed...."

I don't remember the rest of the conversation.

Some of the glamour of what I was doing began fading.

The problem with working "on the line" is that every three weeks or so, you had to work a few weeks in the scullery: kitchen duty. More boring than terrible. And not very challenging.

After a month or so, I made friends with Bard Glass, who worked in the personnel office. He told me the office staff needed someone who could type. I didn't know how, other than plunking on my grandfather's Underwood, but I needed a change. Every evening, after office hours, I went in and practiced typing. I never really learned to touch-type, but I managed to do about thirty-five words a minute, enough to bluff my way into switching from the line to becoming a personnelman. Just like that, I became a paper pusher.

Of course, that meant I had to request a change back to Seaman status.

I soon lost my despondency at not being assigned to the Boxer with my classmates when I discovered I'd been sent to what some called the playground of the navy. The place had an Olympic-sized swimming pool, a tennis court, a library, even a movie auditorium (entertainers like Bob Hope performed there). Almost everyone stationed at Los Alamitos was a reservist who lived in the Southern California area and was called back to active duty because of the Korean war. Since the base served weekend warrior reservists, I had leave on Mondays and Tuesdays. Free to live on or off the base, I felt the navy had blessed me for volunteering.

Friendships with the men I worked with, who had cars and were eager to show me around, became an added benefit. Bard became my best friend while there, introducing me to the best beaches and surfing along the southern coast. He offered me a free place to stay in his parent's converted garage in Huntington Beach, just a short drive from the base. I rode back and forth to work with him every day until I bought my own car.

Eventually, I saved enough money to buy a swiftly deteriorating, uninsured 1935 Ford Coupe that I doubt was even street legal. The roof leaked when it rained, the whole body shook as if it wanted to fly away from its frame, and the muffler blew out the second day I owned the thing. Purchased from some rinky-dink roadside car dealer, I don't remember ever getting a pink slip for it. But the car was all I could afford and I wanted to get around on my own without relying on Bard.

I had no money to get a new muffler, so I got a small piece of fiberglass that Bard used to make surfboards, and with a cork covered with the fiberglass I plugged up the hole. I had to do that about every other week.

Still, the car got me around. Surfing, beach parties, free entries for servicemen in uniform to famous Hollywood sites, and NBC and CBS radio shows became the norm. It was easy to get around the Los Angeles area back then, even in a four-wheel coffin without a lid. Those were truly happy days for me.

Was there a war going on?

The cherry on top came when I was assigned to do the paper work for naval reserve pilots, which necessitated my flying with a squadron commander to these bases in San Diego and Phoenix. I racked up quite a few hours of flight time for a lowly enlisted man with the rating of Personnel Specialist E3.

Let me digress into a story about one of those flights...

I'm sitting in the co-pilot's seat of a twin-engine Beechcraft converted for navy use. The pilot is Commader Alexander Vraciu. We have just taken off from Los Alamitos Naval Air Station on our way to the navy base on North Island, San Diego. The Commander is in charge of a squadron of naval reserve pilots in San Diego. I'm in charge of the paperwork that the Bureau of Personnel needs in order for those reservists to qualify for flying credits and pay for their weekend training.

It's a fairly short flight, but I would be happy if we stayed in the air for hours. Under normal circumstances, I belong in an office down on the ground. But without me, the pilots will not get paid, and I couldn't be any closer to where I want to be: in the air.

We reach our flight pattern altitude when the commander asks me through headphones, "Flown much before?"

"No, sir. Only on a TWA flight back home."

"Where's home?"

"Alton… Illinois. Across the river from St. Louis."

"Ah, mid-westerner. Me, too. I'm from Indiana."

"Oh. Nice." I don't know what else to say, not feeling it customary for an enlisted man to be sitting where I am, let alone chatting with a naval officer, a Commander at that.

"How long have you been in the navy?"

Does he really want to know, or is he just making conversation?

"Almost a year now. Enlisted in January and they sent me out here after Great Lakes boot camp."

"You're regular navy, then?"

"Yessir."

"Why'd they send you to a reserve base?"

"No idea."

"That's navy," he laughs his words. "How do you like it so far?"

"So far, no complaints. I always wanted to come to California." Then I add, "And this is great getting to fly."

"You like flying?"

"Yessir."

"Why didn't you sign up for NAVCAD program? Give you a chance to become an officer and a pilot."

"Didn't know anything about it when I joined. I was going to get drafted, so I just decided to go navy."

"Any college?"

"Year and a half."

Quiet for a minute, adjusting some dials, he then asks, "Want to fly her?"

"Sir?"

"Take the wheel. If you hear a dot-dash, you're veering to the left. If you hear a dash-dot, you're heading right. Just keep it steady on course. The left foot pedal will take you left. The right pedal, right. Get the feel. Go ahead."

My dad had a phrase he used when someone feels ecstatic over something. He called it "being in hog heaven."

Oh, yeah!

I take the wheel and pedals, my body electric with nervous anticipation. After a moment, I ease into it. I am much more than along for the ride; I am flying through the gates into heaven. The Commander leaves me at the controls for a good fifteen minutes. Floating on cloud nine applies. Me, co-piloting a twin-engine aircraft, wearing headphones, like in the movies, my seat a parachute. Let's fly forever...

Over the engine noise he yells, "Good job. You should think about that NAVCAD program. Not too late if you want to stay in the navy." He takes back my airplane. Not even a firefly now, I struggle returning to an E-3 enlisted man again.

"Thanks. That was...cool." Lame words that can't convey the half of it.

He starts talking on the radio with somebody at the North Island tower. The gist of the conversation: it's too foggy to land there, so we are directed to land at Lindberg Field, the municipal airport in San Diego-- if we can.

"Not good news," he tells me.

As he speaks, we enter a thick layer of fog. I'm more excited than fearful. In fact, I envision a wild, unanticipated adventure of some kind, maybe even a forced parachute jump. The plane shudders, drops quickly, rises even faster, more bumpy shudders, my foolish thoughts now challenged.

The Commander plays around with some radio dials and gets in contact with Lindberg Field. We're only ten minutes out.

"Okay," he says. "The fog's rolling in fast. Visibility should improve once we drop a little lower."

He goes quiet, concentrating on our landing. We're both looking out the window searching for something besides fog.

"There." He sees something I don't.

He reaches up for a control lever above his head. Then the lights in the cockpit go out.

We're in the dark.

Now I am worried. The plane is losing altitude. The windshield is sprinkled wet, I don't see anything but fog, and all indicator lights are out. I relive the crash I witnessed.

"Get the flashlight in my briefcase... between the seats," he orders.

I fumble between the seats in the dark and find the briefcase.

"Find it?" his voice beginning to show a little of my own concern.

I find it. Just as I bring the flashlight up from the briefcase, the Commander leans over to look for it himself, and I whack him in the head with the heavy metal.

A moan and a call to Christ and God Almighty echo around the cabin. The plane tips back and forth like a seesaw. The engines offer a feathering sound. There's an, "Oh, shit!" either in my head or aloud. What did I just do? Am I in trouble? Visions of me in the brig for striking an officer zoom out of the fog while other images of me not able to land the plane are thankfully interrupted.

"Turn it on!"

"Sir?"

"The flashlight. Turn it on."

I do as commanded, thankful I didn't knock him out.

"Shine it on the instrument panel."

Why did I need to be told?

The plane steadies. He's back in control. I don't understand the words on the radio, but I understand what he tells me.

"It's too socked in. They don't want us to land here."

I want to ask what we do now, did I hurt his head, but I just wait for him to say something.

He resets the radio frequency, and I hear him requesting someone to respond to his call to the nearby El Toro Marine Air Base. He explains our predicament to someone on the other end, and we get permission to land there. He resets some dials, and I feel the plane sliding east.

"Looks like we'll have to spend the night in El Toro. No fog there."

We are quiet for some time. But I'm anxious to ask.

"Sir. Sorry about the flashlight thing. Are you okay?"

He doesn't look at me, but his face is stone.

I wonder if he saw my stars.

The fog clears away as we head for El Toro. I see the X crossed landing strips down below. We're given permission to land, and within minutes, we are on the ground taxiing to our parking spot for the night.

Before we get off the plane, I wait for the Commander to say something, anything, about my hitting him. He says nothing. I worry. He puts on his dress blue coat with the three wide gold stripes on each sleeve and a hat with so much gold embroidery on the peak it must weight three pounds. The left side of his chest, covered with colorful ribbons, displays evidence of what he's accomplished over his career. I'm in my whites with just three small stripes on my upper sleeve and a silly-looking hat that matches how I feel.

The two marine guards receiving us give the stiffest salutes I've ever seen. The Commander's uniform impresses them. I am now the sidekick of royalty.

The Commander salutes back. "Corporal, show me the way to BOQ. And you," he points to the other marine, "my aide will need some chow and a bunk for the night. See that he gets treated well. He's had a tough day."

"Yes, sir." Heels click.

Before the Commander heads off in one direction, he tells me, "Meet me here at 0630."

"Yes, sir."

"And bring some ice for the goose egg I'll have on my head."

"Sir? Yes, sir."

Is he kidding?

I'm led another way, savoring being called "his aide," not an illegal, stupid co-pilot.

"He must be important, huh?" the Marine asks.

I don't want to ruin his fantasy.

I reply, as any good aide would, "Oh, yeah. You have no idea."

Neither did I --then.

Switch now to 2016 for a moment. I'm watching a documentary on World War II, the Battle of the Pacific. A quick scene grabs my attention. A smiling pilot is just stepping out of his F6F Hellcat fighter plane, like the one I used to sit in. He has just finished what history calls "A Mission Beyond Darkness" during the 1944 Battle of the Philippines. On the fuselage of his plane are 19 small stickers of Japanese flags, signifying that he has shot down that many enemy planes. And my ears prick up when the announcer on the program says, "LTJG Alexander Vraciu has just returned from a mission in which he destroyed a Japanese ship."

WAIT! I know that name! I pay closer attention.

"Vraciu's greatest success took place on June 19, 1944, during what became known as the 'Great Marianas Turkey Shoot,' when he engaged a Japanese fighter squadron in air-to-air combat, downing six Japanese aircraft in eight minutes using only 360 rounds of ammunition. In December 1944, Vraciu parachuted from his downed plane during a mission over the Philippines, and spent five weeks with Filipino resistance fighters before rejoining American military forces and returning to the aircraft carrier USS Lexington."

I am stunned.

I'd only flown four other times with the Commander during my tour of duty at Los Alamitos. He always let me fly once we were in the air, knowing the high I got pretending to be a pilot. He never mentioned his war record, and treated me with respect, always making certain I was well taken care of when away from home base. And as much as I admired him at the time, I had no idea that I had smacked a WWII hero in the head with his flashlight.

I am on Google, researching Alexander Vraciu. During his naval service, in addition to the 19 planes he had shot down, he destroyed 22 enemy planes on the ground. He earned, among 16 commendations, the Navy Cross, the Distinguished Flying Cross with two Gold Stars, the Air Medal with three gold stars, the Naval Presidential Unit Citation with two gold stars, and others—all displayed by ribbons on the coat he wore that night at El Toro. I had no idea what they represented then.

I can hear the echo of the Marine that night: "He must be important, huh?"

What I'd give to answer him again.

Anyway, you can understand why, after two years of high-flying bliss, my new orders-- yanking me from my easy-going, undemanding, fun-packed, California-high environment, that transferred me to the USS Mississippi, a forty-year-old battleship stationed in Norfolk, Virginia-- could stir up a strong hatred toward her before I'd even boarded her.

I despised her even more when I first saw her. No new, sleek naval craft, just a 700-foot- long, 32,000 tons of dull grey metal tied to the pier. Her World War II, 14-inch guns had been stripped and replaced with smaller experimental 5 inchers. Modified in so many ways over the years, she looked like the Frankenstein monster of the navy, which to me made her even more disappointing. They even changed her number designation for BB 41 to EAG 128.

Not eager, I climbed up the gangplank, my duffle bag over my shoulder and stopped when I stepped on deck. The Officer of the Day, a young Lieutenant, gave me a stern look as I set my duffle down to retrieve my written orders.

"Reporting for duty," I said. And handed him my papers.

His face did not express "Welcome."

"Forget something, sailor?"

"Sir?"

"You right out of boot, are you?"

"No, sir. Two years in." I had no idea what he was going on about.

"Where's the salute?"

"Sir?"

"The salute, sailor, the salute."

Then I remembered. The cardinal navy rule: when coming aboard, salute the flag flying at the aft of the ship, and then salute the office of the deck until he salutes back. You do the reverse when you leave the ship.

"I forgot, sir. This is my first-time aboard ship." I saluted the flag and then him.

He didn't release me from my salute, making me hold it while he looked at my orders. He took his time, then stared at me for a minute.

"Two years in and you don't know ship etiquette? What's your rating and what can you offer this ship?" This was not the navy I knew.

Still holding my salute, I said, "I'm a PN3, sir. Personnelman, sir." Of course, he could see that on my papers. And he damn well knew what a PN was.

"Well, Personnelman, it seems there's a huge lack in your naval training. I'll have to check and see if we need any more – Personnelmen." He emphasized the word as though it held contamination. Then he saluted back, at last releasing me.

"In the meantime, I'm assigning you to the duty crew." He turned to a crewman nearby and ordered him to take me below and find a bunk assignment for me.

Once we cleared two decks down, my escort said, "He's an asshole, the LT. He's in engineering so you might not see much of him if you're Personnel."

Nice to hear, but I felt like an ass for not remembering shipboard protocol. We exchanged names, and he took me to the Quartermaster's office where I was officially checked in and given a bunk and locker number, thin mattress and bedding. My guide pointed out my fold-out bunk, a middle one of a three stackers, wished me luck and went back to his duties.

Tossing my bag and bedding on my bunk, I looked around the impossibly small living quarters. Grey metal floor, grey metal bulkheads, grey metal locker, grey metal ceiling. And my mood greyer than my surroundings. I wanted my wide-open airfield and the sound of airplane engines.

I did have one advantage as a PN. I knew my orders and assignment would be handled in the ship's Executive Officer's office. The last thing

I wanted was to be placed on some ship's duty roster swabbing decks or painting the bulkheads. Too scared, yes, and way too spoiled for that.

Asking around, I found my way to the Exec's office. I explained my situation to the guys in the office who invited me in and welcomed me as a fellow sailor and promised they'd take care of my assignment once the Officer of the Day sent them down. One of the guys in the office named Morey seemed to feel sorry for me being so out of my element and helped me get squared away in my new environment.

"Does this old tub ever leave the dock?" I asked.

"Actually, this 'old tub' is shipping out tomorrow."

His tone let me know he didn't care for my calling the ship an old tub. "Oh. Tomorrow. Didn't know that. Where're we headed?"

"You don't know anything about this ship, or what we do, do you?" Morey asked.

"Not a clue," I said, refraining from mentioning I didn't want to be aboard, and that the ship was named after a state I never wanted to see again.

"Here's the scoop. The Mississippi has seen more action than any present ship in the navy. She's been around in various modifications since 1917 and served in a lot of historical events. During World War II, she helped win the Pacific from the Japanese. She earned eight battle stars for all her support in the Pacific and helped support the troops on Okinawa. Twice hit by Jap kamikaze planes, she never sank and continued to fight under severe conditions."

"I saw pictures of kamikaze attacks in newsreels during the war. Maybe it was this ship," I said.

"Could have been. But that's why her designation was changed from battleship BB-41 rating to EAG-128. She's now an experimental gunnery and anti-aircraft missile ship. We've been given the honor of testing the first Terrier missiles."

I received his message loud and clear. Don't say anything negative about the ship.

We did leave Norfolk the next day and, thanks to my fellow officemates, I was assigned to work in the Executive Officer's office despite what the LT had claimed he would do. At least I was somewhat familiar with the type of work, and over the first few days began to adjust and get my sea legs.

I have to admit, being at sea opened up a whole new life perspective. The steady roll of the ship, the expanse of the ocean, the isolation all began to appeal to me. I'd experienced the sky, now I experienced the sea. Plus, what the ship was doing was so secretive, we had to hide from Russian submarines so they couldn't learn what we were doing. During the day, experimental guns fired away at drone airplanes sent out as targets. Timers set on the shells being fired relayed whether or not a round being fired could be counted as a hit on the drone without actually blowing it out of the sky. I later learned that the gunners, when tired of practicing, occasionally set the timers so that they actually did destroy the drone. No more practice until another drone could be sent out which could take a day or two.

During missile quarters, the time when a missile was going to be tested, everyone had a special job assignment. The whole ship seemed to become tense during missile quarters. At that time, the missiles had not been perfected, still very much experimental. I became the Captain's count-down man up on the bridge. By headphone, I was connected to the missile launchers and would relay the last-minute countdown to the officers and engineers on the bridge.

The excitement of a missile launch can't really be described. There's a pop sound seconds before the missile takes off. Then orange flames shoot out as the missile seems pulled up into the air by some invisible force, leaving a streak of orange-grey vapor and a loud swishing sound. Will it continue on up, or will it disappoint and fall into the sea? I witnessed both. And began to understand the importance of the old Mississippi to the navy's future defenses.

When it came time to fire the first missile with a warhead, I again stood on the bridge next to the Captain and gave the count down as relayed to me: ...six...five...four...three... two...one...fire! We watched the missile jerk from the launch pad, the familiar swish and orange streak and cloudy vapor trail lifting off and heading upward. Then I could sense the entire ship, along with me, silent, holding our breath as the missile dropped altitude, arched unexpectedly and headed back toward the ship. It had honed in on our metal structure.

Such silence. It felt as if everyone on the ship watching held their breath.

We were the target!

Then just yards beyond the bow, the missile seemed to sense it was wrong, and dropped into the sea.

The Captain looked at me. "SHIT!"

Did he want me to say something?

"You saw that! Those fucking engineers almost blew up my ship."

He looked at me as if I had words of wisdom. Then he realized I was waiting for his orders to stand down.

"Shit! Secure from missile quarters!" he yelled. I passed the word on.

He stormed from the bridge and headed for the missile launch site.

It never happened again. By the end of the year, however, Terrier missiles had been perfected and variations still are being used, I understand.

The power of the sea often kept us at its mercy and dictated its own terms. I gained even more respect for the old ship taking on one particular hurricane. There is nothing you can do but ride out a storm and hope for the best. But being young and senseless, I felt enthralled by the way the ship and crew would be thrown about. It became a game to try to walk steady while running around to various deck levels until strapping yourself in your bunk became the only alternative. One moment the ship would sway to the starboard, then dig its bow deep into the water while the aft end of the ship rose up from the sea, the screws now useless whirling against the air, only to crash down, jarring the ship's innards, now the waves sucking down the aft end while the bow rises high above the water. A dramatic shift to port, only to repeat its dolphin-like antics, nose down, tail up, roll to the side, nose down, tail up, until released from the ocean's will.

That's when I knew I was a sailor.

One day while in the galley line to eat, the server asked me something I didn't quite catch.

"Gravy on the spuds?"

I looked up from the food tray assortments.

"Say again."

"Gravy. Want some?" On your spuds?"

I looked up at him, dressed in his white T shirt and cap, and noticed his dark skin, a Filipino. I don't know why this surprised me, but it did. I looked at the other servers behind the food line and realized it was the first time I noticed that everyone working in the galley was non-white. I began to realize that I seldom saw a person of color in the navy, not at that time anyway. If there were, I didn't see them. I only saw what I was used to seeing.

Here I was, serving on a ship named after the very state I learned to despise as a child.

At least no one was being lynched from the yardarm.

I have to add something here. By the time my four-year enlistment was up, I was more than ready to be out. I was asked if I wanted to re-enlist for another term, and laughed at the suggestion. I felt I'd done my duty and the navy was behind me. As time went by, I realized my service experience would always be with me. As reports of soldier and sailor deaths mounted, especially those associated with the U.S.S Boxer, I was even more aware of my luck, even a touch of guilt. So many service men died in a futile war that still hasn't been declared over. The navy treated me well. Although most names have been lost to me, I remember with fondness the men I served with on land and sea. I so wish I could see them again and share memories. We lived a camaraderie that is difficult to put a name to. To this day I feel sad-proud emotions when I watch movies that deal with the navy. If I were a talented writer, I might be able to express this better. But then maybe it's nothing that can be shared, only felt, and only if you've served.

A form of love, maybe.

CHAPTER 11

"Unforgettable"

Basically I served on a ship that went nowhere. When the USS Mississippi left port in Norfolk, we headed for open water so all the guns and missiles could fire away for testing and development out of harm's way. The main point was to not let the Russians see our activities. So, what did I see? A lot of sea.

To the crew's surprise one day, the captain announced we would get a shore break by docking in New York for twenty-four hours. I never knew if we were being rewarded or it was strictly navy business of some kind. It mattered not. The idea of having shore leave in the Big City made the anticipation a kid feels on the night before Christmas pale in comparison.

One of my cohorts in the Exec's office, I forget his name, was a New Yorker and promised to show several of us who planned to go ashore the best of the city. He kept his word considering what little time we had.

I'll drop the travelogue and my wonder at the tall buildings and get right to the meat of this story.

I met a remarkable person.

Late in the evening, our group stopped in at Birdland to hear George Shearing's jazz quintet. The place was packed, hot, smoky and standing room only, so we had to spread out. I burrowed my way through the mass toward the bar, thinking I might get a drink and a better view of the band, but got jammed between two women. I didn't realize they were together until they started talking across me.

"Oh, sorry." I started to move away, though where would have been a problem.

"No, stay. We should be listening, not talking." She smiled and turned her attention to the music.

I nodded and did the same, not really giving much thought to her or her friend. That is, until the musicians took a break and the lights came up.

I was book-cased between two attractive young women.

"What's your ship?" one of them asked.

No doubt my uniform prompted the question. When I told them, and my time limit, they expressed their sympathy.

"I'm Charlotte, by the way. This is my friend Diana."

Charlotte, a curly blonde, short and cute, reminded me of Molly in a way. Diana was the taller of the two, with short, dark hair and eyes of a fawn. I immediately was drawn to her.

I introduced myself and offered to buy them a drink, surprising my usually shy self. I casually removed my glasses and slipped them into my pocket. They noticed but didn't say anything.

"No, no. Let us buy you a drink," Charlotte said. "What are you drinking?"

"CC and ginger, please." That came out like I was an old hand at drinking. I wasn't. I just had heard others order it on my few shore-leave excursions. Didn't learn until later that CC was Canada Club whiskey.

Charlotte headed for the bar and Diana asked, "How long have you been in the navy?"

I told her while trying not to let her notice how I was gulping her in.

"My brother's in the navy. Aboard the Boxer."

That prompted me to tell her my bootcamp story, about why I was not on the Boxer, but might have been.

"What about you?" I asked. "What do you do?"

She explained that she had graduated from NYU last year and now worked at Crown publishing as an editor.

"I want to finish my college work when I get out. This damn Korean thing. I was just getting into the swing of it."

Charlotte came back with the drinks and the three of us fell into a conversation about an array of things. I found myself more at ease around these two women than ever before. It wasn't just the drink. Yes, maybe some. We talked music, mostly jazz we liked.

"How'd you get interested in jazz?" Charlotte asked.

"I guess it started with listening to Woody Herman, Stan Kenton, Duke Ellington and those guys, but I really got interested when the father of a girl I had a few dates with found out I liked jazz. He introduced me to Illinois Jacket, Cozy Cole, Dizzy –you know, individual players in those bands."

"Did your girlfriend like jazz, too?" Diana asked.

"No. In fact, she told me I should date her father. Actually, he was more interesting than she was."

"Ooo. Burn." Charlotte laughed.

"I've an idea," Diana interjected. "Charlotte, let's take him to Bennie's."

"Great idea!"

"What's Bennie's?" I couldn't help but wonder why they took a liking to me, if that's what it was. I was just another average guy in a sailor suit.

"I think you'll like it," Diana said. "Unless you'd rather stay here?"

The idea of spending more time with these two, especially Diana, was…of course I said yes, not caring what or where Bennie's was. I liked the sudden unexpected mystery of it all. I'd stepped into a feeling of excitement.

We gathered to leave before the next Shearing set, and on the way out I saw a couple of my shipmates. They noticed who I was with and gave me the big-eye question and then a thumbs up. I gave them a salute back. Just look at me, guys.

It never occurred to me at the time what I might be getting into. Who were these women? Where were they taking me? Alone in a big city I didn't know, would I get back to the ship in time? Would I get back to the ship at all? None of those questions entered my mind. I was dazzled by these two women paying attention to me.

It happened just like this:

I'm sitting between two good-looking women in the back of a taxi off to Bennie's.

As we drive, they point out famous buildings, stores, landmarks, most of which I never heard of or faintly remember from movies. Then we arrive in what they tell me is the theater district. We exit the cab, surrounded by car horns blaring, a cacophony of voices, shoulder-to-shoulder people, garbage smells mixed with street-vendor foods, swirls of colorful lighting and monstrous advertising marquees.

We walk through the crowds for a block or so until we come to a set of steps leading down to an unmarked door. Charlotte opens the door and leads us through as though it's her own home. Inside it's dark, and another entrance is covered by heavy red drapes. We follow Charlotte through and encounter someone sitting at a table exchanging a stamp on the back of the hand for money. The ladies pay for me.

I try to pay, but they tell me they support sailors on leave.

Bennie's, I see, is a dance hall. A quintet is playing "Nice Work If You Can Get It" for the dancers on the floor. There's a bar in the back with a few people standing near. Other than that, it's just a large room with tables along the walls, colorful lights swirling around making lively patterns on the dancers and the floor.

"What do you think?" Diana asks.

I nod. "Nice."

"Charlotte's boyfriend plays the drums in the group," she tells me.

"There he is." Charlotte waves and catches his eye. He gives a quick head movement and smiles acknowledgment while not missing a beat.

"Like to dance?" Diana looks hopeful.

"Like I like to eat."

"Then let's go, sailor."

She takes my folded-up hat I don't know what to do with and gives it to Charlotte to hold. Diana and I are on the floor just as the music stops. We're holding each other in dance mode, neither one letting go even though there is no music. For the first time, I see more than a lovely face. Chemistry is not my favorite subject, but it becomes mine as

I look at her. I see something, feel something, become something, want something. The music starts again, a slow "Let's Fall in Love." And as we move, I swear we do fall in love. I do, anyway. Just like that.

We dance slow dance, lindy, jitter-bug, samba, whatever the music offers, without stopping for I don't know how long until Diana asks, "How much time do you have left?"

I am so mesmerized by our dancing I'd put time aside. I look at my watch. One ten.

"I have to be back by 7."

Her eyes. The way she looked at me.

"Come with me," she said.

I don't ask where. At that point, I am willing to go anywhere with her. I never want to leave her or let go of the newly tapped feelings I am experiencing.

Diana pulls me by the hand to the door as Charlotte throws my hat to me and waves goodbye. I shrug my shoulders as if to tell Charlotte, "I don't know what's happening."

We are in a taxi again headed for an address given by Diana. She still holds my hand and puts her head on my shoulder.

"Okay?"

"Extra okay."

We say little if anything until we arrive at an old brownstone building. Diana pays the fare, not allowing me, and leads me up a flight of stairs to her place.

"Charlotte and I share the place." She unlocks the door and there we are.

I look around. It is a two-bedroom, shared bathroom, the kitchen slightly connected to the living room, books, magazines spread about. A small place, but clean and nice.

"Charlotte will spend the night with her boyfriend."

I understand what she means.

Charlotte puts some records on a phonograph player, and we dance a slow dance or two, negate the idea of a drink, take an enchanted shower together, and end up in bed. I barely hear John Coltrane's

"What's New?" in the background. I tell her my story about Suzanne. I feel nervous, uneasy and clumsy...

You don't need to hear all the details, just know I was swept away in sweet submission.

I made it back to the ship in time. Of course, my shipmates wanted to know how I managed to catch not one, but two women; where we went; what were they like; did I get any? That stuff. But, you know, I did not want to share with them what was the most memorable night of my life up to then. They pressed, but got nothing from me. I didn't mean for it to, but my silence laughably labeled me a mysterious lady killer. If they had only known.

As the ship left the Hudson River dock and headed out into open water, I went aft and watched New York slowly shrink into a watery mist. Maybe it was my eyes that held the mist. It wasn't like I was leaving my heart back in the city; instead, my heart now contained a previously unknown sweetness, warmth, tenderness, even love. I think we both knew we probably would never see each other again, but what she gave me was a gift I can never forget.

Smirk all you want. But for me....

A few weeks later, and to my huge surprise, I received a package from Diana addressed to me aboard the ship, a hardback copy of *The Odyssey*. No note or comment or return address.

I'm not sure why she did that.

Another gift?

A book she'd help edit?

A memento?

A message to me?

Whatever, I still treasure the book.

CHAPTER 12

"Teach Me Tonight"

When my four-year enlistment in the navy ended, I went home and did nothing for a few weeks. I thought about returning to Carbondale and picking up where I left off in my studies. But the more I thought about it, the more I knew I did not want to stay in the Midwest, not after experiencing California. So I applied to UCLA and even though they didn't accept all my transfer credits, to my surprise and pleasure, I was accepted as a sophomore for the next school year. My parents were not happy I was choosing to live so far way, but my dad, especially, was pleased I wanted to finish the education he had pushed me into. A part of me wanted to do it for him, too.

I knew I would need money for the move west. Dave, my old boss at TriCity Grocery, was nice enough to give me a job, knowing I wouldn't be staying home more than a few months. I saved as much as I could while living with my parents. I offered to pay rent or for food, but they wouldn't let me.

When the time came, it was a bittersweet goodbye with my parents.

"You sure this is what you want to do?" my father asked.

"I've been itching to get back to California ever since I left."

"You said you were going to lose some credits by transferring. That okay with you?"

"It'll take longer to get my degree, but I'm in no hurry. I'm not sure what I want to major in yet."

"California's so far away," my mother said. "And it seems like you just got back and you want to leave again."

"I'll write. I'll call. I promise."

"I guess I'm worried you'll get out there and get distracted from finishing school."

"Don't worry, Dad. I've seen what life could be like without an education."

"You don't know anyone back there," Mom said.

"I might reconnect with some navy buddies. Anyway, I didn't know anyone when I went to Carbondale, either. And it worked out." My mind flashed a moment on Molly and her brothers.

The three of us hugged, and I admit I felt a bit of a tug on my heart along with the excitement of starting new.

While the financial support I received from the GI Bill helped pay my tuition and books, it didn't take long for my savings to evaporate. I found a job working part-time for an insurance broker. The job consisted of coming in to the office after hours and calling clients that were letting their policies lapse and asking them why. Basically, I just chatted with them and listened to their grievances and offered to have someone call them to straighten out the problem.

The job worked out well for me and the insurance broker. I managed to help him retain customers, and I earned enough to rent a small, one-bedroom studio attached to a home in a well-to-do neighborhood near the university. I decorated it with a Magnavox phonograph set-up and some jazz records. Happiness, incorporated.

I needed a way to get around LA besides buses, so I daringly bought a used Triumph T100 having never before ridden a motorcycle. It seemed practical at the time, and it didn't take long to get used to riding it and developing a manly pride in it. Whew! Look at me!

It took me a few weeks to get used to my class schedule and work routine. Learning to study and concentrate didn't come easy after four years away from it. But I began to fall into a busy, solitary pace. I lost track of Ted after we split, and I was often tempted to try to locate some of the friends I'd made at the Los Alamitos Naval Station two years ago, but had no way of contacting them now. That was probably to my advantage, as I had little time for socializing that would have kept me from my studies.

In the beginning, I decided not to carry a full class load and had no idea as to what major I should pursue. I was in no hurry. I took the usual requirements that covered the liberal arts: biology, history, sociology, French, English. But as the first semester passed, I found my interest in English and American literature growing. I hadn't realized it, but I didn't really know how to read, not for college, until one of my professors threw this lesson at us.

Listen in:

PROFESSOR

Good morning, class. Let me present a poem which I'm sure most of you are familiar.

Humpty Dumpty sat on a wall.
Humpty Dumpty had a great fall;
All the King's horses
And all the King's men,
Couldn't put Humpty together again.

Can anyone tell me who Humpty is?

STUDENT 1

--He's an egg.

PROFESSOR

What in the rhyme tells you he's an egg?

STUDENT 2

--That's how he's pictured in children's books.

PROFESSOR

Show me anything in the rhyme that says Humpty is a male or female or an egg.

Class is quiet a moment.

STUDENT 3

--Isn't the rhyme about some English king? Richard the 3rd or something?

PROFESSOR

Possibly. But how would that relate to the point of the rhyme? In fact, what is the point of the rhyme?

STUDENT 1

--Some things can't be fixed once they are broken.

PROFESSOR

How do you know?

STUDENT 1

--The last line says it: "Couldn't put Humpty together again."

PROFESSOR

So who is Humpty?

STUDENT 1

--An egg!

Class laughs. Me, too.

PROFESSOR

Let's really look at the rhyme. First line. What are the key words?

STUDENTS

Voices from around the room.

--Sat.

--Wall.

--Humpty.

PROFESSOR

Right. And what does "sat" suggest Humpty is doing?

STUDENTS

Voices from around the room.

--Sitting.

--No, it's past tense. Was sitting.

--He was immobile. Not moving.

--Didn't do anything.

PROFESSOR

Right. Immobile. What about "wall"? What does the word bring to mind? What types of wall are there? And I don't mean "brick" or "rock..."

STUDENTS

Voices from around the room.
--You mean like a barrier?
--A wall has two sides.
--Something that you have to climb over?
--A problem, maybe? Something that you can't decide?
--Like that phrase "sitting on a fence."

PROFESSOR

Yes. So we know Humpty sat on a wall, another way of saying Humpty was passive, perhaps undecided about something that has more than one side to consider.

STUDENT 2

--But that's not what the line says. It just says he sat on a wall. Aren't you reading too much into the line?

PROFESSOR

Am I? Or, am I reading beyond the words, trying to find out who Humpty is? The little poem may have more to it than a simple nursery rhyme. We won't know until we really examine what's below the surface. See what you think when we finish.

Professor turns back to the board.
What are the key words in the second line?

STUDENTS

Voices from around the room.
--Humpty fell.
--Yeah, but it was a "great fall," so the wall was high.
--If the wall represents a problem or situation needing an answer, Humpty's "great fall" may mean he didn't solve the problem, or made the wrong decision.

PROFESSOR

Very good.

STUDENT 2

--I still think that's making a big deal out of simple words.

PROFESSOR

Perhaps. But you still can't tell me who Humpty is, can you?

STUDENT 1

--He's an egg!

More classroom laughter.

PROFESSOR

You won't give up, will you? Well, let's keep looking.

He points out the next two lines on the board.

The key words here are "king" and "horses and "men." Do they suggest anything to you?

STUDENTS

Voices from around the room.

--A king is the one with the power. It could mean anyone in power.

--The President.

--A dictator.

--A boss.

--Anyone in charge.

--Horses refer to power. Horse power. King's horses could refer to the strength and power a king or leader has.

--The king's men could mean his advisors, the ones who help him stay in power.

STUDENT 2

--So, you're saying that Humpty's fall, or the decision he made, or whatever he did when he left the wall was so bad or wrong, that nothing, even the ones with power, could help him. Nothing could be the same again after his fall.

PROFESSOR

Am I, or is the poem telling us that? We put no outside thought in the rhyme that isn't there if we look deeply at the words in the poem.

STUDENT 2

---We still don't know who Humpty is. I just assumed it was a man...

STUDENT 1

-An egg!

STUDENT 2

Smiles and continues...

...but nothing in the lines say it is a man.

PROFESSOR

You're right. We don't know who Humpty is as a person, or even if Humpty is a person. Does it matter?

STUDENTS

Voices from around the room.

--This is frustrating.

--Then, who or what is Humpty Dumpty?

--And so what, anyway?

--Humpty might be a specific person, but Humpty could also be anyone who makes a bad decision that can't be changed or made better. A decision that could change your life forever.

--I think the author makes up the funny name, Humpty Dumpty, so it doesn't refer to anyone in particular, and maybe not even a person, but an idea, even.

--Oh, I get it. Humpty could be someone who's pregnant and doesn't know whether to have an abortion, you know? Then when the person makes the decision, it turns out to not be the right one and you have to live with it.

--I don't know about that. Kind of far-fetched.

--No. I mean, Humpty could refer to any wrong decision you make that has a negative, irreversible effect on you or others.

--So Humpty is you or me?

--Could be a person. Look at General MacArthur. He sure made a bad decision by trying to overrule Truman and take the war in Korea into China. And look where it got him. President Truman fired him, and he lost his power and was forced to retire after a life time of service. None of his friends who wanted him to run for president could put him back in power after he made a bad decision.

PROFESSOR

What's my point in all this? I want to illustrate that reading contains at least three components: the literal, the critical, and the aesthetic levels. Reading "Humpty Dumpty" at the literal level requires an acknowledgment of what's obvious: "Humpty Dumpty sat on a wall...had a great fall..." and so on. You can even memorize the lines and repeat them.

That's a literal reading. A critical reading requires you look a little deeper. Who is Humpty? Why was he sitting on a wall? Why did he have a great fall, and what is a "great fall"? Is it nothing more than a memorization rhyme for children, or is there a meaning behind the lines? These are critical questions that go beyond the literal level. Then we get to the aesthetic level, our personal reactions and connection to what and how the author has written what we've read. Do we think the rhyme scheme is clever, well-written, or just silly? Has the author made us think about something we never thought about before? Or, maybe our feelings or opinions are being shared and reenforced by the author. Maybe reading the lines brings back memories of our childhood, or a major mistake we've made in our lives. Humpty was just a little exercise to make you aware of the type of reading I want you to do in this course. As I said, read beyond the words, but don't insert ideas, opinions or feelings that you can't prove if they are not found in the words of the work you are reading.

STUDENT 1

--I still think Humpty is an egg.

Maybe. While I was not one of the voices in the discussion, this was my first lesson in reading since Dick and Jane.

CHAPTER 13

"Falling in Love with Love" (Again)

I tried applying the Humpty Dumpty advice to my reading materials. I read voraciously, often feeling a lack of necessary background for class discussions. Compared to me, some students seemed to have read everything, already knew everything. I did my frustrating best, but didn't raise my hand much.

At the time, I was taken by the idea of learning and I wanted to be a thinker and enter the minds of men like Socrates, Plato, Locke, Rousseau, but I could only read about them, rather than think like them. I wanted to feel "educated," but my mind wanted to wander to music and literature. Even there, I drifted toward the arts that dealt with the loss of love that contains a sort of romantic touch of tragedy. Maybe an effect of all those love lyrics I grew up with? What have they taught me about love?

Between classes, studying, and work, I had little time for social engagements. I attended a few drinking parties and tried study groups, but most of my classmates seemed younger and smarter than me and I felt it. I had a few flings but nothing serious developed. I only met three or four others like me on the GI Bill and they were married and busy with their lives. I accepted myself as a kind lone wolf.

Wait. Now that I think on it there was this student in my American Lit class. Yes. I had a crush on her from afar. I'd spend more time looking at her in class than paying attention to the instructor. I imagined what she was like, what being with her would feel like. Harper, I think was her name. Maybe that was her last name. Doesn't matter.

I finally got nerve after class one day to ask her out "for coffee or something." I remember she asked what the "or something" was. I struggled to come up with a retort, but we ended up eating pizza at some place in Westwood Village. We talked about our class, the instructor, and our assignment to write a pretend introduction to the collected works of some American author of our choice. I admitted the task seemed daunting. She suggested I pick Katherine Ann Porter, since her works were short stories and novellas. I took her advice, read all of Porter's works, and felt good about my paper. (I'm thankful Porter's only novel, *Ship of Fools*, hadn't been published yet!)

When my paper was returned marked with an "A," I asked Harper to dinner as a thank you for her recommendation. I picked her up at her sorority house on Gayley, and we walked to a nearby steak house. At first, I thought there might be some chemistry between us to explore, but the more we talked about anything but our lit class, the more I realized how wide apart our interests were. She leaned heavily into that sorority society menu, and I had no taste for it. I decided to admire her from afar once the evening ended.

After dinner, we went to some performance at Royce Hall. I forget what, but when it was over, we started walking back to her sorority house when she stopped and asked me if she could see my apartment. Did she mean what I thought she meant?

Yes, as it turned out.

Now, after Diana, I'd had a few, not many, sexual flings or what one partner called "releases" -- but Harper? I'd never experienced anything like her lack of sexual performance. She wasn't interested in any foreplay, just in a hurry for insertion, then surprised me, if it was real, with a blaring *la petite mort* almost the moment I entered her. And that was it for her. She just lay there thinking about who knows what while I finished, then told me that was nice and that she should be getting back to Gayley.

No argument from me.

I never saw her again after the class ended, deciding I'd best go back to studying and insurance.

One night after work, I decided to give myself a break and rode my Triumph over to The Lighthouse, a jazz venue in Hermosa Beach where Howard Rumsey and his All-Stars played. I hadn't heard any live jazz since my New York adventure. Rumsey, an original member of Stan Kenton's orchestra, freelanced for a while and then formed his own combo that made its home at The Lighthouse.

The group was in the middle of "How High the Moon" when I arrived. A woman was imitating June Christie on vocals. At least that's the way it sounded to me. The place was not overly spacious. With every table packed, I stood by the door until my eyes acclimated to the smokey dark and spied a vacant stool by the bar. As I listened more, I gave her voice more appreciation. When she dropped the scat singing and let go of the lyrics, she proved she belonged on the stage. She also belonged in the black form-fitting dress she wore.

Her performance ended a set. I looked around for a waitress, but they were all busy filling orders. Then the singer I'd just heard came straight toward me and smiled, sort of.

"You're in my seat."

I gave a witty answer. "Oh, sorry. Didn't know."

I slipped off the stool and she took over.

First look made her between twenty-five and thirty, about five-five, a beach tan, cropped curly hair, pleasant face, almond eyes, small nose, not much makeup, if any, but light pinkish lipstick on thin lips.

"They keep this stool for me so I can get to the stage quickly," she said by way of apology.

"Right. No problem." Another witty rejoinder.

A waitress approached us. "Abbie, you want anything?"

"Club soda, please."

"And you, sir?"

"CC and ginger." It just came out.

The waitress left. Abbie and I smiled at each other.

"I enjoyed your singing."

It wasn't a lie.

"Thanks. I don't get to sing in public much. Howard gives me a gig here a couple of times a month. I've had a few sets at Shelly's Mann Hole, but trying to break in to the jazz world.... Not easy."

"I can imagine."

We were silent for a minute.

"You've got a great voice."

"I'm told I sound too much like June Christie. My Achille's heel."

I didn't want to tell her I agreed.

"Good group of musicians. You like working with them?"

And we fell into a conversation about some of Rumsey's All-Stars like Conti Candoli, Shorty Rogers, Bob Cooper and how they encouraged her. I'd heard of most of them, even had records with some of them playing, and was now elated realizing I was actually watching them perform. Our drinks came, and I leaned against the wall admiring her crossed legs. Suddenly school and work seemed far, far away, and I felt like someone in love.

The musicians started milling about the stage and she had to leave to do another set.

"You hanging around?" she asked.

"I'll save your stool." No way was I going to leave.

Once the group settled down on stage, Rumsey did a little riff on the bass and then they went into "Here's That Rainy Day." As soon as Abbie came in with "Maybe I should have saved those leftover dreams..." I was in music heaven. And when Cooper entwined his soft, sinewy tenor sax behind her voice, I didn't want the music to ever stop.

During the set, Abbie did an upbeat "Almost Like Being in Love," which became my sentiment exactly. Then she finished with a sultry "Where or When."

When she came back to her stool, she thanked me and asked how I liked the set.

"Have you made any records? I'd buy them all."

Abbie laughed. "I wish. I have my agent working on it."

She told me she worked at Capitol records as a secretary. She had hoped the job would help people who could help her gain a recording contract, but so far nothing.

She didn't seem to mind my hanging on to her, so I enjoyed another drink and even though she was through singing for the night, she stayed on her stool. When the group finished, I asked her if she was going to be here tomorrow night.

"I don't have a gig tomorrow, but I'm coming to hear Chet Baker."

The way she said it. Was that an invitation of sorts?

"Coop told me he's going to be here," she continued. "You know his work?"

"Oh, yeah. I have a record with him, Gerry Mulligan, Bob Whitlock and Chico Hamilton. Unusual recording. No piano, just trumpet, baritone sax, bass and drums. Great counterpoint between Chet and Mulligan."

"You a musician?"

"Next life, maybe. I just like jazz."

The place began to empty out. But I didn't want to leave what up to then had been my best night since New York.

"Maybe I'll see you tomorrow night?" Abbie asked.

"Hope so." I wanted to ask if I could give her a ride, or go somewhere for more music, but at that moment I didn't quite see her on my motorcycle. Besides, she left with one of the musicians.

I don't remember what route I took on my way back to my place. The entire evening replayed in my head. I realized how much I wished I could make my life music. I fantasized asking Abbie out. I kept hearing her singing "Maybe I should have…"

When I got home, it was late, but I was far from tired. I was jazzed and put on my "Chet Baker Sings" album. A weak voice, yet he knew how to make the lyrics reflect romance. With every song he sang, I tried to imagine Abbie singing it. When he got to "But Not for Me," I thought: Exactly! Get real.

I went to bed, restless as that willow in a wind storm.

The next morning, I started work on an essay due for my poetry class, trying to remember everything my English professor had taught me. I picked Shelley's "Music When Soft Voices Die (To-)" because it was short, dealt with music and soft voices, and reminded me of Abbie. but I couldn't think of what to write. Then I got the crazy idea of comparing the poem to the lyrics of "There will Never Be Another You." To me, they both offer the power of music and memory of a loved one. Diana?

Diana.

Abbie.

All day, both class and work felt like pulling a Mac truck. All I could do was think about going back to The Lighthouse and seeing Abbie. Fool's errand, I kept telling myself, but was not listening.

I had to work later than usual and by the time I got to the club, it was jammed. I paid and pushed my way through the crowd. Recorded music was playing, so the band was on a break. I looked for Abbie on her stool, but someone else was sitting there. At first I thought maybe she had come and gone. I'd already missed the first set. Then I saw her at a table over against the wall sitting with two men, very animated and engaged.

Like an electrical jolt, I saw myself as the disappointed fool I was. What was I expecting? That she'd be sitting on that stool waiting for me? I was nothing to her, just a part of the audience. I told you so, didn't I? Man, I hadn't learned anything.

I started to leave, but decided to have a drink and wait for Chet Baker to play. I kept looking her way, but she was too involved in conversation. I didn't recognize her table partners but figured they had something do with music.

So, I stared and drank my CC and Ginger.

The recorded music stopped and the place quieted down as the audience watched the musicians drift up to the stage. That's when I saw one of the men at Abbie's table make his way to the stage and pick up a tenor sax. Based on the album cover photo of "Chet Baker and Crew," I realized it was probably Phil Urso. Rumsey was on bass, but I don't remember the rest of the players. But I do remember that musical night. Baker, for me, is at his best when he plays standards. And he loves to sing them. I knew most of his recordings at that point in time, but to see and hear him live embraced me. And when he did "I Wish I Knew" and "I Fall in Love Too Easily," I felt he was playing and singing for me.

I left after Baker's set and took a slow ride through the night letting the music take over my thoughts and reprimanded myself for being a silly romantic. I excused myself realizing that my formative years were filled with lyrics from love songs. I'd been brainwashed into believing in sappy love lyrics knowing nothing about love.

Is it possible to be in love with love?

CHAPTER 14

"I Wish I Knew"

"A bit of a stretch, don't you think?"

That, along with a B grade, was the only comment on my poem-comparison essay when the instructor returned it. So different from my mentor's encouragement at SIU. He didn't offer much help. In truth, my attending college began to seem a bit of a stretch. I wondered if I was learning anything useful or even if I belonged. What did I want to do? What was I doing with my life? Of course, some of my self-questioning had to do with my depression brought about by my foolish thoughts over Abbie.

When I thought of dropping out, I remembered my discussion with my parents before I left home. Quitting school would hurt my parents, especially my dad. So far, I'd been writing or calling home and telling them how well things were going. In a way, they were. What would I do if I quit? Become an insurance agent? I'm not getting any younger, and my mom keeps asking me if I've found a girlfriend. I know she's waiting for the day I get married. When will that be?

They've put a lot of faith and trust in me. Pressure. Confusion. Doubt.

I got on my Triumph and started riding nowhere in particular until I realized I was heading toward Huntington Beach, a place with fond navy memories. I wasn't sure I'd ever thanked Bard properly for letting me stay at his parents' converted garage. What I knew of Huntington Beach then was this small oil-well town on Highway 1 with a long pier and perfect surf.

When I got there, I was disappointed to find he no longer lived there. His parents told me he lived in Hawaii working on his doctoral degree in environmental studies. I'd met them a few times and they remembered me. When they asked me what I was doing, I played up my college attendance not letting on I was thinking about dropping out. I felt a tinge of jealousy that Bard had managed to achieve what I hadn't, a worthwhile goal.

After a short visit, I went over to the beach and walked the pier, thinking about the times Bard and I would break the rules and jump off into the surf. After I walked the pier, I took off my shoes and strolled the wet sand. I thought about the abalone and lobsters we used to catch and cook on the beach. The parties at night with Bard's surfer friends. And bad sunburns in attempts to get as tanned as we could.

I sat on a large piece of driftwood and watched as one wave after another rose, crested, then dropped with a thud, the water rushing, slushing toward me, only to sink and disappear into the sand. The waves seemed to know what they were doing. They had a goal.

So, too, had the sandpipers as they raced with short legs toward the receding water digging their sword-like beaks for food before retreating from an incoming rush of a broken wave, back and forth, back and forth.

And the pelicans heavily lumbered away with flapping wings only to smoothly stretch them out and seamlessly skim long and low over the water like it all belonged to them, guarding, searching, doing.

Seagulls, some sitting on the water off shore, others hovering on the beach sitting in groups, squeaking and squawking, waiting to see if I had food they can steal. They had their goal.

What was mine?

I don't know how long I sat on the beach watching and listening to the natural music before I headed back to my place. When I got home, I played Billie Holiday singing "You Don't Know What Love Is." It seemed to fit my immature mood. I scrounged up some leftovers, and while I was munching, I thought of the line from Shakespeare's Twelfth Night, "If music be the food of love, play on..." Then I substituted the word "fool" for "food" and laughed at myself, thinking that would make a great line to use in an essay, reminding me that I did have an essay due next week for one of my Lit classes.

On a whim, I decided my decision to stay in college would depend on the grade and the reaction I received from my professor on this one essay. Silly, but that's how I felt at the time.

I don't remember exactly how I approached it, but the theme had to do with the role of music and love. I wrote about a correlation between Orsino's unrequited love song in Shakespeare's "Twelfth Night" and the role music played on our emotions and how music inspired dance. I used as many lines from love songs I knew to support my thesis. I put everything I had into that essay.

Once I turned it in, I continued to attend classes and go to work. But my mind was never far from that essay and what it would bring. Would I actually base my future on that one essay? The more I thought about it, the more inane it seemed. Maybe I wasn't cut out for college. My dad would be so disappointed.

Maybe that essay guided my next move, maybe not. Either way, the A grade and the comments on my originality proved a huge ego boost. The professor's comments also included the question "Are you a music major? Your references show signs of musical knowledge."

A music major? I could recognize musical instruments and their sounds, but I couldn't play a one, though I wished I could. I didn't know a C note from an E note, if there was such a thing. All I really knew about music was in my ears and stacks of records. But I needed music in my life. Music let me know I was alive and in the present moment, in the here and now. Yes, I loved music, especially jazz, but....

Well, why not learn more about what you love?

I told myself I didn't need to major in music, but I could take classes in music theory, music appreciation, history of music, maybe even take singing lessons. I could carry a tune. Why not learn more about vocal skills and learn to read music?

Why not?

CHAPTER 15

"Comin' Around Again"

After I received my BA degree, it took me over two more years of various classes to get my MA in liberal arts. In addition to the required courses, I took a few unnecessary ones just for my own pleasure: creative writing, intro to journalism, art appreciation, music theory and world literature. One of my instructors recommended I take photography, and I began to see how it could benefit journalism and art appreciation. It took longer to get my degree, but it was worth it. I picked up a potpourri of knowledge that together helped me build my future.

I began to understand what musicians did with their instruments to create the sounds I was hearing. I learned music terms and how to really hear music. For instance, I don't know how many times I listened to Miles Davis's recording of "So What" before I heard what I was hearing. Now when I listen, I'm aware of the recurring pulse or 1-2-3-4 beat pattern. The first seconds open with Paul Chambers playing a soft bass line that Bill Evans joins with a two-note response on the piano. The two seem to ramble, searching in no particular key. Then the bass and piano combine for faster tempo melody. The bass drops a step while the piano drifts around between chords. Slight pause, then the bass grumbles into a low register. Then suddenly the bass plays a repeating riff while the piano comes in with the two-note "So What" cord in quartal harmony. Jimmy Cobb comes in on drums. Then the trumpet and two saxophones join in as Cobb hits the cymbal. Chambers goes up a half step while horns play the riff in a new key, then all the instruments drop back to the original key. Drums take over and then Miles begins his solo.

This kind of knowledge opened up my ears, giving even more meaning to my love for music, which I confess at the time was mostly cool jazz. That's not to say I ignored classical or popular music. Several classes gave me a good dose of the masters, my preference leaning toward Mozart, Ravel, Debussy, Copeland. One course introduced me to Spanish classical music, which I immediately took to, especially Juaquin Rodrigo's "Concerto de Aranjuez. Miles Davis plays his version of the second movement on his "Sketches of Spain" album.

Sorry if I'm going overboard here. I'm just trying to show the excitement I felt when I began to feel my feet where finally on the ground.

I did learn to read basic music, took voice lessons (nothing professional, played with my timbre) and kept up with the different music scenes around town, classical, blues, pop, expanding my musical knowledge which eventually paid off and led to my new career: freelance writer.

That came about when I wrote an essay attempting to compare West Coast jazz with East Coast Jazz. I even attached a few photos I had taken at various jazz clubs. My instructor knew an editor at *Downbeat* and suggested I send it in. Surprise! They published it, paid me, and that was the beginning of my writing articles and critiques for various publications for a living, a meager one at first. I started by writing reviews, nothing too technical, and sending them to newspapers and magazines. I collected mostly rejections in the beginning, but I persevered along with help and encouragement from John Horn, one of my professors. I studied the way critics like Nat Hentoff, Leonard Feather and Stanley Crouch covered their subjects. Mainly, I tried to get readers to feel the music as much as I do.

In the beginning of my new career, I held on to my part-time job with the insurance brokerage. But the writing assignments began to grow. At first, I covered just jazz, but began to spread my interests to performing arts in general in order to get more work. I began to interview prominent artist either in person or via phone. Some of the publications paid my travel expenses to events in Las Vegas, New York, San Francisco and New Orleans, and much, much later, cities in Europe where jazz seemed more popular than here. In time, I was able to say goodbye to the insurance business.

During my first assignment in New York, I forget now what my subject was, I thought I'd try to find Diana. Even though I'd been to her apartment, I had no recollection of where she had taken me. I felt compelled to look up Crown Books. It was somewhere on Park Avenue South in a building complex, and I walked all around it trying to remember Diana's last name, thinking I might find her, see her. I would just walk in to their office and ask for Diana. A fool's errand, of course, but emotions of the heart do strange things. What would have happened if I had found her?

Between assignments, I wrote a novel, *No Way In*, about a writer who struggles to create writing that reflects the images, sounds and feelings he personally experiences when he listens to Miles Davis. I gave all the knowledge I had about Miles at the time to my main character who eventually realizes it's an impossible task and ends up sitting alone in a room listening over and over to "Ascenseur pour l'echafaud," the sound track Miles did for the French movie of the same name. I think I tried to emulate Virginia Woolf, who claimed she heard the sound of her sentences in her head before she wrote them. You can especially hear sound and rhythm in her book *Waves*. Or maybe I was influenced a little by Dorothy Baker's *Young Man with a Horn*. Probably both.

Anyway, it made me think that Flannery O'Connor might be right: Only those with a gift should write for public consumption. My book was not a big seller. Eventually I earned enough royalties to equal my advance money. For sure, the book wasn't going to change my life in any way. Still, I was proud of the book and fantasized that maybe Diana or Abbie or maybe even Miles might get word of it.

It took over a year, but I became fairly accepted with *Downbeat* for what I did and obtained contracts with a few major magazines, like *Esquire, Rolling Stone, and Vanity Fair*. Occasionally they bought some of my photos to accompany an article. Between traveling to attend performances in small clubs and huge staged events, movies, theater and writing up what I saw and heard, I imprudently began writing another novel trying not to be influenced by anybody. I didn't want to be another Kerouac or Kesey, popular at the time. I wanted to find me in my writing. So I was busy and enjoying myself doing what I wanted and liked. I even began to make money. My social life had more acquaintances than friends and had no serious romantic relationships. The lone wolf. And that was alright with me.

When *Downbeat* asked me to do a cover story for an upcoming singer named Abbie Hart, I expected fate was playing with me. In my work, it wasn't news to me that Abbie had finally received a recording contract a few years ago and was on the charts. The idea of seeing her again after so long mixed me up emotionally. But another part of me couldn't wait to do the story.

Her latest album was getting good play on the airwaves. I noticed in listening her voice had lost that raspy lightness of June Christy and now had a touch of smoky vibrato. She used her voice like an instrument and added nice counterpoint to Al Connor's tenor sax sound that seemed to envelop her on most of her songs. And she could hold a note forever.

Abbie was singing at The Carlyle Café, so I flew to New York to interview her. I knew I could do a phone interview, but I called Monty Higgins, her manager, who loved the idea I was coming and told the Carlyle to let me in for any show when I arrived. I like the Carlyle. I'd been there before. It has a feel of sophistication and intimacy, plus great acoustics for small jazz groups.

Abbie was in the middle of an upbeat "Just One of Those Things" when I arrived. I was led to a small table lit by a tiny shaded table lamp with a straight view of Abbie and the quartet backing her up. Monty and I did our greetings then turned our attention to Abbie. She looked and sounded like she belonged up there on the stage. Her once cropped curly hair was still curly but longer, and her fair skin had lost its tan. Otherwise, she looked like the Abbie I remembered who had confiscated my heart without knowing it. Would she remember me? I doubted it. As I watched her, old feelings I knew I shouldn't permit were happening again.

When her set ended, Monty brought her to our table and introduced me. Then he left us alone to get acquainted for the interview.

"Nice to meet you. Monty tells me you're going to do a story on me for *Downbeat*."

She didn't remember me, as well she shouldn't have.

"Nice to meet you... again."

"Again? We've met before?"

"A while back."

"Where...when?"

"I love that song."

"What?"

I smiled at her confusion. "That's the last song I ever heard you sing. 'Where or When'."

She laughed. "You got me. Where? And when?"

"The Lighthouse. In my young and foolish days."

"The Lighthouse? In Hermosa Beach?"

"Mm."

"That *was* a while ago."

"You were working at Capitol Records, hoping for a break."

"I did for a while. Some memory you have."

"I remember every song you sang, both nights."

"Both nights?"

"The first night you bumped me from your stool. The second night you sat at a table with some musicians playing with Chet Baker and sat in on a set."

"I'm embarrassed. I don't remember you."

"Why would you? But I confess you stole my heart."

"That's sweet and sad. Was I nice to you, at least?"

"Very nice. The first night. The second night I just looked, disappointed I didn't get to talk with you."

"Well, we can make up for it now."

She smiled and I started getting that old feeling.

After Abbie finished her last set, Monty invited me to join him, his wife Sophie, and Abbie for a late dinner. I accepted, not realizing how much more than a dinner I was agreeing to.

Most of our dinner talk was about approaches to jazz music, the varied tastes from New Orleans jazz, bop, straight ahead jazz, to fusion. We discussed albums we owned of jazz greats we loved: Dizzy, Chet, Ella, Sarah, Billie, Coltrane, Bird, Miles, Hubbard, Clark Terry. We never ran out of names, spilling into classical and rock figures as if in a game of who knows the most. We agreed that jazz seemed to be on a decline, replaced by more popular styles drawing large crowds who liked to dance and scream above the performers. I told a story about the night I was in St. Louis for a George Shearing show at Peacock Alley and he stopped playing because the crowd was too noisy. The audience finally realized he'd stopped and went quiet. He refused to play unless people listened. I've always liked that about most jazz aficionados. They listen.

Monty and Sophie turned out to be not only fun, but two of the most handsome people I'd ever met, the image of the perfect couple. She'd been a stage actress but quit after marrying Monty. He taught English at a city college for a while, then played the stock market, making a small fortune, then quit to manage Abbie and three others whose names I didn't know, but he was sure they would make it big in the future. While I liked Monty from the beginning, I sensed an ego that demanded attention, and noticed Sophie deferred to him a bit too often. But he seemed well-read and appeared to know the music and theater business. I liked that he paid for our very expensive dinner.

Afterwards, we went to the Blue Note to hear Paul Desmond. Everyone there listened.

After the Blue Note closed, Monty and Sophie, slightly drunk, went home.

After they left, Abbie and I, slightly drunk, went to her room at the Salisbury Hotel.

CHAPTER 16

"My Foolish Heart"

I did more than write a cover piece on Abbie.

I married her.

Not right away. Seven weeks later.

I say I married Abbie, not "we got married." I'm sure I pushed for it, and to my surprise she agreed, or maybe the right word is surrendered. I could see she had real feelings for me and I went with those. At any rate, we had in my mind a whirlwind seven weeks of amusement and diversion. We spent a lot of time with Monty and Sophie, who witnessed our marriage, making the rounds at jazz bars, seeing a few Broadway plays, finding dance spots (my idea), and taking in some city sights. It seemed Abbie and I shared in our taste of nearly everything. I felt unhinged with happiness. When her gig ended at the Carlyle, we found more time to be alone and personal.

We rented a small beach-front cottage on Fire Island for two weeks, never leaving sight of each other. Walking the beach and building sand castles became a daily routine. We bought a few groceries, but mostly we ate out. No, mostly we stayed in bed. Just as her singing voice drew me to her, so did her being. Our bodies fit and craved each other, wanting little but to be joined.

"You only want me for my body," Abbie said after sex one morning.

"True."

"That's all I'm good for?"

"Well, you can sing a bit."

"That's it?"

"What more could a man want?"

She sat up in bed, pulling the sheet up to her neck.

"Come on. Seriously. What do you see in me?"

"I told you."

She kicked her leg against mine and gave a small snarl.

"Okay. Okay. I see a beautiful, talented woman who has cast a spell over me twice now and has made me very happy."

"Are you happy?"

"Couldn't be happier. Or luckier. I feel alive with you. I don't know what it is. Maybe that chemistry Guy Masterson sings about in "Guys and Dolls." All I know is, you make me happy."

She snuggled up to me and gave me a kiss.

"I'm happy, too."

And she showed me.

After, she asked, "Will you love me when I'm old and can't sing anymore?"

"You'll never be old and you'll always be able to sing."

"Liar."

"Even if that should happen, I'll always love you."

And that sums up what we called our two-week honeymoon.

My parents were shocked when I called them to tell them I got married. Abbie spoke to them on the phone as a way of meeting, and we received their well-wishes. Despite my excitement, I could feel some restraint in their reaction. I knew my dad wanted to say, "I hope you know what you're doing." And I knew my mom wished she had been at the wedding, as simple as it was.

When Abbie and I returned to LA, we found a decent two-bedroom condo in the Wilshire area. We didn't need anything too permanent since both of us traveled. Monty saw to it that Abbie kept busy with club and media spots. The article I did about her brought attention and demand for more studio work.

She played LA spots for a few months and then got a gig in Lucca, Italy, her first of several European tours. Because I could write anywhere, I went with her wherever her bookings or tours took her. Over a course of years, we found ourselves in Paris, Madrid, London, Montreux, Helsinki, Belgrade, Heidelberg, and places I've forgotten. Because of other musicians in some of the jazz festivals, I got to meet and write some well-knowns like Pat Metheny, Freddie Hubbard, Wayne Shorter, Alan Broadbent, Charlie Haden, and get interviews with them. I even met Miles once and dared approach him to compliment him on a performance, and he looked at me and said, "Yeah," and walked away. I took that to mean he agreed with my good taste.

The travel, after time, started to wear thin and had an unsteadying effect on our marriage. Sometimes I couldn't travel with her because of my assignments, separating us for weeks. We seemed to be on a merry-go-round of airplanes, trains, buses and waking up in hotels not sure where we were. Drugs and drinking found their way into our lives. Abbie and I experimented with some Ecstasy, cocaine, mostly grass. We stayed away from the really hard stuff after seeing what it did to greats like Chet, Bill Evans, Coltrane, Russ Freeman, Art Pepper. Too many others. But I could feel I was again tilting in the wrong direction, as was Abbie.

When Abbie's last European tour ended, I suggested we take a break for three or four months, find a place on the coast of Spain, and clear our heads and bodies. We had enough money to afford it. Drugs weren't helping us do better work. I thought I might even get back to working on my novel.

Reluctant at first, she agreed, and we found a place on the coast of southern Spain. At first, we both felt the relief from schedule pressures. She had four months before another recording or booking, and I completed all my outstanding assignments. We were free to be carefree. As it turned out, too carefree.

Then the morning I remember only too well...

One bloodshot eye opened to a yellow Madrid that squeezed out red spider-leg veins into the gray plains, northward to Santander, south to Granada, west to Portugal, east to the Pyrenees. The huge Michelin map taped on the dull white wall dared me to focus on where I was.

I couldn't.

With effort, I rolled over on my back, blinking at the cracks in the ceiling to clear my scratchy eyes. I closed them again, pressing my hands hard against my aching temples. Too many *sol y sombras* still mingled in my blood. Abbie had warned me I should go easy on the stuff, but I felt a need to prove to that damn crowd I could handle their challenge. Plus I was a little jealous. A lot jealous.

My left arm stretched out across the bed. She was up already.

"Abbie?" Even speaking hurt.

Maybe she didn't hear. Probably didn't want to after last night. I didn't remember most of it, but it couldn't have been good, not the way I felt.

Raising on one elbow, I leaned back against the wobbly headboard, squinting through the half-shuttered window. Was it gray out? Rain, perhaps? God, how welcome that would be. My eyes cleared. No, just more hot blue skies.

I slid back down and pulled the sheet up to my chin, closing my eyes. *Sol y sombra*. Light and dark brandy. Who thought up that one? Well, goodbye CC and Ginger. Brandy and I certainly have gotten acquainted since coming here.

A steady hack, hack, hack began outside, someone using time, being productive. Productive. Not a word I could lately apply to myself. The rhythm of the axe didn't match the steady thumping in my head. I tried to massage the pain away.

What had happened last night? Probably best not to remember. Not yet. Guilt might overwhelm me. Too early for that.

I forced myself to sit up.

"Abbie?" Still no answer. Get up; go see.

The cool tiled floor awakened my bare feet and the mid-morning air gently covered my nakedness on my way to the bathroom. But the bright whiteness there encouraged my headache. I sat on the toilet rather than stand. "Ah, polluted powerless pee," I mumbled. "My life won't end with a bang, just a dribble."

I stood and squinted into the cracked mirror over the sink. I saw something I might see in a wavy carnival mirror. A stubbled double chin depending on how I moved. Sunken, dull brown eyes surrounded by a watery red, surrounded by fatty tissue. Bags under more bags. Nice tan, though. I blinked a couple of times, watching those little hair-like things the ophthalmologist called "floaters" painlessly slide up and down in my vision. I looked older than I remembered.

"Mirror, mirror on the wall, who's the dumbest shit of all?"

I grabbed a towel, wrapped it around my increasing middle and went out on the patio framed by blood-red bougainvillea. Every day, for over two months now, I looked down at the growing village of La Herradura, set on the horseshoe-shaped bay, its white buildings stacked like huge dice, making their way from the shore to the top of the surrounding hills. From here, the Mediterranean blue didn't show its pollution, but it did show directly across the way, at the other end of the horseshoe. New and taller construction terraced upward and would soon block the clear view of Andrés Segovia's hill-top house.

When we'd first arrived and the guitarist's home had been pointed out, I had secretly considered it a good omen, a symbol of creation, a reminder of artistic purpose and accomplishments, a part of what I had come for, sitting there just across the way.

"It's not happening, Andrés. I'm as dead as you are and much less accomplished."

My eyeballs throbbing, I turned back into the house. The living room, sparsely furnished, was uncomfortable. I wanted to blame my lack of accomplishment here on this environment, but that would be a lie. Anyway, the view was great and the rent was right.

I stopped, a little dizzy, and leaned against the wall-to-wall bookcase, empty except for a dozen or so of their books and some yellowing paperbacks left by past English-speaking owners. On one shelf lay my folder and journal of creative writing ideas. I threw a kiss toward them.

"One of these days."

As I walked through the hall back to the bedroom, I sang out her name, played with it, knowing she wasn't there.

"Abbie! Oh, Ab –bee! Abbie, Abbie, ABBIE! Where are you? I'd be so nice to come home to." I plopped down at the foot of the bed, staring at the big map on the wall. I'd hung it up because there were no pictures in the room, just a small wooden closet with no door, and the bed with a noisy headboard that banged when we made love, which, I realized, we hadn't been doing much of lately.

I started singing hoarsely to myself, making up a tune. "*Sol y sombra, sol y sombra,* my soul is somber, my body's not sober, my legs can't samba, it's so unfair, and oh, oh, oh, what am I to wear?"

I picked up the shirt and shorts I'd worn last night and sniffed them. They were wrinkled, but they didn't smell, so I put them on.

A quick look in the kitchen verified that Abbie had not made any coffee. Probably down at Sarita's place. Sarita made great cafe con leche, better than the poor excuse for coffee our own little pot dripped. And I definitely needed coffee this morning.

After slipping on my deck shoes, I left the house. Our rental car wasn't there. Maybe she'd driven to Sarita's.

Normally a pleasant ten-minute jaunt down the hill, the walk to Sarita's jarred with every step, and even with my prescription sunglasses the brightness invaded me. *Todos el dias. El sol.* I was sick of the sun and heat. It sapped my energy. The days were too hot to work on anything. So we slept by day and played by night. And that was the trouble. We played too much.

Everything looked familiar and yet still foreign as I followed the road that curved from one end of the bay down to the other. A flat, blue-green this morning, the Mediterranean on my right lapped quietly at the sand and rock beach with its scattered array of soppy potato chip bags, beer bottles, and soda cans. It looked better from a distance. Like most things, I was discovering.

I walked past the six-story bloques on my left that were slowly devouring the empty spaces, obscuring the olive-treed hills that eventually led to the mountains that separated La Herradura from Granada. At one time, I'd been told, the beachfront was all farmed land. Most of the apartments stood empty this time of year, but in July and August, they would all be taken at triple the normal rent, the beach a swarm of oiled, near naked cancer candidates. I certainly didn't want to be here then.

Weekends were bad enough. Anyway, the rent on our place would go up, and we couldn't afford to stay. Just as well, just as well.

Sarita's felt dark when I first went in. I saw only three people and Abbie wasn't one of them.

"*Buenos dias*," I offered to all three. I heard a faint "*Buenos*" from Sarita, nothing from the two men who stood at the bar looking me over. Strange the way Spaniards stood at a bar and drank as if to say, "Just one and I'll be on my way." I had yet to see a Spanish bar that had stools.

Feeling the men's stares, I went to the other end where Sarita sat behind the counter reading the newspaper. I ordered my usual: *un grand cafe con leche y una tostada*. While she fixed my order, I offhandedly asked Sarita if Abbie, *mi esposa*, had been there. She examined me, as if trying to place me.

Hell, lady, we've only been coming here for months.

She shook her head, shrugged one shoulder, and made a "no" gesture with her face.

I took my coffee and toast over to a table by a window and sat down, too tired to stand. I placed my head between my hands and squeezed at the pain, wondering where Abbie had disappeared, feeling a touch of worried anger. She didn't have to disappear without a word. Still, she probably had a right to be mad after last night, although I couldn't remember what I'd done. What had I done?

I squinted out at the blue sea and a wave of guilt hit me. Abbie never truly wanted to come here. This was all my idea—my dream, really—since college, since that day the music professor played Joaquín Rodrigo's *Concierto de Aranjuez*. Other than my acquaintance with jazz, I'd never heard or felt anything so moving, never realized the power classical music held. Even Miles gave it a try. A doorway opened, I entered, and my love affair with Spanish music grew. Mañuel de Falla. Frederico Torroba. Albeniz. Segovia -- their music displayed such powerful passion, feelings I felt might be shared in my writing. Oh, foolish man.

I had told Abbie living in Spain would be cheaper. We'd experience another culture; we would travel the country, visit Aranjuez, Granada, Seville; learn to speak Spanish like the natives; live on the Costa del Sol for a while; swim in the sea every day; we'd sip sherry watching fantastic sunsets; Spain would inspire us, provide me time to write the novel I kept saying was in me; she could adapt the culture in her singing.

But the writing wasn't coming. And my Spain didn't feel at all like its music.

I flinched. A little warm coffee spilled on my leg. I noticed the toast plate was empty but didn't remember eating.

Finishing my coffee, I walked across the street to the beach, my head still aching, now feeling more despondent. I tossed a few small stones into the flat water. Was that the "dark continent" on the horizon? Someone at last night's party had told me on a clear day you could see it.

Last night.

Why could I remember that comment but nothing more? I must have been pretty obnoxious. That last *sol y sombra*...

I threw another rock at the sea and started back to the house. The sun was already at work and the walk up the hill was not shaded.

Where the devil was Abbie, anyway? Maybe she'd gone to the market in Nerja with Peggy.

Peggy.

After we'd met Peggy and her husband Paul, nothing had gone the way I had envisioned it. When we first arrived, the couple had befriended us, introduced us to a small circle of ex-patriots. At first, we were grateful to be shown around, to communicate in English. It made settling in easier until our Spanish improved. Trouble was, our Spanish never improved. As newcomers, we were invited to dinners and parties and escorted to the bars with the best tapas. Then we felt obligated to invite people over. Life had become one big party. And Peggy and Paul were always there, like expectant social vultures.

I was sick of them both. Paul was always flirting with Abbie. And Peggy was coming on to me, getting a little too friendly, making suggestive comments.

Peggy sure came on to me last night. I did remember that.

Oh, god, did I...?

No, I could never hurt Abbie. Not intentionally. Damn, why couldn't I remember? Well, we had to quit the partying, that's all.

The walk back up the curved road to the house cleared my head some, but the heat had started. My shirt stuck to me and before I was halfway back, my heart was pumping like a captured rabbit.

Distant church bells broke the quiet. Glad to stop, I listened, trying to put a melody to their uneven tempo. The sound reminded me of the power of music, what it could do for and to the soul. But it made me melancholy, uneasy, nostalgic for some thing or some place that didn't exist. I wanted to create word sounds that would touch people's souls. So, why wasn't I trying?

The car was still gone when I reached the house. I didn't know whether I should be mad or worry. Where the hell was Abbie? She must really be pissed. Still, part of me was glad she wasn't there. It prolonged having to deal with last night. What ever happened must have been pretty hurtful.

Thirsty and hot from the walk up, I took a San Miguel from the refrigerator and walked out on the patio. For the hundredth time, I looked through the flowering bougainvillea down at La Herradura, then across the bay to Segovia's place.

How easy it had been to slip into a lazy, nada existence here. Was this who I was?

After another sip, I stared at the brown beer bottle. My thumb peeled the damp label up the middle.

Face it. There would be no new novel. My only word music came from the sound of tinkling ice cubes, popping corks and caps, and pouring fizzing foam in a glass. And I had only myself to blame. I was blowing my chance. Soon it would be back to Abbie's bookings. and I would continue waiting for moving music to provide the words I'd never write.

Feeling a little sorry for ourselves, are we?

Come on, drama king. Here's your chance. Be operatic here. Dump the bottle's contents while singing a moment of epiphany in basso profundo. Turn the bottle upside down, watch the amber liquid spill over the green bougainvillea leaves. That's it. Good scene, very thespian. Nice directing, but I'm wasting beer. So what? Throw the empty bottle against the wall? No, no, move to the bookcase and put it on the shelf next to the large brown folder with your notes for your novel. Stare at it. That's right. Ah, the music swells. Now pick it up. Hold it as though you're weighing it. Play up this moment to the audience. Hold it against me. Hit a high note. Now hold it away from me. Hit a low note.

I smirked and tossed the folder back on the shelf, knocking a sheet of paper floating to the floor. It wasn't one of mine and I started to ignore it. Curious, I picked it up...

Couldn't face things - you. Stayed in Almuñecar with Paul. Back around when? Really sorry about last night. Really. You have every right to be angry with me. We'll talk when I get back. I need time. I don't understand it myself. I don't know why it happened. It just did. Sorry, sorry, sorry! Forgive me..
Abbie.

I read it again. A knot slowly twisting as unwelcome understanding began to tighten somewhere inside me. I looked at Abbie's note again, but my moistening eyes blurred. I couldn't focus on the words, only experience discordant emotions I'd never felt before. My throat went dry, constricted. I sank into a chair, motionless but for the swirling dissonance inside my head.

Then my heart heard it-- the rough, raspy, wailing timbre of a tenor saxophone, not the music I'd been waiting for.

**

Abbie and I left Spain a week later.

We didn't talk much while we made travel arrangements and packed. Abbie moped around sheepishly, crying occasionally, and I couldn't find anything but mean words to say when I did talk. The hurt was deep. It wasn't until we got home that we talked the talk.

"Why, Abbie?"

"It just happened."

"Not good enough. I guess I'm not good enough. That it?"

"It's not that. You're fine."

"Then why?"

"Things happen. I don't know why. It's not you. Blame it on booze, drugs, me. I don't know. I did what I did and I'm sorry. I didn't set out to hurt you."

"I've been faithful." I sounded pathetic. "Is Paul the only one?"

"Oh, god. What's the difference?"

"Does that mean there were others?" My heart skipped some beats. I didn't really want an answer.

Yes, I did.

"Well?"

"Christ, can't you leave it alone?" She looked at me with a face I'd never seen before. Anger? Hate? Defense? Shame?

"No! I can't! Tell me."

"I don't want to hurt you more." She put her face in her hands.

"Then there were. Who? How many?"

"How many? How many? What do you think I am?" Abbie shrieked.

"Unfaithful!" I yelled back.

"Yes, that's me. Unfaithful. I did everyone in the band. Every night!!"

That threw me. I gasped, grabbed my chest and wanted to die.

"Jesus! You believe that? You actually believe that of me?"

I drew some breaths and turned in an unsteady circle, no control of mind or body. It slowly sank in that it was her anger talking.

"Connor. The only other one. Satisfied? You were off on an assignment somewhere."

"The sax player?"

She nodded. "I was lonely. We smoked a joint. We had sex. End of story."

I said nothing.

She looked at me. "All this has made me see what I've not been honest about. I love you in a way, but I don't think we should stay together.

Our work, well, doesn't work together. I need to feel freer than I do. I don't like hurting you, but that's the way it stands. I'm sorry."

"You don't love me."

"I do, just not the way you need me to."

We decided to separate for a while. We both knew the separation would turn out to be divorce. And that's how it ended.

My first reaction was to blame Abbie. But I had to share the blame. I was the one to push and rush into marriage when neither one of us was ready to commit to such a long-term togetherness. We were sexually attracted to each other, and that's what really kept us together for over four years. For all that we travelled together, we were more often apart. Not conducive for a healthy relationship. Our lifestyles required it. She was a true part of the music scene, a member of the band. I was an outsider, the admiring audience. She made music; I wrote about it. And I went along with the excitement of being with music makers, but I didn't like what it was doing to us as a couple. I didn't like what it was doing to me, drugs, drinking to excess, wasting time with people I didn't respect. I was tilting again. I had hoped maybe in Spain we could regain the feelings we had experienced on Fire Island. Instead, it brought out the truth.

But, oh, the hurt, the pain. Time may heal old wounds, but you're left with nasty scars.

My parents never met Abbie. Now I had to tell them we were divorcing. Without giving too many details, I explained it was over. Our jobs interfered. We just fell out of love. They had little to say, and I felt somehow I'd failed them, too.

CHAPTER 17

"Bewitched, Bothered and Bewildered"

Abbie wasn't interested in keeping the Wilshire condo and wanted me to have it. So I re-furnished it to my taste. I built a wall of shelves for my record collection and another for books. I bought a new computer and desk and turned one of the bedrooms into my office. Thankfully, I had several writing gigs to keep me busy and to help fight off the limp and lonely feelings hanging over me.

After a few months, I started to lose my despondency over Abbie when a malignant melanoma on my left side took precedence. Those fun, sunny days at the beach finally caught up with me. The doctor just happened to catch it during my yearly physical, warning me it was life-threatening and might have progressed more than he could determine without surgery. I needed an operation yesterday, he stressed. It freaked me out. I'd never thought about death before. Might I die? Suddenly I was caught up in blood tests, CAT scans and pamphlets explaining cancer. Then I was in an operating room.

The cancer was serious enough the doctors had to carve out part of my left side up into my arm pit and remove all my lymph nodes there. They felt they'd removed all of the malignancy, which was a relief. I spent a week in the hospital and then had a few months of radiation and physical therapy recovering the use of my left arm. It gave me too much time to think about my life and what I was and wasn't doing with it. I fell into a deeper funk when the doctors told me to stay out of the sun.

I didn't feel like seeing anyone but began writing my parents regularly. I needed some kind of human connection. I didn't want to call them and let them hear depression in my voice. Plus, I didn't want them to worry about me. When I finally wrote about my cancer episode, they called me, and I felt like a school kid again as they reprimanded me for going through it alone. "You should have told us..." and all that. I should have. I have quite a few "should haves."

When *Travel* magazine wanted to know if I was available for a long-term traveling assignment, I jumped on it. They wanted me to journey through Mexico and Latin America focusing on Mayan and Aztec ruins to obtain photos and information that the magazine could use to serve as a series guide for tourists. It wasn't just the money that appealed, it was the idea of getting busy and doing something different. I needed the adventure.

The magazine wanted me to travel with one of their professional photographers. That didn't appeal to me. I showed them some of my photography work and convinced them to save money by letting me take the photos. I wanted to travel alone.

I'd sold my Triumph before I went to Spain, and happily I hadn't yet bought a replacement. I decided to buy a VW pop-top Camper for this job, which would probably take a year to cover so many countries. I could live in the camper when I couldn't find good hotel accommodations or stopped in jungle areas. It had a nice bed, stove, sink and would be roomy enough for me. And much better than those Boy Scout camp tent cabins.

I had a month before I was to leave, so I visited my parents for a few days. My stay was an emotional boost for us. They worried about my traveling alone, but I promised I'd write, call or get in touch as often as I could. I also used the time to read as much as I could about the Maya and the Aztecs and studied what I hoped would be passable Spanish. I obtained maps for all the countries I would be traveling through and worked out a route that looked passable, at least on paper. The VW had a tape deck so I could listen to tapes I wanted to bring. Then I did what

I'd been vainly wanting to do for a while. I got fit for contact lenses. To this day I find myself pushing up invisible glasses off my nose.

I leased out the condo for a year. The only thing I asked of my tenants was to be nice to my record collection. After dealing with loose ends, I was off.

I'm not going to bore you with my itinerary--you can find that in *Travel*-- except to say as I began my way through Mexico, I found my Spanish needed help, so I stayed for a month in San Miguel d'Allende for a crash course at The Instituto. Of all my Latin America travels, two events stand out: one very physical and one very spiritual. The first one took place while in San Miguel.

I met a woman in my Spanish class who had recently moved to San Miguel permanently. She approached me after class, introduced herself as Sade (like the singer, she said) and invited me for a drink at her apartment. Flattered, I accepted, though cautiously and curiously as to why me since there were several men in the class.

Turns out my Sade's background was similar to the singer Sade's background. She, too, was born in Nigeria, but moved to England when a child. Her wealthy parents sent her to a boarding school in France until she was old enough to attend Barnard College in New York. After graduation, she traveled the world, "has lived everywhere and has sown her oats," she told me, and was ready to settle in San Miguel.

Her apartment, very expensive-Mexican designed and furnished, had two bedrooms and two baths, a spacious living room with fireplace, and a dining room with attached kitchen. A small, private patio sat just outside large sliding doors. Besides various plants, the place was decorated with candles of all sizes and sorts.

Sade was probably the most gorgeous woman I'd ever come in contact with. Her body movements caused you to never want to take your eyes off her. I seldom did. But I was most astonished by her interest in sex. She was upfront from the beginning. She invited me for a drink, yes, but made it immediately known what she wanted. You can understand why initially I might have felt a little skeptical, but curious, and, of course, willing.

I hadn't had but two sips of my Brave Bull before she handed me a worn copy of a book.

"Are you familiar with this?" Her black eyes looked deep and expectant into me.

I looked at the cover and nodded. *The Kama Sutra.* I also probably blushed as I handed it back.

She held the book against her chest. "I'm on a quest."

"A quest?"

"Yes. My quest is to have tried every position in this book with three different men before I die."

Where was this going?

"I'd like you to be number three."

I almost dropped my drink.

"Why three?"

"It's a solid number, sacred, a triangle of power."

"Oh."

All I really knew about the Kama Sutra was that it contained descriptions of sexual positions. My mind flashed back to Bill and his sex-position flip books and Ted and I sneaking peeks at different copies of the Kama Sutras in the local library. She wants me to be number three...

"Don't look so shocked," Sade said, slightly frowning. "I've found that's a problem with Americans. They are too shy about the subject of sex. They want to keep it under the blanket, so to speak. I see you are shy." She took a deep breath and continued to educate me. "The Kama Sutra is misunderstood. It's more than a manual of sexual positions. It's a guide to the art of living well, explains the nature of true love, how to find a life partner. Better put, it's a philosophy book dealing with the power of love."

She stopped and frowned. "You think ill of me."

"No, no. I...I'm more intrigued by you. You've caught me off guard. And I guess I am a bit shy. Always have been around women I'm attracted to."

"You're attracted to me?"

"Of course." I'm sure I reddened again.

"I should have let you finish your drink. I sometimes move too fast, but I don't like to waste time. You've made me anxious to be clear up front. You see, I am attracted to you, too. I've noticed you in class. Something special in your aura."

I didn't know I had an aura.

So that's how I spent my time in San Miguel. She offered one of her bedrooms to me so I wouldn't have to live in my VW van; plus it made it easy for both of us to study Spanish and the Kama Sutra together.

I found studying the Kama Sutra much easier that studying Spanish. Let's say I majored in one and minored in the other. And, curiously, some of those Kama Sutra positions strengthened my left arm still stiff from the operation. She never asked about the scars, but liked to trace them with her finger.

When the time came for me to leave, it was both difficult and a relief. Sade's personality was as intense as her beauty. She told me her physical quest was filled, but that now she needed to find her spiritual center. I didn't think I could help her with that one.

So I was off once again on *my* quest, happy I was able to help her with hers.

From there, I began to cover every Mexican and Latin American country down to the Big Ditch, stopping at ancient ruins large and small.

But a stop in Guatemala is where I received my second most memorable puzzle...

I was told by a fellow traveler that I must go, that there is nothing like it. Well, there are many things for which there is nothing like it. But I decided to see for myself. One Sunday, while in Guatemala, I visited Chichicastenango in the highlands. Little did I know what lasting effect my visit was to have on my life and my future travels.

Chichi is a few hours north of Guatemala City and home to one of the largest, most colorful native marketplaces in Central

America. Sundays and Thursdays bring together not only local Maya vendors, but scores of artisans from all over Guatemala hawking mixed-matched woven textiles in anomalous color combinations; ornately carved wooden masks and costumes depicting various Mayan gods and animals; pottery of various shapes and purposes; machetes, knives and other tools; exotic candles; incense; medicinal plants; myriad grains, fruits and vegetables; pigs, goats and chickens; and small eateries offering anything that would fit in a tortilla.

The thick air felt old and tired, swirling with greasy cooking smoke, mixtures of strong incense, and the residue of fireworks from rockets and firecrackers exploding periodically for no particular reason I could discern. The smells volleyed from putrid to sweet and back again as I made my way through the market, all my senses entertained.

I meandered through the city with my heavy-lensed camera slung over my shoulder at the ready, though no device could have captured my visceral enjoyment of the thriving foreign life and cacophony of languages and music surrounding me. There, at the top of the eighteen worn rocky steps leading up to the entrance, sat the 400-year-old Santo Tomas Catholic Church that housed *Popul Vuh*, the sacred book of the Maya, before it was stolen years ago. Men and women in their vibrant indigenous dress, some selling flowers, some waving burning incense and chanting, some burning candles, one scattering something on a small fire, commandeered the steps as they meshed their thousand-year-old traditional Maya beliefs with those the Spanish brought hundreds of years ago.

I started to climb the steps to enter the church, but had difficulty making my way through the crowd. Someone spoke to me in a melodic language I took to be K'iche' Maya, a soft, soothing sound. I smiled, not understanding, and attempted to continue through the mass. Halfway up, I was stopped by a native Spanish speaker who told me the Church was a sacred place, and that I could not go inside with my camera. Best to obtain a guide, he suggested. I looked around and sensed everyone on the steps was watching to see what I would do. I saw myself as a trespasser and turned back down the steps.

As I continued to roam the streets, an inexplicable feeling of apprehension and premonition came over me. I can't say why, neither will I try to describe it. But something compelled me to wander deeper into the narrow market streets as though on a quest. Like a magnetic force, I felt drawn to something yet unfound.

I stepped aside at one point as a procession of men, some dressed in jaguar face masks and brown and black spotted costumes, others in simple everyday clothing, marched by, a ragtag group, not particularly in step with the sounds of wooden flutes and drum beats. I almost started to follow them, but I held back until they passed. Moving on, I stopped at various stalls halfheartedly examining the offerings of each and became aware of the market's organization: all wood merchandise in one area; all pottery in another; condiments in another, and so on. At one point, a vendor, a small man dressed in simple dark pants and a white opened-neck shirt, held out a small, plain pottery cup to me.

"*¿Quieres una bebida?*"

Taken aback, I peered into the cup of brown liquid he offered, which reminded me of the kava I drank in Fiji, a lightly numbing, narcotic-like drink.

"*¿Qué es?*"

"*Una deliciosa bebida.*" He smiled, nodded and pushed the cup further toward me.

I looked at the drink, then back at him, my skepticism obvious. I searched for the right words.

"*¿Qué hay en ello?*"

"*Una bebida de Maya,*" he said with pride. "*Ixcacao con guaro.*"

"*¿Qué?*"

"Ish-ca-ca-o." He gave me a wan smile. "Chocolate and sugar rum."

"You speak English?"

"Some." He continued to hold out the cup.

I examined him more closely. His face, dark Mayan chocolate itself, appeared as smooth as polished leather; greenish-black, cat-like eyes seemed to search for something in mine. I felt a slight unease and reticence to accept.

"How much?" I asked, stalling.

"*Nada, señor.* An offering."

I didn't want to seem impolite and felt compelled to take a sip, even though all travel books warn tourists to be leery of such drinks.

Forgetting caution, I took the cup and sipped. A not unpleasant taste. I nodded approval and offered him the cup.

He gestured for me to drink more.

I felt sure I shouldn't, but sipped some more. Slightly sweet, yet peppery. My mind told me I would regret this, but my taste buds encouraged me on as I wondered what this was going to cost me.

After a few swallows, I handed the cup back, feeling I'd finished my unnecessary obligation.

"Very...different. Graçias." I wasn't sure what I was supposed to say.

"*Ah, de nada, señor.* A pleasure."

I started looking in my pocket for some quetzals to pay him. "*¿A como?*"

He waved his hand. "*Nada.* Nothing, señor."

Odd, I thought. "Well, gracias again."

I started to walk away when the vendor called back to me.

"Señor, I show you something?"

Of course, I thought. Now comes the reason for the drink. What does he want me to buy?

"I don't know," I hesitated. "I need to get back to the city before dark."

"I promise, not long takes. And never you forget what you see."

Before I could answer, he offered his hand and name.

We exchanged a loose handshake.

"Sorry, say your name again?"

He repeated his name. Ish something. It did not sound Spanish.

I still had trouble understanding him, and decided the closest I could come to pronouncing his name was to call him Ishmael.

"Follow please," he said as he slipped into the crowd.

Things were happening too fast. I thought he wanted to show me something in his stall. Where was he taking me? Should I trust him and follow? I hadn't felt comfortable around him, yet here I was being led to…where? And to what?

I trailed behind him through and around many vending stalls, almost losing him on occasion in the crowded streets, then realized we were leaving the market. I caught up with him as we headed across a clearing and up into a wooded area.

"How much farther?"

"Soon."

Whoa, wait, I told myself. You're walking into a trap, stupid. Turn around. Some gang is in the woods waiting to take your camera, your money, your clothes, maybe your life. I tried to shake off these negative thoughts, and noticed I was feeling a bit lightheaded. Was it the mountain air? Fear? Or, maybe it was something in the drink he gave me. Of course! He's drugged me!

I stopped walking. He noticed and looked at me with a face that offered no surprise, no danger, no threat.

We caught eyes.

"You hold fear."

"Yes, I have fear." I wasn't about to pretend I didn't.

"*Si, entiendo su posición.* As I would, *tambien.*"

"What do you want me to see? Where are you taking me?"

We stood in quiet a moment. I still felt a bit dizzy and my tongue felt tingly.

"Did you drug me?" I blurted out, then felt silly, rather pathetic.

"Señor, how to tell...*no quiero hacer daño.* No hurt do I make you."

His face seemed innocent, but those deep, cat-like eyes....

My mind raced. Should I believe him? Who is he? I should go back. Be sensible. But if I turned around now, what would I miss? I might never have an occasion to witness something off the tourist track like this again. Is my paranoia unwarranted? I'm physically bigger than he is. But if there are more of them in waiting? Oh, come on. Ease up. You're being overly cautious. Go with the man! Maybe this is that expectancy you felt earlier.

I nodded. "Okay, okay. Let's go."

Showing no emotion, he continued walking, his footsteps seemingly soundless on the dirt path.

I stayed on my guard as we went deeper into the woods, never seeing another person. He stopped at a small clearing just outside the opening of a small cave entrance at the rise of a mound and pointed to the remains of a fire. From my various readings in preparation for my travels, I learned that Maya shamans used fires for all types of sacred ceremonies, believing fire is a living, breathing organism, some saying fire is God itself. Shamans make a circle of sugar or grains around the ring of the fire and divide the circle into various parts, placing items like incense, corn, cocoa beans, copal, or whatever they deem useful for a particular ceremony. Four tall candles representing the four directions are often placed within the circle. Then smaller candles of different colors are placed flat around the center of the fire. Yellow candles represent peace; red, love; green, earth; white, purity and so on. No doubt I was looking at a recent ceremonial fire. I was certain of it when I noticed some small feathers around the circle of melted candles burnt to the ground and dark spots I assumed to be dried blood.

The grey ash still let off an occasional bit of smoke. As I stared into the ashes, I thought I saw the lively, crackling fire, the blood of the sacrificial fowl being dripped into the sugar around the fire, the colored melting candles oozing into the wood beneath them, odd smells, a shaman chanting something. A vision came. I saw it all, but understood nothing.

His voice brought me back from wherever I was.

"You have stood here before."

"What?" In a flash I awoke to where I was. "Here? No, never. This is my first time in Guatemala."

"*Si*, you here before," he insisted. Then he said something unintelligible I assumed was K'iche. "I told to bring you back here."

I breathed a nervous laugh, but the way he said it made me shiver, and my skin felt pricked; my breath skipped. What kind of deceit was this turning out to be? I looked around and saw nobody. What was he talking about?

"Who told you to bring me back?"

"The I'x-Balan spirits."

Right. Spirits now. Spirits ready to jump from the woods and attack me now while drugged.

We just stood there, each of us looking down at the ashes. No spirits or human bodies came running at me out of the woods or the cave. Baffled, mesmerized, really, I just waited for his next move.

Slowly, in a low voice, eyes closed, he again started to mumble in K'iche or whatever. He repeated what sounded like sound, "Ish. Ish." He kept blowing his breath into his hand. What was that about?

He's got to be setting me up for something. Why did he say I'd been here before? Spirits told him. Does he expect me to believe that? The only spirits are the ones in the drink he gave me, and I foolishly drank myself into a world that's playing with my perception.

While my mind groped for normalcy, I remembered my camera. I needed pictures to prove this incident was happening. I started to take a photo of Ishmael standing by the fire, but he stopped mumbling, raised his hands and shook his head.

"No."

"Why?"

"Sacred place. No take." He pointed at my camera.

"Well, can we go in the cave? See what's in there?"

"No. A shaman must cleanse you first."

"A shaman? What's in there?"

"The spirit of the jaguar."

Now I knew this was all a con of some type. Could this get any more preposterous?

"Well, can I take a picture of the outside?"

"No."

I relented, too baffled and annoyed to argue.

Through my travels, I had learned to take hip shots of people who didn't want to be photographed or who wanted money for a snapshot. Never raising my camera to focus, I just aimed the camera from my hip which self-focused when I clicked. And I wanted proof of what was happening to me, so I managed to snap six pictures of him and the fire area on the sly as I questioned him.

"I don't understand. Why do the spirits want me here?"

"They have reasons."

"But why me?"

"You are of the number twelve of the Day of the Jaguar."

I knew the jaguar held a special place in Olmec, Aztec and Mayan traditions. In many of the places I had traveled, Chichen-Itza, Palenque, Uxmal, Tikal, jaguar symbols were etched in stone, formed in ceramics, temple mantles and wall paintings. A totem animal, the jaguar represents power, confidence and energy. It has the ability to live not only on the flatlands and the mountains, but also in the trees and in the water. No other animal can kill it, only man. Its spirit, Maya believe, can enter a person and give that person power.

But it was his reference to the number twelve that caught me up. My birthday is December the twelfth. How could he know my birthday? Just happenstance? Maybe no connection at all. I wanted to know more.

"What does that mean, the number twelve of the day of the jaguar?"

"Is one of the 20 days of the sacred Mayan calendar. You are of the Day of the Jaguar."

"How do you know?"

"The Spirits."

This fiasco was getting nowhere. I shook off the idea I was drugged, and felt in some way duped. Unsatisfied, yet intrigued, I wanted him to get on with whatever scam this was leading up to, curious as to why he picked me to bring here. He could not know my birthday. This was one mysterious carnival con, and I was more than ready for it to come to an end.

"You must allow the Nawales to enter your being, or you will miss the core and become depressed, angry, mean, jealous, lonely. You no find road to wisdom. Look. Up that tree. A black jaguar looks at you. Accept her spirit."

I looked up where he pointed. I saw nothing. I searched the trees nearby. There was no jaguar, black or otherwise in the trees.

"I see nothing."

"Allow it. Then you will."

Unsettled by Ishmael's insistence the Spirits wanted me, I decided I'd had enough. His clever deceit pushed my discomfort button. I began to feel a touch of panic. "I think you have me confused with somebody else. It's getting late. I need to get back to the city."

In a steady voice of confidence, he said, "The jaguar sees you. You will see if you allow."

"Sorry, I'd like to see a jaguar, but I don't."

His eyes and face held a look of disappointment in me as his body slumped. Yet he did not seem to want to hold me there. He nodded, looked at me sadly, and turned to go.

He started back to the market and I followed. He didn't look behind as we walked, but seemed to read my mind.

"No photos."

When we got back to the buzz of the market, Ishmael disappeared into the crowd. I tried to find his stall again, but it was impossible in the market melee. Who was this Ishmael? Why had he picked me to dump all that business about sacred Mayan ceremonial places, spirits, a jaguar in a tree? I felt confused and unsatisfied, even used somehow.

On my way back to Guatemala City, I tried to convince myself that I'd been entertained in some way, but had no idea why I had been picked to participate. And participate in what exactly? Then I began feeling foolish that I was in such a haste to get away and wished I had stayed and asked more questions. I'd missed an opportunity -- for what exactly I couldn't be certain. I'm certain now he never wanted money or planned to rob me. But I realized it too late. I was left with the impression I'd cheated myself of an inexplicable experience.

Over the weeks, as I finished my travels in Latin America, the experience vacillated in my mind between a lost sense of adventure and an acceptance of being seduced by a clever Guatemalan, whoever he was and for whatever reason. That is, until I got back home and developed my photos of the journey. Curiously, while every other picture I took on my trip revealed its subjects, the six forbidden hip shots I took at the "sacred place" in Guatemala were all solid black. Never one to believe in the supernatural, I admit the black, not just blank, six photos gave me pause. Coincidence? Perhaps. Still, my mind failed to make sense of it.

My confusion was further tested a year or so later when I was on a night safari on assignment in Botswana, and I took a photo of a leopard sitting in a tree. Because of the poor lighting at the time, I wasn't certain the picture would reveal much. But in the enlarged photograph, the leopard's shining eyes seemed to be staring directly at me, and I shivered when an unanticipated image of Ishmael came to me. Instead of a spotted body, the animal in the tree appeared in the photo as a black jaguar. In fact when others, not aware of my story, viewed the picture, they assumed it was a black jaguar.

Maybe I'm making too much of these oddities. But taken together, I'm still having trouble making sense of my encounter with Ishmael, because in a way he was prescient. As he predicted, I never will forget what he showed me. The forbidden photos had not been permitted. His mysterious reference to the number twelve, my birth date, still puzzles me. And I eventually did see what looked something like a black jaguar in a tree. \

In an awakened, spiritual, metaphorical way, as I write this, I find myself returning to that sacred place in the hills near Chichicastenango and wishing I could relive my meeting with Ishmael. Who was he? Himself, a shaman? I realize now that he sincerely wanted so much for me to "see" something that I turned my back on. Obviously, the episode continues to haunt me, and I worry I missed an opportunity to be made aware of ...what? An enlightenment or insight of some kind? I need to know what he offered me that I passed up. My moment was lost by my own narrowness and fear of something I didn't have the openness to explore.

I'm coming to believe that my travels have mostly been superficial. I ask myself what I have learned or personally gained by visiting other countries that couldn't be found in travel books. Yes, I've immersed myself in other languages, learning bits of words and phrases, witnessed a variety of dress styles and customs, listened to musical styles and instruments, stayed in the recommended hotels and inns, eaten a variety of culinary treats, visited the museums and art galleries, climbed the steps of ancient ruins, relaxed on sandy beaches, hiked exhausting mountains, shared space with wild animals, moved about in taxis, vans, buses, planes, boats, on horses and foot, and come home with souvenirs. Sometimes traveling was exhausting, a strain, only to arrive at my destination wishing I were home. That's not to say there weren't times of pleasure and unexpected excitement. Of course there were. And I've been privileged to be able to travel. But it seems my experiences are nothing more than those gained by following a trail made by others before me, a collection of information for yet another Lonely Planet edition. And if I add it all up, is there much difference between a traveler and a tourist?

How many "days of the jaguar" have I squandered in my worldly travels? What really do my collection of travel photographs say about me if photos of places and people are nothing more than photos of places and people? Look, see, I was there at one time. But something in those pictures is missing, and I can't help but feel that given a chance, Ishmael might have led me on a path to formulating an answer.

Still, I wouldn't trade my travels for anything.

CHAPTER 18

"This Can't Be Love"

After several years of working for *Travel* and other magazines, I'd had enough of moving around. I managed to save and invest most of my money, so I felt I could coast for a while. But I wanted out of the Wilshire condo and bought a place in Belmont Shores. The town had grown so different since I had been there in the '50s that I wasn't sure it was the right move. But I took a fancy to a bungalow, about 1000 square feet. It was a small framed stucco, tiled roof, arched doorways, fireplace, the usual California-Spanish style, one bedroom, but large enough for me. All the houses were cramped together, but this one had a small private Japanese-maple-treed-backyard with a two-person hot tub. It cost more than it should. But I felt like I needed to live in a neighborhood near the beach, where I could walk to stores, bars and theaters. I didn't need my Mazda Miata much.

I kicked back my first month there and acquainted myself with the whole Long Beach area. I familiarized myself with the downtown area and nearby Bixby Knolls and Naples. I even spent one night aboard the moored RMS Queen Mary, a famous ocean liner now a hotel and museum. The waterfront Aquarium of the Pacific has a shark lagoon and touch tanks. The Museum of Latin American Art displays some contemporary works I like. A 19th-century adobe house, Rancho Los Cerritos, turned into a museum, is set in large, lovely gardens. I felt content with my move, even though so much of what I remember from my navy days at Los Alamitos was changed or gone.

On a stroll, I happened to walk by a Scuba Dive Shop, and impetuously, I signed up for a PADI course. I'd actually been wanting to learn scuba for some time. Now seemed like the right time. I wasn't getting any younger.

Six other people were in my class: two young married couples and two single women, obviously friends, about age thirty or so. I was the oldest in the group. I can't say I didn't notice the two women, but I had no real distracting thoughts other than to keep my attention on the class work. Over several weeks, we had lessons on diving safety, then some diving practices in a pool, then a beach dive. The final test involved an open boat dive.

On the day of the final, one of the single women bailed on us, confessing she was afraid to do the ocean boat dive and had only joined the class because her friend had begged her. The class had been working in "buddy" teams, and until then the instructor had been my "buddy." The other woman still wanted to finish the course and be certified, so she became my partner.

Her name was Connie. She had an appealing, knowing, competent look, an inner radiance I hadn't noticed until then. The more we interacted, the more her attractiveness expressed itself. Blond hair surrounded an angular face, and open, light-blue eyes that drew you as soon as you looked at her. Her nose was thin as well as her lips. Just short of my height, she had an athletic look and graceful movements. At one point before the dive, I started to help her move two heavy oxygen tanks. She lifted them quite easily, letting me know she needed no help from me.

In truth, I was happy her friend dropped out. Like that line in the song...*I'm so happy we met/I'm strangely attracted to you.*

The boat took us out near Anacapa Island for our test dive. The instructor first took each one of us and had us take our masks off, show how to clear the mask, follow hand signals, and whatever else. I don't remember. What I remember is Connie and me going through the buddy routine and diving together after we passed our test. When we found an interesting-looking fish or an eel or a lobster hideout, we would tap the other and point and nod. I found myself enjoying her enjoyment. For me, it became an underwater dance and romance.

After the boat dive and our certification, I overcame my shyness and invited Connie for a celebratory drink. She accepted and said she knew a place close by called The Song Is You, a Karaoke bar. We settled in a booth, and after each ordering a vodka martini on the rocks with two olives, we took a long look at each other.

"So, who are you? Besides my diving buddy," Connie asked, smiling.

"Who am I? Excellent question. In truth, I don't always know."

"Sounds sad."

"Didn't mean it to."

"I'll try the usual tack. What do you do?"

"I'm a writer, a freelancer. Mostly music, theater, lately travel writing. How about you?"

"Real estate. I have my own business, so maybe I'm a freelancer, too."

"I wish I'd known you when I bought my place. Maybe I could have gotten a better deal with you."

"Definitely would have."

I saw her lower her eyes as if she hadn't meant to say that aloud.

"But," she added quickly "whatever you paid, hang on. The prices in that area are going to go up."

Our drinks came and Connie raised her glass. "Congratulations, you're now a PADI diver."

"And to you," as we clinked glasses.

After two drinks, we opened up. We discussed why we were interested in scuba diving (she thought it sounded exciting; I confessed it was a long-term whim) our opinions of our diving instructor and classmates, her friend who dropped, our divorces, our favorite foods, the gym classes she attended four times a week, (I should join, I said) our preference for dogs over cats (except for my jaguar; I tried to explain that one), where we attended college, and of course, our music preferences, the fact we liked to dance. I don't think I ever was so open to a stranger.

I don't remember why, but it happened. Connie challenged me to sing with the karaoke machine. I agreed, but only if she sang a song, too. There were only three or four customers in the place, and we'd had just enough to drink to accept the challenges. I hadn't sung in so long I'd forgotten how good it felt. I started out with "This Can't Be Love" and then she joined in. We sang every standard on the list.

The easy conversation and the relaxed singing with her caused unfamiliar stirrings in me I hadn't felt since maybe never. I wanted to see more of her, but I worried the worry regarding the age difference. Our conversation revealed I was ten years older than Connie's 35.

I blurted out fast before I lost my nerve, "Listen, Karrin Allyson is playing the Catalina Bar & Grill in Hollywood next Saturday. Will you join me?"

"Let me check my calendar. Yes."

"I like your calendar."

"I love her voice. She's one of the best. How could I not say yes."

I felt something in her yes, and it was more than her appreciating jazz music. I didn't want to go home. I wanted to stay and drink and sing with this woman forever. I was hooked. But she turned down a third drink offer, and we exchanged phone numbers to make arrangements for Saturday. I tried to herd in my feelings and be more rational, but no go.

Like a smitten teenager, I couldn't wait to see her again on Saturday. I made reservations for dinner and the show at the Catalina before I even called her to make sure she still wanted to go with me. When I did call, Connie told me to pick her up at her office in Long Beach.

I picked her up on time Saturday and discovered she had a sizable office with four spaces for realtors to work. She was dressed in a black tailored pants suit and white blouse, understated pearl earrings and matching necklace. She looked ever the professional…and desirable. On the way to Hollywood, she told me she had never been where we were going and was excited to get to hear Karrin Allyson in person. I doubted her excitement was half as strong as mine.

When we got to the Catalina, the woman who showed us our table actually remembered me from my days of covering jazz. I was flattered, and Connie was impressed.

I watched Connie as Karrin sang and played and knew she felt the music the way I did. The last number Allyson sang was a touching version of "Here's That Rainy Day."

"Whew. That gave me chills. Love that song." Connie said.

"I love that you love it. It's one song I'd want to have on a deserted island."

"Whose version would you want?"

"Good question." I thought a minute. "I'd have to take Wes Montgomery's, for sure."

"What about Karrin's?"

"She's in the competition, but don't know if she's recorded it."

"What about Carman McRae's?" Connie challenged.

"True, but what about Kenny Rankin's?" I asked.

"What about Natalie Cole, or Nat?"

"Okay, but what about Bill Evans?"

"Wait. What about Ella?"

"So true. And what about Stan Getz?"

"And there's Paul Desmond."

"Okay, okay. You got me. I'll take them all with me."

We laughed, then she said, "Oh, and don't forget Abbie Hart?"

I went silent. A windmills-of the mind moment.

"What?" Connie looked puzzled.

It just came out, "Abbie Hart broke my heart. She's my ex."

"Uh-oh. Sorry."

"Nothing to be sorry about. All over and done."

That wasn't an exact truth. I may have been done with Abbie, but not the residue.

When Karrin returned to the stage, I listened ...as best I could.

Then I looked at Connie, not sure what she sensed, but without looking at me, she placed her hand on mine. With that, she became part of the music that filled my body and soul. If you don't know the feeling, you never will.

CHAPTER 19

"Getting to Know You"

Because she'd left her car at her office, I took Connie back there after the show. Before we parted, she kissed me, gently, during my awkward moment of wondering if I should do the same, and that was enough of an encouragement. I didn't kiss her back, but her kiss opened the door for me to ask to see her again.

I invited her to attend a 1962 French movie that interested me, "Cleo from 5 to7," with Corinne Marchard. I knew from our first conversations that Connie spoke French and thought she might enjoy it. I was also interested in Michel Legrand's musical score. The film is about a selfish, occupied-with-fame singer who has two hours to wait for the results of a biopsy that might reveal cancer. Free-wheeling and experimental, the film follows Cleo around the streets of Paris as she meets and talks with various people and finally senses her selfishness when she compares her troubles with a soldier she meets on leave from his duties in Algeria. It's an example of the French New Wave film making period.

After the movie, we huddled in the corner of a nearby bar to discuss our reactions. Looking back, I find it interesting that both Connie and I would, in a later time, share Cleo's fretful concern in the film. Our conversation went far beyond the movie. We somehow opened up to our most personal feelings, concerns, desires. We connected, aware we both had lone wolf syndrome.

After I opened up about my previous marriage, Connie told me about hers. She and her ex married right after graduating from Cal State

Long Beach. He became a financial consultant who worked with one of those major stock trading firms, and she took a job in a bank, not sure what she wanted to do. Things went well between them for the first three years until they discovered that she couldn't have children. He didn't like the idea of adoption or artificial insemination, but he wanted a child.

"Did you?" I asked her.

"Interesting question. The fact that I couldn't have a child naturally upset me at first. But it did make me question if I even wanted to be a parent. I'd never really thought about it, you know? At the time, I didn't feel I'd lived much. I needed to know more about who I was. If I'd gotten pregnant, I suppose I would have accepted it as part of marriage. Interesting question, though. The more Gil and I talked about adoption and all that, the more I realized I didn't think I was cut out to be a mother. I was right. Not with him anyway. So it put a strain on our marriage."

"I can only guess. My life with Abbie didn't allow us to give it much thought. Her career wasn't conducive to family life. Mine either, for that matter."

"Are you sorry?"

"Not the way things turned out, no. Better we didn't. I didn't know it back then, but we both were too young, inexperienced."

"Well, things got worse when Gil made some bad investments for clients and it turned ugly. He turned nasty and abusive, taking his disappointments out on me."

"Physically?"

"Mentally...then physically."

"How bad?"

"Bruises mostly. Broken wrist."

"Jeez, Connie. How long did you put up with it?"

"Too long. It got to the point where I started taking self-defense classes." She gave an embarrassed chuckle. "The good thing about it is that it got me to join an athletic club, and I've been going regularly ever since."

"I can't picture you in that kind of relationship."

"How do we ever know? Well, I found a good lawyer, and bye-bye Gil."

"Is he still around? Do you ever see him?"

"I haven't seen him since the divorce, four years now. By law, he's not to ever contact me. And he hasn't. I have no idea where or what he's doing…and don't want to."

"Quite a story."

"Do you see Abbie?"

"No. Not since the divorce."

"Are you friends at all?"

"Friends?" I had to think a minute. "Not friends. Not enemies. We parted okay. I think at first I mostly blamed her, held the most resentment. Infidelities. You know. But I should have been more aware. We had lots of time separated. No one's fault. Our jobs. And I did some drugs until I became aware of its destruction on some musicians. On me. Her. And I admit when we were apart, I had desires, opportunities for flings. But I never followed up. In some crazy way, I think I was jealous of her doing what I didn't do. Yeah. I was devastated until time helped me think things through. I understand and accept what happened."

Connie nodded. "Past lives."

"Definitely."

As we talked, I learned Connie slipped into selling real estate through contacts in the bank where she worked, eventually forming her own company. She found her niche, as she put it, and made her job her life. Her bank and real estate connections allowed her to make some excellent investments.

"So, I won't be after your money," she quipped.

That's not what I'm after, I thought to myself. But the question I was thinking just popped out.

"So what do you see in me?"

"It's what I *think* I see in you. I've not found many men I've been comfortable with since Gil for one reason or another. I'm picky.

Something's different about you. You're not pushy. You don't smother me. You're a bit shy, but open, sensitive, a romantic, and I like that. We'll see if I'm right."

"So, I'm on trial?"

"Yep. So watch your step, mister. I'm judge and jury."

"You're scaring me."

And so it was that Connie and I began our relationship. We went scuba diving every possible weekend, unless she had an open house to show. I started photographing undersea scenes. Connie bought a camera and began taking photos of her own. Her photos showed a talent as she captured the abundant sea life subjects from fish to plants. Once out of water, we would research what we had photographed and began a photo journal. We developed an impressive knowledge that enhanced our diving.

Her business demanded much of her time. She had three employees who required attention. Sometimes we had lunch together, sometimes dinner, mostly out since neither one of us could be labeled cooks, even when we tried. My job gave us excuses for going to jazz clubs, theater, or movies and became even more fun because Connie was sharing it with me. Fun. That's what it was. How-high-the-moon fun.

The age difference bothered me more than it did Connie. She tried to put me at ease by saying she "appreciated my maturity." As the song says, "she made me feel so young." I began to forget the difference.

We held so few disparities in our views and tastes, from books to politics, that we trusted our relationship all the more as time went on. Sometimes we'd spend the night at my place, sometimes hers. We both had business associates we'd mix with on occasion, but other than seeing Monty and Sophie periodically, none we would call close friends. We were comfortable with ourselves.

We talked about moving in together, but decided to keep our separate homes, giving us some time alone so that we always were happy to get together. We talked of marriage, but saw no reason for it. Maybe we didn't trust it after our experiences, but for whatever reason we had a relationship we appreciated and felt safe in. Two loners who had found each other. Rilke said it: "two solitudes that protect and border and greet each other."

An aside here:

Connie and I were in bed in some hotel on one of our weekend jaunts switching channels for something to watch. She noticed there was a listing for Adult Movies.

"What do they mean by adult movies?"

"Porno."

"Pornography?"

"Un huh."

"They show porno movies in hotels? Is that legal?"

"Why? You interested?"

"I've never watched any. Have you?"

"Yeah. Some. Do you want to watch?"

"Why not? I don't like to be undereducated."

"Pick one."

She did. We watched a while.

"I can do better than that," she said.

Yes.

I tell you this only to let you know what you might be wondering about our sex life.

As years passed, I took as many writing assignments as I wanted. We managed some traveling when Connie could take the time off, sometimes diving trips to Cabo or Hawaii, sometimes weekday or a weekend getaway somewhere. We'd drive up to Santa Barbara for theater or music events, or head further up to Esalen in Big Sur. Sometimes Las Vegas, if someone we liked was performing. One year we took a month-long trip to Europe.

Connie, a fine skier, taught me how, and when the snow was good, we'd spend the weekend on Mammoth Mountain. We'd downhill and cross country. Over time, I advanced to the blue ski runs, but Connie could handle most black ones. She was a natural athlete.

I remember one time we were cross-country skiing off the trail into the woods. Connie had gone ahead and I stopped. The only sound in the silence was the light rippling of water under a creek iced over. I looked around at the thick snow-covered trees and ground. An ecstatic feeling of oneness with nature came over me. I had a moment of realization. I would not be there experiencing what I was feeling if it were not for Connie. She'd brought me a new life.

And the more time we spent together, the more we eased into our commonality. To use my dad's old phrase, I was in hog heaven.

Connie had never been to New York, so I convinced her to take a break and fly with me to the big city. I had to discuss a travel book I was working on with my publisher.

We stopped on the way to visit my parents in St. Louis where they had moved when my father switched insurance companies. They found every reason to like Connie. And Connie, an only child whose father she never knew and her mother buried, appreciated my connection to my parents with a touch of envy. Within hours, she and my parents bonded, interacting as if they were old friends. In asides, my parents expressed their happiness for me, assuming, I think, that Connie and I would marry.

"Your mom and I never met Abbie, but I think you've got a real winner here, son."

I got the feeling my dad had a little crush on Connie.

"I know I do."

"I assume you two have worked out the age difference?"

"You mean children?"

"Hmm. That and the future."

"Connie can't---and that's okay with me."

My dad looked off and nodded.

"I know you and mom wanted grandchildren, but it's not in the cards."

He nodded. "Well, enjoy your lives while you can. Time catches up to you too fast.

I know. Believe me, I know."

I should have pursued what he was getting at, but I let it pass.

"Be good to her," he said.

"You don't have to tell me that. She's keeping me young."

While there, I learned that the pianist Herbie Hancock was playing at Peacock Alley and managed to talk my parents into coming with us to hear him play. They said they enjoyed it, but I could tell they were being polite. My mom, I know, preferred music with a melody she could sing and dance to. She was up on her pop music. My dad still liked the music of the Grand Ole Opry. His idea of "good listening music" was along the lines of Eddie Howard's "To Each His Own." When I was a teenager and played my Stan Kenton records, they left the room. But Connie and I tried to turn my parents into jazz aficionados explaining what Hancock's group was doing with melodies they knew. We failed with my parents, but we loved what we heard.

Since we were only an hour or so drive away from Alton, I took Connie to see where I had spent most of my youth. Thomas Wolfe was right: you can't go home again. Time had taken its toll on downtown Alton. Nothing I grew up with was there. No Tri-City Grocery, no Grand Theater, no Vogue, no Young's, no dime store, or Hart Schaffner and Marks, no banks. A gambling showboat sat on the river bank, the only new attraction among the empty buildings. And the old river road and train tracks Ted and I knew so well, gone; replaced by a modern paved road and bike path. I couldn't find Blue Pool. The Piasa bird, mostly neglected in my day, now a painted tourist site. Most of the city had moved north toward Godfrey, away from downtown areas hit hard by major floods and hard times. I hear Alton is now being renovated and having a growth resurgence. Nice for the folks who live there. My Alton no longer exists. Everything must change, no?

We stayed with my parents a day or two more, then said our goodbyes.

In New York, once my editor and I put the finishing touches to my book, we did the rounds of all the places I thought Connie would like, Birdland, The Blue Note, Dizzy's Village Vanguard, Smoke. It felt good to be back. The tight city always electrified me and was so different from spread-out LA.

As they say, we did the town.

On return, our living arrangement went on seamlessly and timelessly; while she did well in real estate, I continued writing some critiques, magazine articles and travel articles. On travel assignments, I couldn't wait to get back to Connie, so I accepted fewer and fewer. I was in good financial shape and didn't need to work continuously. I kept chipping away at that novel I maintained I was going to write. My travel book did fairly well, for what it was, with sales fairly steady for a few years.

The music scenes were changing. Jazz took a back seat to newer music as it came along: Elvis Presley, Ray Charles, The Beatles, The Beach Boys, The Rolling Stones, Elton John, Michael Jackson, Madonna, so many others I can't name them all. Big stage venues became popular where more screaming than listening took over. Some jazz performers made the big stage, too, like Pat Metheny, Dave Brubeck, Sonny Rollins, Charlie Haden, but certainly not like the overwhelming pop groups. I was offered work, but often for performances not my taste. I preferred the intimate jazz clubs that were growing fewer.

Because Connie and I liked diving and being on the ocean, we bought a used Islander 30 sloop we saw for sale at the Bay Marina that included a slip. The name of the boat was also a draw for us: In the Moonlight. Connie loved Billie Holiday's recording of "A Sailboat in the Moonlight." Connie had more sailing experience than I did, having crewed on racing boats out of Newport Beach. In buying the boat, we no longer had to rent one or pay fees on diving boats; plus we could go whenever we wanted.

The boat gave us still another dimension to our relationship. We had fun taking her out for day spins, weekends to Catalina, daring trips to Santa Cruz Island. Sometimes we'd spend the night on the boat without leaving the harbor. Jokingly, it became our home away from our homes.

Life was unbelievably good to us. A good dozen years, at least, just went by in a fast, sort of thankful bliss for what we had and sorry for those who didn't.

CHAPTER 20

"Smoke Gets in Your Eyes"

Somewhere Hemingway wrote, "If it is all beautiful you can't believe it. Things aren't that way."

So true.

They say, whoever *they* is, that trouble comes in threes. Trouble number one: me.

I was diagnosed with bladder cancer. I won't go into all the details here; maybe I'll want to later, but it took a good six months of going nowhere and another six before going anywhere. I could never have managed it without Connie. She went through hell with me, and I know it wasn't easy for her.

Trouble two: my dad's death. Because of my own illness, I could not travel while he was in the hospital sick with his own cancer problems; an inoperable tumor behind his heart was wearing him out. But I was well enough before the end to visit him one last time while he was in a hospice facility. I'm grateful for that, because I was able to tell him how much I appreciated what he'd done for me growing up and pushing me to go to college. I remember our last conversation when he mentioned how time catches up with us too fast. I didn't pick up on it then. He must have been sick and didn't tell me. He wanted to know if I'd married Connie, and I know he was disappointed when I told him, but he accepted it when I explained our closeness and love for each other.

"That's good. That's what matters. Like the song says, "The greatest thing is just to love and be loved."

Those were his last words. He fell into a deep breathing spasm and unconsciousness. My mother held one of his hands, and I held the other as we watched him leave us.

I wanted to tell him...

I know I didn't always live up to your expectations. You often worked late when I was young. I know your job required it, but it did mean I saw little of you my early years. But one event stands out for me. I think it was a company picnic or get-together of some kind. I was about seven or eight. A ball game made up of father-son teams was organized. When it was my turn at bat, an important run was needed for our team. I could tell you expected me to do something to save us, to make you proud, but I struck out. Disappointment covered your face, a look I remember now, and I cried making it all the worse. I've borne a type of guilt for that, even though I can qualify my actions by reminding you I never played ball before that day. Didn't own a baseball bat. Never had a father throw me a practice pitch. How could you have expected me to make you proud? I'd like to think maybe that look wasn't just about me.

But that's a big minor in our lives.

Remember, Dad, what was I? Ten? I was scooting around on the concrete basement floor with one foot on the back of my tricycle when I rammed into the basement door. The glass half of the door shattered and a large hunk dropped loose and stabbed me in the wrist. I don't remember it hurting much at first, just the wonder of the changing dark patterns splattered on the concrete floor as my blood gushed and spurted from my wrist. I knew Mom would want to put iodine on the cut and it would hurt, so I didn't want to go upstairs and show her. But you heard the noise from the crash and called down, "What happened? What are you doing down there?"

I didn't answer. I felt mesmerized by the flood of dark red leaving me. I felt nothing of my slashed wrist, only that I wanted no iodine.

"Son, what's going on? Answer me!"

When I didn't, you came partway down the stairs and saw me holding out a leaking arm.

"Oh, my god! What have you done?"

You came all the way down and had me sit on a step while you examined my wrist.

"Oh, good lord!"

After that, I don't remember much. I went lightheaded and only recall spotty moments. You must have put some kind of bandage or tourniquet on me; I don't remember. I do remember you had to carry me up a long, narrow flight of stairs to a doctor's office. God, that must have been a strain.

I was stitched up and told I should be thankful you, Dad, had been swift and saved me from more blood loss, and that the ligament to my thumb had been saved. I also remember you had to carry me down those stairs and eventually to my bed, where I was ordered to stay for three weeks while I recovered from blood loss.

At least I avoided the iodine.

The next day, when you came home, you brought me a couple of comic books to read and set our only radio next to my bed for my entertainment. When I said I was sorry about breaking the door window and not telling you right away, you scoffed, "Ah, don't worry about it. Just thankful you're going to be okay now." Then you added, "Don't be so afraid of iodine next time, okay?"

Dad, look. You can still see the scar on my wrist.

I know you had my interests at heart. Remember those lace-up boots I wanted, the kind that lumberjacks wore? How I wanted those! But so impractical, as Mom pointed out. I'd out grow them before the heels wore down. And costly; more than two good pairs of shoes. But as I remember, you won a contest at work by signing on more new clients than anyone else. You used the prize money to buy those boots for me when it could have been used to pay off some of your debts.

And I'll never forget the time I pretended I'd found a fifty-cent piece on the sidewalk. It was right after my cousin Patsy had visited and had lost hers. I did find it where I said I did, but I knew and you knew it belonged to her. When you confronted me, god, how ashamed and embarrassed I felt. But you reprimanded me without anger, more by explaining your disappointment in my lack of honesty, and how I should come to you if I needed money or anything. It was more than a lesson in humility.

Then there was the time I came home from junior high school with a very sore tailbone. Our one-armed PE teacher ruled with a smoothed oak paddle with holes drilled in it so that it made a whistling sound just before making contact. If our class did anything out of line, we got to meet his paddle. I don't remember what I did wrong, but that day I bent over as directed and heard the wind passing through the holes in the paddle just before it struck. He aimed too high and, oh, I received more than a message.

When I told you what happened, you came to my PE class the next day and spoke with my teacher.

"What did he say?" I asked when we were home, worried that he told you I deserved the paddle for whatever it was I no longer remember I did.

"It's not what he said. It's what I said," you answered.

"What?" I wasn't sure I wanted to hear.

"I told him if he ever hit you with that paddle again, I would personally show him what it felt like."

The teacher never used that paddle in my class again.

And remember when I had that newspaper route? What was I, thirteen or so? True, it didn't last long, because you saw me struggling with it. The winter months were severe, and you saw me battling my way through the cold wind or deep snow, trying to keep my papers dry. I had trouble collecting from people, some hiding from me when I came to collect. Enough, you said. Quit. You've proved yourself. You don't know how happy I was at those words.

You and Mom get high marks for the way you provided my introduction into the teenage mystery of sex. I was down in the basement shoveling coal into the furnace and noticed an open book on a table. Why was the book there? It never had been before. It was a nurse's handbook. I couldn't believe what I was seeing: pictures of a woman's private parts in various stages of giving birth. I don't know how long I stayed down there reading and looking at pictures of the female anatomy and drawings of sexual intercourse. It dawned on me that you had put the book there for me. Did you do it because you were too embarrassed to bring up the subject, or was I not asking you the right questions? I didn't know what I should do. Leave the book there or take it up to my room? I left it there, checking to see every day if it was still there. One day it was gone and no mention of it was ever made.

Well done.

You were proud of me when I turned sixteen and landed a job working after school at Tri-City Grocery. I gave you part of my pay every week to help with household expenses. You wanted me to learn responsibility and the value of money. It wasn't until after I graduated that you told me you had put the money aside for my college education. You and Mom had never discussed college attendance with me. Neither of you had gone to college, but suddenly you insisted I should take advantage of the scholarship.

And so I did. And it was one of the best things that ever happened to me. I entered a world I never knew existed. I became excited about learning for the first time I could remember. You are responsible for that. Did I ever thank you?

But after a year and a half, the draft board had my number, and I was about to be called to the army. So I joined the navy. You were proud of me for enlisting, but worried I might never finish college. I promised you that I would. And I did.

I remember after graduating navy boot camp, I spent about two weeks in misery because all of my buddies got their duty orders, but I didn't because of some clerical foul-up. I was left at boot camp knowing no one, doing the odd shit details, having no idea when my orders would come in. I wrote home expressing my misery and wishing I'd never joined the navy. Ironically, when my orders did come, I was sent to Los Alamitos Naval Air Station, at that time the playground of the navy. I fell into a "hog heaven job," as you would say.

I was called into the chaplain's office one day and asked why I was so unhappy in the navy. I had no idea what he meant. Unknown to me, you had written to the Bureau of Naval Personnel after getting my letter from boot camp telling them how unhappy I was. The Bureau contacted the chaplain at the naval base to check up on me. Once I explained the background of the letter, we had a good laugh. I couldn't believe you were so disturbed on my behalf that you would write a letter to the Navy Department sharing my misery. While I was embarrassed, as well as appreciative that you were looking out for me, it opened my eyes to how much you loved me.

Thank you, Dad...

CHAPTER 21

"There Will Never Be Another You"

Trouble number three showed itself when I returned home after dad's funeral. Connie learned she had breast cancer. Fortunately, the cancer was caught in an early stage. We read everything we could, got several doctor opinions and checked out the best facilities. Connie had to choose between breast conserving surgery or a mastectomy. She chose BCS and was able to keep most of her breast, but she had to undergo radiation treatments. It was my turn to pay her back.

Our lives slowed down for a while. Connie didn't feel like traveling, or doing much of anything. I tried to get her to do something publishable with her photo journal, but she never held a strong interest. We took one last sail and decided to sell In the Moonlight since we weren't using it much anymore. We'd do take-out once in a while, but mostly we became stay-at-homes, putting together less-than-gourmet meals, though we did improve over time. We found our entertainment in watching old movies like "Singin' in the Rain," "Guys and Dolls," all the Fred and Ginger movies, and French movies just to hear the French. We selected books and poetry to read to each other (Connie loved Mary Oliver), and took long walks on the beach. My record collection got well used as we listened and compared and commented on the way certain musicians improvised songs from standards. We challenged each other at chess and Scrabble.

And it was lovely in its own terrible way.

Slowly, as Connie gained strength, we began seeking outside entertainment and some light travel again. Two years whizzed by, then

Connie's cancer resurfaced and she began chemotherapy treatments knowing the doctors felt it was a lost cause. She took the news better than I did. She accepted the inevitable and sold her business and her home, retired, and moved in with me. Her decision seemed practical since we didn't need a lot of room, and we were no longer gadabouts. Connie, often feeling sick or down, wanted to stay close by me, and I felt the same.

One day, Connie surprised me.

"Will you marry me?"

Neither of us had ever mentioned it since the beginning of our relationship. I was surprised, but then, not so much. I could feel what was behind the words.

"What took you so long to ask me?"

"I told you once you were on trial, remember?"

"Does this mean I can finally be myself?"

"Oh, no. Now you have to pass the marriage trial."

"God, woman, you're a hard case."

"Are you sure you want to?" she asked. "We never..."

I put a finger to my lips to silence her and gave her a "wait a minute" sign. Then I looked through some CDs and played Nora Jones' "The Nearness of You."

"Here's my answer."

We listened.

"God, you're such a sappy romantic."

"That's why you love me."

And so, in a very simple civil ceremony, we married.

I quit pretending I was going to write a novel. When she felt well enough, we traveled short range, but mostly we remained sedentary. Her energy came and went.

I convinced Connie that we should look through our diving photos and form them into a book. She needed something to occupy her that required little energy. Reluctant at first, she agreed. We began forming what we tentatively entitled *Sea Creatures*. I contacted my publisher with a book proposal and he sent us a contract. That excited

Connie enough to want to finish our project. It gave me another year with her as we worked on the final page proofs.

Connie never got to see the printed book.

I thought I'd be better prepared for her death than I was. We talked enough about it beforehand; she set her affairs in order so I'd have no worries, expressed her desire for cremation and definitely did not want a memorial service. Who would come and for what, she said.

"Hey, come on. You have people you worked with who admire you. And there's Monty and Sophie, and…"

Connie snapped at me. "I said no one. Especially not Monty and Sophie."

"Okay. Okay." In her condition I didn't want to press her reason. "No service."

She was physically dwindling before my eyes, and I knew the pain medications caused her not to be herself. And it pained me, too.

I still can't believe she died before me. I feel guilty. I know you can't catch cancer from someone; still, all that time she was around me and my cancers. But cancer has its own rules. Her cancer came back swiftly and decidedly. Cancer just teases me with one kind after the other, but here I am and she's not.

Grief comes in all sorts of packages, constant, or in waves, or in physical hits from hard shots you can't duck, and your knees buckle and you fall into depression. Devastated, thrown into a foggy life style, I seemed to get strange pleasure in my depression by playing all the music Connie loved and all the music that supplied more sadness. My constant thought: Why Connie and not me? I had ten years on her. It didn't seem fair, but I know there is no such thing as fair. For a while, I couldn't concentrate, or read, or watch movies or television– unless they fed my heartache. Everything felt lackluster. I was the anguished lone wolf now, a stray, with no one close to share my grief. Connie and I had become so dependent on each other being there. And when we did talk about death, it was always about me going first. We should have paid more attention to reality.

I had another problem. I'd signed a contract with a publisher to write one of four volumes on the history of jazz. I was to do the volume on jazz from 1940 to 1960. It would be a real feather in my cap to be part of the project. But I couldn't get moving on it.

I knew I needed help. Superficial (I can say that now) thoughts of suicide came and went. Did I really have it in me to continue? I wasn't sure. I decided on a psychiatrist and attended a number of thoughtful therapy sessions.

One night, I had a vivid dream. In it, Connie and I were having an argument, almost a shouting match.

"You're not listening," she kept repeating.

"To what?" I'd yell back. "What for?"

"You complain when no one listens to the music. Now you're not listening!"

"What music? I don't hear any music There is no music!"

"To the music of life, damn you! You're not listening to the music of life!"

"The music of life? What are you talking about?"

"Just listen, dammit!"

And the screaming back and forth went on until I woke up, tangled in damp covers and sweating.

I sat on the edge of the bed unable to shake the dream. I looked at the side of the bed where Connie would have been sleeping, half expecting her to be there.

"Connie...."

The sun started peeking through the curtains, and without any thought or direction, I got dressed and found myself at the beach. The tide was low, the winter rocks and ridges exposed, expanding the moist sand. A few others were about, checking the tide pools or jogging. What was I doing there?

I ambled for a time, watching my thin beach shadow shrink as the sun rose higher. I heard the soft sounds of the collapsing waves. Watched the scurrying curlews, willets, and sandpipers having a feast in the low tide. White and grey feathered gulls flew and fought and stared, waited. Awareness. A V-shaped squadron of brown pelicans skimmed over the water's surface, followed by a group of black cormorants, necks stuck out like arrowheads. Awareness. Two joggers startled me from behind as they passed. The voices of excited children playing in the tide pools declared they'd found a star fish. Awareness. Off shore, paddle surfers tested their balance skills, while above I noticed two hang gliders looking for a landing place on the beach. I observed a man throw a stick into the water and his dog smashed through the waves to retrieve it over and over, the dog showing so much joy. Awareness. A group ahead of me stood around something on the beach. When I got closer, I saw a dead, emaciated seal had been washed ashore. Voices dealt in speculation of the cause of death. Should some nature service be notified? Look at the flies! And that smell! Poor thing!

And with that reminder that death is a part of life, I realized what Connie meant in my dream. Listen to the music of life, she had declared. It was all around me, and I had been ignoring it. I was wallowing in self-pity. It took a dream to wake me up.

On my way home, I had a good reckoning with myself. Connie would be devastated by my lost in mourning. She had spent her life living, and if things were reversed, she would mourn and then get on with life, not withdraw from it. I wasn't honoring her death, I was grieving selfishly, thinking only of my loss. She would want me to "get with it, old man."

I didn't immediately jump back into life. Moments existed when I'd catch myself staring into space, crying; mornings when I'd reach across the bed to touch her and feel cold sheets; looking through *Sea Creatures* just to feel her presence. I'd catch myself about to ask her a question about something I was reading or doing. "Listen to this, Connie..." How many times did I hold her box of ashes, wishing them to magically leave the container and reform into my love. My love. I never said those words enough to her. Why not now?

I needed to bring Connie's ashes back to life, so I sprinkled some around the base of the Japanese maple tree in the backyard, mixing them in with the mulch. Together we had watched the leaves change colors as weather came and went. She had even pressed some gold, yellow, brown leaves in a book. (I must look for that book.) The rest of the ashes I gave to the sea after renting a small sailboat in the marina. I felt I needed to say something. I remembered a line a minister offered at my dad's funeral: "In the midst of life, we are in death."

Step by step, I slipped away from my mordant shell and felt her nudge me into an awareness of the time I had left to live. A void in my life existed and I had to accept it. I had to pretend Connie was the lucky one because she didn't have to deal with the power of bereavement.

Pretend. Yes.

Then one day, I sat at my computer and began working on the jazz volume I was assigned to write. I looked through some of my past writings and photographs I'd done for various magazines and books. I began organizing and selecting what I could use and what form it would take. I established a list for research. It was a first step back into life.

Once I got fully into the project, I couldn't help but remember some of the unforgettable music venues and talents I got to witness. I was so fortunate to hear and meet some of the greatest jazz musicians of all time. But I also couldn't help remembering how some of them were treated if them happened to be black. Too often I saw black musicians touring with whites who were not allowed to eat or sleep in the same places even though they made up most of the band. Or they just got hassled if they were Black. Like, back in 1959, Miles Davis, well-known then for his album *Kind of Blue*, was playing a gig at Birdland. He stepped out for a cigarette during a break when a policeman came by and told him to move on. When he asked why and told the officer he worked there, even pointing to his name on the marquee, the policeman handcuffed and arrested him for not moving on. Another officer hit him hard on the head. With blood gushing over him, they dragged him to the police station. Miles was known to say, if you're black there's no justice. I could understand that at the time in some places I visited, but not New York.

R. D. McGee Yes, I remember.

One night watching the news or something on TV, I saw an advertisement asking for donations to an organization that helped save animals. The ad showed some terrible pictures of shivering dogs looking sad and lonely and needy.

I saw myself.

On impulse, I went to the local animal shelter. The sad, compelling advertisement had worked its magic. So many dogs of all breeds and size surprised me. My presence seemed to send every dog in the place barking. I didn't know what I was looking for, or even if I really wanted one. If I got one, I knew I didn't want a small one. Small ones are cute, and I see quite a few men walking little dogs, but I didn't want a lap dog. Besides, I find the barking of small dogs grating and want to put them out of their misery.

As I walked the cages, several dogs made themselves known by barking, tail wagging, or jumping at me. Then I came to a cage where an adult golden retriever, sat down in front of her cage door and looked at me, head cocked, quiet, tail sweeping the floor behind her like a windshield wiper. She contacted my eyes.

"About time you got here. Where've you been?"

Yeah, I know.

Her name was Lady, and I discovered in short time that name fit. Two needy beings, we connected in short order.

I went out shopping for all the necessary dog accouterments; bed, feed bowl, water bowl, leash, food – and actually enjoyed it. When I brought her home, she inspected the place and seemed to approve. After her inspection, she sniffed around my desk and plopped down as if to let me know this was where she wanted her bed. So that's where I placed it, and her dog home was born.

The two of us became part of the beach-walking populace on the beach. I also noticed on our walks that women of all ages began paying friendly, conversational attention to me, attention I never received before Lady accompanied me. I even received "Invites." I accepted a few. Nice, but no thanks.

Lady and I developed a routine. In the morning, I'd have a coffee and biscotti while she ate her breakfast, then off for a beach walk. Never did Lady ever pull at her leash. She more or less kept pace with me. When other dogs approached, she was friendly, but a bit aloof, as if she wasn't interested in being sociable. As to chasing after a thrown stick? Forget it. She'd look at me as if to say, "Nice toss." (I know; that's anthropomorphic.) When I let her off leash, sometimes she'd take off in a run for a bit, but soon would turn around and walk with me as if she preferred being with me. Maybe she stayed close because she feared being left a stray again. I could relate.

Afterward, I'd grab a breakfast at Ziggie's while Lady sat at my feet. I'd sneak her in places claiming her as a service dog. Well, she was a service to me. When we got home, I'd work at my computer, checking email and reading the news before trying to work on my jazz manuscript. When Lady found nothing to do, she'd put her head on my lap letting me know she was bored or wanted affection.

I'd try to work until lunch. Usually, if the weather was fine, we'd eat in the backyard. In the afternoon, I'd do a little reading or play chess online. Lady would make herself at home at my feet. In the evening it was another beach walk. Back for dinner, then music time or television or more reading. I usually listened to music lying on the floor, and Lady would either curl up beside me, or if I watched television, lay her head on my lap.

I discovered Lady had music preferences. Her classical tastes ran to piano concertos, preferably Mozart. She endured Ravel and Debussy. If I played hard jazz, Bebop, or loud big bands, she'd leave the room. When I played soft singers like Nat Cole and Diana Krall or quiet instrumental solos, like Bill Charlap or Wes Montgomery, she would stick her nose close to one of the speakers. She loved any version of

"Here's That Rainy Day." It made me wonder about former lives, though I believe in no such things. Still...

At bedtime, it was a scuffle to keep her from sleeping on my bed, but despite my demands that she go to her own bed, in the morning, she was often on one side of me.

I managed to finish what would become Volume Three in the *History of Jazz* project.

I dedicated it to Connie and Lady.

Not a wild life, but we're a sweet old couple and we managed to muddle through the days.

CHAPTER 22

"When Somebody Loves You"
Then my mother died.
I found someone to take care of Lady and flew back to St. Louis. It wasn't easy for me to travel, plus I hated leaving Lady, but I had to.
And there I found my mother...

Yes, there in that shiny, silver-grey vessel designed for longevity under the ground, the top half of the lid open providing assurance that the occupant would rest for eternity on soft cream-white, velvet-like fabric. I did not want to look, nor had need to. I held no desire to observe the artificially decorated lifeless body of someone I love; no, not a vision I wanted to carry in my mind or my heart.

But grief, pulled me in, and I stood before her one last time. I refused to look at her face, but my eyes were drawn to her hands, despite the cosmetics, still gnarled, arthritic skeletal fingers covered in wrinkled, blotched blue-black skin, almost hidden under the closed half of the casket lid. Those hands held much of the story of my life.

Those hands changed my messy diapers, tenderly bathed me, held me to her breasts, helped me as she taught me to walk. Her hands soothed when my cheeks and brow held fever. Her hands turned the pages of the books we read together. Her hands took me as she walked me to my first school, assuring me I'd be fine. Her hands played the music that made me dance and sing. And as I grew too youth-embarrassed to hold hands, her hands put up with me, pointed me in the right direction when I needed it, and continued to hold nothing but love.

They deserve this rest, those hands that threaded the needles that sewed all those clothes I took for granted, washed and ironed them, mended them when I roughed them. For years, those hands managed to open jars and cans, hold those heavy pots, stir the thick sauces, pit the cherries, peel the potatoes, clean the messy dishes, scrub the toilet bowls, deal with all my clutter.

How did she manage to fasten those tiny necklace clips, and do it from behind her back?

Those hands never deserted me. Never ignored me.

Remember when I was what? Six maybe?

"But it tastes bad," I said, pushing away the tall, brown bottle of cod liver oil, the one with a fish molded in the glass on one side.

"I know it does. But the doctor thinks you need it," you said.

"No. I hate it."

"Tell you what. If and when you finish this bottle, you can have anything you want."

"Anything?

"Anything within reason," you said, adding, "If we can afford it."

A gag and a frown with each daily spoonful, I managed to empty it.

Wouldn't I have wanted a train set, toy soldiers, a dump truck? But there's a photograph of me in a family album, dressed in a tuxedo (you no doubt made for me) and shiny black patent leather shoes, grinning after a dancing recital. And another of me with a five-year old girl dressed in a formal gown, with white tap shoes, my dancing partner. You were so proud when the dance instructor asked me to show a much older student how to do the Buffalo Shuffle. How you managed to get me to think I wanted tap dancing lessons is hard to fathom, even today.

Ah, Mom, you put one over on me. Such a rush of mixed memories.

Remember that little grocery store in Webster Groves, the one with baby alligators in a fenced pond in back? As a four-year-old, I couldn't wait to go to the store with you. Imagine. Alligators. And those frozen Milky Ways the storeowner kept from melting in the summer heat. It's a remembrance that comes with an image of a white stucco bungalow along with a white spotted Great Dane that bit me when I wanted to play and it wanted to eat. The teeth scars on my hand serve as a fleshy monument to a dog that didn't live with us for very long.

A raggedy-looking man came to our door one day, it must have been before I started school, looking for yard work and payment in food. If I remember correctly, he carried a hoe or a tool of some kind over his shoulder with a bandana tied to the end of the pole filled with his meager belongings. He scared me at first, but you put me at ease when you gave him peanut butter on bread and a piece of the cherry pie you had baked for me. He was so thankful. You gave him something to drink and he was on his way.

"Why did you give him a piece of my pie?" I was not happy about that.

"Did you get a good look at him?" you asked. "The poor man's down on his luck and hungry."

"But you said it was my pie. You made it for me."

"You'd rather let a man go hungry than share what you have?"

"Why doesn't he get a job?"

"I'm sure he'd love one. You should be grateful your father has one and doesn't have to go from door to door to feed you and me."

I missed your message then, and could only think about that piece of pie, my pie, being given away. While you were downstairs doing the laundry, I put some of my toys in a handkerchief, and tied it to the end of a stick I'd found.

You were wringing some wet clothes through the two white rollers attached to the washing machine tub. For some reason those two rollers squishing out water stick in my head.

"I'm running away from home," I announced.

You didn't look up. "Where will you go?"

"Away. Somewhere." I hadn't thought very far ahead.

You still didn't look at me. You just continued running wet clothes through the rollers. I wanted you to see my pole and stuffed handkerchief that kept irritating me by sliding down the stick.

"Well, if you're not happy here, I guess you should leave."

"Okay. Goodbye," I said, hesitant.

"Goodbye." You still didn't look at me.

"Goodbye -- forever," I said, angrier than ever, and left. I doubt I made it to the end of the block. I saw the man with the pole being turned away from a house down the street. I watched as he went to several houses, turned away each time. Within minutes, my plans did not look promising. I went home.

"Did you find what you were looking for?" you asked. I don't remember how I answered, but at some level and over time, I understood what you were trying to teach me.

I still can't look at a Hershey's can of cocoa without remembering the many times we made fudge together, you letting me lick the bowl, waiting what seemed forever for the mixture to harden before being cut into squares.

On special days, we'd take a streetcar downtown, mostly window shopping; we had no real money, but we always lunched at Woolworth's, sat at the lunch counter where I was treated with a mayonaised ham sandwich on white bread, cherry pie and a cherry Coke. Ah, but I excuse you. You were a young mother without the advantages of today's advertisements warning you about food causing everything from tooth decay to cancer.

And the radio. We lived radio. You ironing to those soap operas – "Ma Perkins," "The Guiding Light," "The Romance of Helen Trent." In the evenings I remember listening to "Your Hit Parade," with Dorothy Collins and Snooky Lansen. Who could forget a name like "Snooky?"

Somehow, you always seemed to have the latest sheet music so we could sing along with the top ten songs of the week.

I smile when I think of the time I thought I was protecting you when during a yard party some friend, a stranger to me, picked you up in jest and pretended he was going to toss you in the ash pit out back, and I kicked his shins and beat his thighs, screaming, "Put her down! Put her down!"

You laughed, but he may still have scars.

Remember when you sent me to the dime store to buy some thread or something you needed for a sewing project. I must have been ten or eleven. (Those were days before frightened helicopter parents.) You said I could spend a dime on something I wanted as a reward for running the errand. But what I brought home and showed you, I've forgotten what, a toy airplane perhaps, cost more than the change I brought home revealed. Your blue-green eyes held a look you'd never given me before and caused my eyes to fill.

"Did you steal that?"

Did I say "yes," or did I nod? I know I confessed.

"Why did you take it?"

Struggling for a defense. "It cost more than a dime."

"And you needed it badly enough to steal it?"

"No. I...I just wanted it."

"Have you ever stolen anything before?"

Did I say "no" or just shake my head in disgrace?

You looked at me for an eternity without saying a word. At last, "I want you to take it back and tell the salesperson that you took it without paying for it and that you're sorry." Then she added, "You are sorry, aren't you?"

More than you knew.

I don't know who was more surprised, the woman behind the toy counter when I told her what I'd done, and then thanked me for being honest, or me, for not being reprimanded or arrested.

You became a den mother so I could wear the blue and yellow Cub Scout uniform. And I hope you'll forgive me for being embarrassed when you volunteered to chaperone those junior high school dances. You helped me select a birthday present for my first girl friend who was so important to me at the time but whose name I don't even remember right now...

Too many thoughts, as I look at those hands... unordered, rushing pieces of memories ... long separations buried under time gone by, events and distance ...

You were visiting from St. Louis. We went sailing, just the two of us. You'd never been to California or on the ocean before, and I could tell you were surprised your son knew how to handle a thirty-foot sloop. You were nervous when you stepped on the slightly swaying deck, expectant, not sure of what you were getting into, worried that you might get seasick, yet excited, trusting. You put yourself in my hands.

How I enjoyed watching you ease into the feel of sailing, shifting sides to duck under the boom when we'd come about, you relishing the wind on your grinning face, taking pleasure in the frequent silence interrupted by the occasional slapping of the waves against the boat, the wind straining to stay in the sails.

A wave spray hit you lightly in the face. Startled, you recovered quickly. "Ooo. Salty," you said, with a good sport smile. I noticed grey in your hair.

You forgot about seasickness when you saw the seals piled on top of one another on the signal buoy, barking at us as we slipped by. You laughed at the lumbering, flapping pelicans in flight, yet commented on how serene it would be to ride on their backs when they eased into their long, effortless glide skimming over the water.

The breeching whale took you off guard. Will it ram us, you worried; it's so huge, look at that, look at that, as it dove under us, then showing off by sending a fountain of watered air high above the surface. You looked at me for assurance, and I laughed.

A school of dolphins surrounded us, challenging us to go faster, faster. I had you haul in on the jib, tie it off, shift to the starboard as we heeled low in the foamy water, the dolphins racing alongside, turning their bodies, eyeing us as if to say, "Give up; you can't win."

You felt the exhilaration, dared to lean over the side, trying to touch the smooth skin of a friendly dolphin. They soon grew bored with us and went their way.

We didn't say much out there. No need. Mother and son together.
The next day, you went back to St. Louis.
That was the last time I saw you. So now, I look and see.
You're still here, in my hands.

CHAPTER 23

"That's What Friends Are For"

You can imagine my state of mind dealing with my mother's death after Connie's. Dark days, people say. Yes, and darker nights. But it wasn't the end of darkness.

Katherine Anne Porter's "Granny Weatherall" came whoosh-washing over me as I visited Monty. I hadn't seen him for some time. Like the dying Granny in the story, Monty's unsound mind floated back and forth between delusion and reality, making it one of those how-real-fiction-can-be moments. Too real for me.

I would run into Monty every once in a while when I was still writing jazz articles. I introduced Connie to Sophie and Monty at one of the jazz venues we were attending. In fact, Sophie and Connie became friends. The four of us saw a lot of each other for a time. They were cool enough to never bring up Abbie in our conversations. Then time and space interfered.

Monty, some years younger than I am, was in terrible health and bedridden. In fact, as I learned on my visit, he was dying and could be dead by the time I write this. Sophie called to ask if I would come visit, an unusual request at the time. I knew Monty was sick, but he'd hung out a no visitors sign, so I had stayed away. I knew the feeling at times myself. Sophie's tone of voice when she called sounded a little harrowed, boosting my suspicion something was amiss.

When I arrived, Sophie greeted me with a hug and thanked me for coming. She looked worn down. A few other people were there: their son Jonah and his wife Jennifer, neither of whom I'd seen for years since they lived abroad; a nurse whose name I never caught; and a minister named Foster from some Congregational church. Since I never knew Monty and Sophie to be church people, it reinforced my concern for Monty's state.

After a somber acknowledgment of everyone, Sophie explained as she took me to Monty's bedroom that he was indeed dying and had asked for me. After Connie died I retreated a bit, then Monty got sick and slowly became a recluse, except for occasional brief texts that fell eventually off.

A hospital-antiseptic-like smell shocked my nostrils as we entered his room. My knees went weak when I saw Monty pillow-propped up in bed. Indisputably the most handsome man I have ever known, with a body to go with the looks, he bore little resemblance to his former self. Almost bald, little scraggy hairs going every which way had replaced his once thick, black, well-groomed hair. His tanned skin had given up to pale splotches of brown and grey on a puffy, unfamiliar face. No eyebrows now, thick skin covered closed eyes. Was this really my old maverick friend? Seeing him as an invalid, I must have looked like a surprised child.

"Monty? Are you awake?" Sophie approached him prudently.

"Hm?" came with a soft crool.

"You have a visitor." Her tone tried to imply, "Isn't that nice?"

Monty opened his eyes half-hidden under the thick lids, and I stepped closer so he could see me.

He seemed to recognize me at first look. A raspy, "Took ya…long 'nuff."

He sounded angry with me for some unknown reason. Maybe he thought I was someone else.

"Pay no attention to Monty," Sophie said. "He's become a quarrelsome in his old age."

"Yeah," rasp, "yeah. So ya' say… old nag." Phlegmy cough.

"See what I mean?"

I wasn't sure Sophie's smile was genuine.

"Yeah, well, you...woman...you've turned into a...an... old harpy." A wheezy cough. "Leave. I want...to talk to...this (what he called me was indistinguishable) ...alone."

"Yes, your high and mighty." Sophie looked at me with raised eyebrows that implied what-can-you-do and left the room closing the door.

I couldn't tell if the two of them were being playful, or I was witnessing accrued anger between them, but I felt regret for having come to visit.

"How you doing, Monty?" It just came out before I realized I'd asked the obvious.

"Ha!" Rasp. "Good one, buddy." Cough.

"Yeah. Pretty stupid. Sorry."

"Oh... you meant it? I...thought you... being... a smart ass."

"No. Unthinking. I'm nervous to tell the truth. I didn't expect to see...well, this."

I waved my arm at him and the bed. His night table was surrounded by different sized pharmacy bottles, small boxes and a pitcher I assumed was water. An oxygen bottle on wheels stood by the bed side.

"What... did you... expect?"

A slight knock on the door saved me from an answer and the nurse entered. She moved around to the side of the bed with all the pills. I guessed her to be about forty, short grey hair, and a professional air. She wore a solid dark blue uniform just like I'd see in many doctors' offices.

"Sorry, gentlemen, but it's time for Mr. Monty's meds." She pulled one of those thermometers you run across the forehead from the table drawer and ran it across Monty's brow. She wrote something on a pad.

"She calls me... Mister Monty... (heavy breaths) because she can't... remember my...last name. She's a bit ... dim." Rasp.

"I call you Mister Monty because you don't even know my name. I'm just 'nurse' to you."

"Well, that's what...what you are...nurse." Cough.

She fiddled with some of the bottles, took out some pills, handed them to Monty whose hand shook as he raised the pills to his mouth. Then she poured some water in a glass for him.

"W'ad you just...give me?"

"The usual."

"Poison... again."

"The best I could find," the nurse said as she took the plastic tube attached to the oxygen tank and inserted the other end in Monty's nose. He tried to slap her hand away, but she fought him and he gave up. "I told you to keep this up your nose."

Monty had a hard, painful-sounding coughing jag.

"That's what you get for fighting Big Nurse. Now don't let me catch you taking that hose out."

Monty recovered as she started to leave the room. "Yeah? Or...what?"

"Or else. That's what. Now, you boys enjoy yourselves." As she closed the door to leave, she looked at me and said, "He might fall asleep on you. Those meds are pretty strong."

The banter between Monty and the nurse was pure Monty. Always the provocateur, he loved to tease. He could be a sarcastic asshole without trying. But it was usually in his idea of fun, and his way of testing a person's bait level. He appreciated a good rejoinder.

"Can't help...lovin' er," Monty wheezed.

"You love all women," I said it jokingly, but truth lay under the surface. Monty shared many of his "conquests" with me, many of which surprised me. And some I wanted to doubt. I wondered what he wanted to prove by bedding as many women as he could. It seemed there were plenty who wanted to accommodate him.

He responded with a throaty rasp and something unintelligible.

"So, bring me up to date," my awkward way of starting a conversation that would lead to his telling me why he asked for me. Plus, the situation made me uncomfortable and I wanted to get out of there.

"You can see ... for yourself. Shit ... I'm a dead man."

"Yeah, well ...." What's to say after that? Don't be dramatic? You'll get better? Don't talk like that? There's always hope? Be positive? "Shit" says it plain enough.

Monty didn't say anything and his eyes closed.

Silence.

"Monty?"

No response. For a moment, I thought he was dead. I stood up and looked closer, ready to call Sophie and the nurse, but his eyes opened as he took a rattling breath and blinked at the ceiling.

"Sorry ... old sport ... guess ... went somewhere ... for a... minute."

Relieved, I sat down in silence, reflecting on his calling me "old sport." He had picked up "old sport" from reading Gatsby and he found great pleasure using the term on me as an irritant.

He fell into mumbling. "Jonah... have to... forgive me... just... me... know I can be... real shit sometimes... not perfect..."

He apparently thought I was Jonah.

"I... just couldn't... see you marrying that... religious girl... you know how I feel... about that Jesus claptrap... (cough) not just that... any religion... didn't need it... don't need it now... (deep breathe) hope you'll grow... out of it... but no... do you really... believe that... (rasp) church stuff or just doing it... for Jennifer..."

I felt I was intruding on a family affair I knew a little something about, but had no business listening, so I interrupted Monty.

"Hey, old sport, it's me. You wanted to see me, remember?"

"Huh?"

I stood up and let him see me.

"Ya' old... fart. When... you get here?"

"Just now," I said, not wanting him to drift backwards.

"About time," sarcasm back in control.

"So sue me." I tried to stay on his level.

"No... no...you should sue me. No I don't mean sue... I mean... kill."

"You invited me here to kill you?" I gave a false laugh.

"To... tell ya' why."

"Please do."

He closed his eyes and fell silent again.

Then Monty groaned and wheezed, but I couldn't tell if it was a physical pain or a sign of remorse as he started talking to someone in his head.

"Told you... I was sorry... can't help... guess I came on to her... I know... I know that was... sick... but..."

"Came on to whom?" I had no idea who he was talking about or why.

"Daisy's... such a bitch...Zelda... maybe *Tender in the Night*... best one... the way he made... the Doc... the weak one in the end... the end... hell... I'm sorry..."

Monty gasped, fell silent, eyes not blinking, and I thought once again maybe that was it. I stood over him and couldn't tell if he was still breathing. I thought it best to call the nurse.

She rushed into the room with Sophie and Jonah following. I stepped back while the nurse began checking Monty's vitals. "Pulse is there, just weak." She kept calling his name while she examined him.

The three of us just stood there, blanks, then sighs of relief when we heard Monty's voice scratch out, "Thirsty... water..."

I figured that would be a good time for me to leave, so I told Monty I'd come back another time, feeling sure there probably would not be another time and certain the nurse and family would be happy with my getting out of the way.

I was saying goodbye when Monty managed to be heard. "No... can't go yet... have to talk...to him. Alone...all alone... get out... out."

I looked at Sophie and then the nurse, shrugging my shoulders and silently asking what they wanted me to do.

The nurse said it would be best if we granted Monty's wishes. It seemed important to him. So once again I was left alone with him.

His fading in and out of consciousness pushed me to get to his point.

"Monty, what are you trying to tell me? What's so important and secretive?"

"O whan that Aprille with his shoures soote the droghte of Marche hath perced to the roote..."

At first I didn't understand his rambling, then I realized he was quoting the beginning lines to the Canterbury Tales in middle English. Damn.

"Monty!"

"Hm?"

"I'm leaving, okay?"

"Alysia ...remember Alysia... god help me...'m such a romantic... you know."

It took me a minute, but I did remember Alysia. Years ago, she was a singer from Saudi Arabia, I think. A real beauty. At first, I thought his desire for her was pernicious, but it turned out he was prepared to leave Sophie for her. But it never would have worked out. If Alysia's father, some prince or other, found out she lost her virginity to an American music manager, he'd have had her stoned to death, had Monty assassinated and started a war with the U.S.

I'd never seen Monty so smitten. I liked Monty, in spite of his seeming need to have sex with every female who caught his eye. Intelligent, a good friend, and a quixotic iconoclast, he had a kind of attention-grabbing appeal. But he could be hard to take sometimes.

My impatience overruled Alysia. "Monty, look at me. What did you want to see me about?"

Deep breath. "Kill me."

"Okay, let me go get a gun. What the fuck, Monty!"

"Mean it... kill me."

"Shit. You're talking gibberish."

"You promised."

"And when would that have been?"

"We promised... each other... if... ever...this shape, we'd help... the other... end it."

He was right. A few years ago, we watched a famous musician die in misery, and we made a pledge we wouldn't let the other of us go through a ragged ending. Timely talk, both meaning it, but not knowing we'd ever be in that position; more wishful thinking than anything else.

"Yeah, well, that was different. I can't do anything like that now, Monty. I mean, even if I did, everybody would know I did it. I'd be called for what it is."

"Promised... friend."

"No. Sorry. I can't. I...couldn't." I figured his meds were ganging up on him.

"Pillow... over... head... nobody'd know... can't breathe... anyway."

"Don't be dramatic. This isn't a movie."

Deep breath, then a rush of words, "I had... affair... with... Abbie."

I didn't absorb it at first. Why was he telling me?

"Yeah... did."

"I'm not surprised. So did a lot of people."

"Connie, too."

"What are you saying?" Was he delirious again?

"True."

"With my Connie?"

"Yeah."

"My Connie, Monty?"

"Ya'."

For a weak, dying man, he had a powerful punch that knocked me to the ropes. What was I to make of this confession? Was it a confession? Knowing his sexual exploits made it difficult to dismiss immediately. I felt my body turn to flame. He had to be lying. Connie wouldn't have done such a thing. No. Wouldn't it have come out? Would Monty betray me like that? Had I not really known him all these years? What did he mean by "affair?" How long did it go on? Have I been cuckhold?

I tried to bounce back. "You're shittin' me. You want me to be angry enough to actually kill you, right?"

"No... kill me...now."

I had a moment when the idea of putting a pillow over his head and holding down hard had strong appeal.

"If it's true, I ought to kill you. If it's not true, I should kill you for telling me such a despicable thing now. Is this the sick you talking, or are you a sick human being showing your true colors?" He knew the story of Abbie which made this hurt all the more.

"I'm...sorry. I didn't..."

"Sorry? You're sorry? I know you're sick and dying, but this... this is unforgivable."

Too stunned and confused to say anything meaningful, "asshole" was all that came out.

"I want... to die. Help me."

"Kill yourself."

I needed to get away. I didn't want to hear anymore. I left in a fog as Monty mumbled something I didn't get and didn't want to. I said goodbye to the family, gave Sophie a quick hug, and told the nurse Monty was all hers.

When I got home, I was unable to sit down, a body without bones. Lady seemed to suspect something wrong and curled up in a corner, watching me.

I made a hefty gin and tonic and journeyed through every room in the house, I don't know how many times. I finally brought myself under a semblance of control and stopped to stare at a photograph of Connie sitting on the mantel taken a few months before she died. I knew her well. She wouldn't have. I wouldn't doubt he came on to her. She was adamant that Monty not be invited when we discussed a funeral service. Doesn't matter anymore. Why listen to a dying man's waggish twaddle? It's a lie, a sick lie. He just said it to get me to kill him. Did he really expect me to kill him? Maybe a lousy attempt to get even with me for something I did? Never did I stray. Tempted, but never. A time or two, I thought about Sophie that way; never did I go beyond thoughts of wondering what it would be like. Old faithful me. He knew it. No, he found it important to brag even o his death bed. Had to prove he bested me. I should go tell Sophie what I know. Let her know what I'm feeling.

But why hurt her? I just can't allow myself to believe Monty. No. No. He's planted a seed, yes, but I choose not to allow it to grow, not now, not ever—ever—ever—please.

I had another drink, and maybe even another, I don't remember. I started having strong, incessant, vivid visions of despicable Monty lying in that bed, grinning, and me, standing over him, pillow in hand, thinking, yes, oh yes.

I drank myself under and woke up the next morning with Lady lying next to me on the floor.

CHAPTER 24

"Down Here on The Ground"

I started having trouble sleeping. My visit with Monty didn't help, but it was more than that. I still mourn Connie. I don't believe him. I can't. She just wouldn't.

My doctor had me on some medications for high blood pressure and arthritis that I think weren't working well together. In general, I seemed to struggle for a strong purpose for living and often catch myself having unusual mind experiences.

I remember one night, dressed in my terrycloth robe, I stepped through the French doors into the backyard for a nightly hot tub and thought I saw something dash around the corner of the house. I stopped and listened but heard nothing, saw nothing. I felt hesitant about going out if there was something prowling around. But because the moon lit up the yard, it was easy making my way to the hot tub; still, I almost stepped in something. My eyes being what they are made it difficult for me to make out what jarred me. I bent lower and grimaced. It was the head of an opossum with almost nothing left but its skeleton and clumps of hair, or whatever it is that covers an opossum's body. No doubt it was the same one I'd seen the other night outlined across the rooftop with three babies following it. It appeared I wasn't the only critter who saw them. I wondered if the babies would survive on their own, or if whatever attacked their mother had left them dead somewhere else.

I made a note to remember to clean the mess up tomorrow before it began to smell and proceeded to the tub. I removed the cover, hung my robe on the stair rail and eased into the 105-degree water. The moonlight pierced the water and exposed my nakedness. At least my body still had flesh on it.

I gave in to the hot water as it worked on my aching muscles. I stared at the October moon and tried to remember what a friend of mine, an astrologer of sorts, said about full moons. Each new full moon has some astrological meaning or power. The one I stared at supposedly contained a spiritual energy offering a time to reflect on our past relationships and mistakes, a chance to heal any wounds we felt inflicted upon us. Perhaps she's right, but to me a harvest moon has always had something to do with farming, a time when the moon gave off more light for extended periods giving farmers longer days to work their fields. But it wouldn't hurt to self-reflect, would it?

My relaxed eyelids closed out the moon.

I know you're up there, moon, while I'm down here on the ground. Ah! "Down Here on the Ground." Lalo Shifrin composed it for the movie "Cool Hand Luke" and Wes Montgomery recorded one of the best versions ever. The chords he uses to play the melody take me elsewhere, then he breaks into improvisation and his chords slowly rise and build and build and more chills, then back to the melody, clever Herbie Hancock piano chords throughout, soft drum brushes in the background, and a playful ending. If only I could find words like Lorca uses to describe Manuel deFalla's music, to describe the *duende* I feel when I listen to that recording, that emotion that comes from somewhere deep and inexplicable. I hear it without sound so clearly and soak it up like this water. I wish you could hear it, moon, but you're not down here on the ground.

Something, I have no idea what, made me open my eyes, an unwanted interruption of mind thought. Did the moon want something? I sat up and saw a scraggly coyote standing over the dead opossum. The splashing of the water made the coyote turn and look at me. We played possum and stared at each other. I saw my childhood dog, Spot; same grey-brown fur sprinkled with cinnamon, pointed ears erect, but this one had a long, bushy tail, its eyes almost slits.

I saw you on my walk two days ago, I said.
Yes, you did.
You stared at me as you are right now.
Yes, I did.
We both just stood there, surprised, like now.
Yes.
Then you trotted off.
Yes.
You killed that opossum.
Obviously.
You've been killing people's cats in the neighborhood.
Why do you say that?
I've seen posters on telephone poles saying cats are missing.
Could be a fox or a bobcat.
No, not around here.
Yes, around here. You're not the only ones dealing with a drought.
But this close to the city?
I'm not going to argue with you. You can't read my mind.

Tired of communicating, the coyote grabbed what was left of its prey and moved out of sight. It seemed to know I was not about to rise nude from the water and go after it. Smart coyote. But I wanted to talk more with this one, to ask what brought it to this neighborhood. Had it always lived around here and this was just the first time I'd seen it? Was it a male? A mother? Old? I'd only seen one other up close, in Death Valley. It, too, had nonchalance about it.

The coyote was right. I can't read its mind. But it must have a mind. What must it be like to be in the mind of a coyote at the moment of our awareness of each other? I'd like to know. What did it think of me? How did it perceive me? "Oh-oh. There's a human. I'd better be careful." No, more like, "This is my catch and you can't have it."

How did it perceive the opossum? "I'm hungry. Oh, there's a meal. I'll catch it and eat it." And what was in the mind of that poor opossum? "Don't move. Maybe it won't see me."

I saw what my mind was doing. And it was all conjecture. Those animals have a mind, but I have no idea how their minds think and work.

I know many Native Americans believe the coyote is a hero-trickster, both funny and fearsome, and a major character in many of their mythological stories. Coyote existed before man, in some stories, even responsible for creating different tribes of people. He can change shapes, even become a raven in some stories. He outwits his enemies, but is often a buffoon and foolish, like the cartoon character, Wiley Coyote. This one did not look like a buffoon.

Would this coyote sit in wait in the shadows for me to leave the hot tub and attack me? Silly. But what if it was rabid? Maybe I should sit in the tub until morning and play possum. It didn't play well for that poor opossum did it? My mind at work again.

I slid back down in the water up to my neck, hoping to regain the ease I felt earlier. The moon was still up there. I could see the form of the face of the so-called man in the moon if I looked closely at those grey spots against the bright white. But no cow jumped over the moon. Not while I was looking and hearing Moon Over Miami. Racing with the Moon. Bad Moon Rising. Moon Dance. Moonlight Becomes You. Moon River. How High the Moon. Fly Me to the Moon. Oh, yeah. You're no paper moon, you old devil.

It must have been the moon glow, because the dead opossum and coyote image kept reoccurring and for some unknown reason I wonder if they had souls. Souls must be important. We certainly refer to the soul enough: soul mates, soul food, soul sister, soul music, sell your soul, bares his soul, rest his soul, lost soul, soul stirring, soul searching, to have soul.

Buddhists believe in Anatman, a denial of the existence of a self, or soul, but belief in a cycle of death and rebirth based on one's karma. Is there animal karma? Were my coyote and opossum once humans in a previous life, but downgraded this time around because of past bad lives lead? And who is to say that rebirth as an animal or bug is a downgrade? We humans are animals. But can animals like coyote and opossum lead a life that allows them to self-reflect? Isn't that anthropomorphizing?

The Hindus, contrary to the Buddhists, believe every living thing has what's called Atman, a true self, one's true essence, a soul. Does that apply to my opossum and coyote? But if they are good Christian animals, they won't reincarnate; they'll be reborn. But as what? And who decides? To confuse me even more, I'm told some Maya believe humans are born with two aspects of a soul. One is in the body and dies upon death. The other can roam around while we are asleep and never die, allowing it to enter a newborn or even an animal. Ishmael, was that you?

Where does this thing called a soul exist, and do I have one? If so, where is it? In my head? That could make it a figment of my imagination. In my heart? Although many Hindus would say it is, it can't be in the heart because too much is made of doing something with heart and soul. What's its shape? Is it an amorphous shroud that envelops me, my future as a ghost? Is it some chemical in the body? Is that why we talk of body and soul? Is it separate from what we call our being? What happens to what we call the soul when one dies? Does it hang out in the Bardo, waiting for judgment? Judgment by whom? Some believe the soul separates from the body upon death and moves on in search of perfection. Where, then, does that perfection exist? Does it go into a newborn, biding its time until it's capable of self-reflection? Jesus asks what does it profit a man to gain the whole world and lose his soul. He puts importance of the soul pretty high up there. But what does he know and what makes him right?

Keats, sure he knew what the soul was, said, "Some say the world is a vale of tears, I say it is a place of soul-making." In her poem "Bone," Mary Oliver says about the soul, "... our eyes have never seen it, nor can our hands ever catch it ...I believe I will never quite know." According to the Smithsonian, during the Great Depression, WPA writers, such as Zora Neale Hurston, Vardis Fisher, Richard Wright, and Ralph Ellison, discovered the "Soul of a People." That's a big soul. For Plato, the soul has three parts: reason, spirit, and appetite. Well, if chicken soup is good for the soul then it must be fed. But is soup food enough? And are these examples of what is meant by writing with soul or just writing about soul?

I think there's nothing spiritual about the soul; nothing more than mind play; nothing that disembodies after death. The soul is nothing more than how others see us and what they project on us. When we die, the memories others have of us collectively become what we call the soul. We live on after death, not as some ethereal entity, but through the recollections the living have of us: what we did, what we were to others, what we left that affected those we leave behind, good or bad. That's how I feel Connie's still with me.

But what do I know? I'm just some weary-year-old soul sitting in a tub of hot water.

Ah, you old devil moon. Maybe my astrology friend is right. You did your duty. While my body was being eased, my mind was working overtime wandering among the stars I couldn't see because you were too bright for me. You caused me to reflect beyond my intellect, offering more mind enigmas regarding life and death on which to dwell.

The moon seemed to cool the water; it didn't feel as hot anymore. My body and soul were tired. It was time to rise from the water, go in and to bed and to dream of coyotes and me howling soulfully at the moon.

I guess I'm still hoping to see the jaguar.

CHAPTER 25

"Stop the World, I Want to Get Off"

Another blood test. Another MRI scheduled. Another round of possible cancer. In my eighties, for god's sake.

My body winces and knots up when I think about what they'd found the last time...yes...the last time...I think I can tell you now...I couldn't before...it's still vivid...

"Stop! Please! Let me out. I can't breathe!"

"Stay calm, sir. Don't panic. It's okay. We're bringing you out now."

The faint, metallic voice cracking through the miniature speaker calmed my panic some, but my loss of self-control slipped into embarrassment as I felt the slab table I was lying on slide out into the open. The whirring noise stopped, but a humming sound stayed in the background. Blinking eyes welcomed the bright, white space of the room, the poster of snow-topped Mount Whitney pasted on the ceiling, a ludicrous attempt at soothing actually working.

A green-uniformed body bent over me, took out the plugs in my ears, unharnessed my head and smiled. "Okay now, hon?"

"Sorry." Shame, shame kept me from looking in her eyes for long. What must she think? A man who has lived this long, racked with anguish by a machine!

She looked down at my humiliated face. "Don't worry about it. You're not the first to get a little spooked. We're used to it. Just lie there for a bit and take some deep breaths." She noticed my dry lips and offered to get me some water.

When she left, I turned my head, looked around and shivered at the coldness of the apparatus that just released me, a huge vanilla donut, with a hole big enough for my body to slip into where magnetic machinery I would never understand waited to scan my insides for foreign invaders. I shivered again, the warm blanket that covered me in the beginning now cold.

CAT scans I knew well. But this MRI, Magnetic Resonance Imaging procedure, threw me. In a backless gown with blue dots, I was placed flat on my back on a narrow morgue-like gurney, my head fastened in some kind of bar vice to keep it immobile, plugs inserted in my ears for protection against the loud, jackhammer sounds they warned would come. Like a large rag doll, my body surrendered as they folded my arms corpse-like over my chest, shoved a cushion under the backs of my knees, and covered part of me with that now cold blanket.

The smiling technician's clear, but tired-looking eyes had stared down at me, warning me, nicely, of course, to be absolutely still, or I might have to go through the scan again. For her, I'm a job. After me there will be others out there in the waiting room, sitting in an open gown tied at the neck, flipping through dated *Golf* or *Sunset* magazines. Over and over, she will repeat the same instructions to all of them. I'm nothing but a daily routine.

"Remember, hon, movement is our enemy. Don't swallow much; breathe as lightly as you can. You'll hear me, and I'll be able to hear you if you speak. Ready? Here we go." She left the room, and soon I felt myself sliding head first into the heart of darkness.

I tried to relax. But when my head began to enter a confined space that grew narrower as my body was pushed farther into the doughnut hole, I began to tense. I closed my eyes, fighting my sudden anxiety. Then BAM BAM BAM...the jackhammer sound and I opened my eyes.

I'm not in a doughnut hole. I'm in a sickening, yellow lit, velvet-lined coffin with the lid shut, my nose only inches away from the top. Discovering the yellow light didn't go out when the lid closed didn't help. I was trapped inside a coffin! My heart searched for more space. Despite the cool air from somewhere, my lungs burned with rapid constrictions. I wanted to stand, to run. I couldn't move my head, and I had no room to move my arms to push open the casket lid even if I tried. The pounding noise became dirt being thrown on my casket. This is my eternity: tombed. A far away, tinny voice asked if I was okay. Crazy question! How could I be okay six feet underground, buried alive? Pride go to hell. I slipped into my real being and pleaded, "Stop! Please! Let me out. I can't breathe!"

Oh, what relief!

"Here. Let me help you sit up so you can drink a little of this." The technician skillfully helped me sit up with one arm while she juggled the paper cup of water in her hand. My worn-thin patient gown came untied and slipped off one shoulder. When I took the cup, the technician adjusted the gown and tied it at my back. I had never in my life felt less of a man.

"Sorry about this." I apologized again, mostly to make myself feel better, less shamefaced. "Don't know what came over me. Claustrophobic, I guess. Didn't know I was."

"I'd say about every fourth person or so gets rattled once they enter the machine. Some patients get a prescription for a mild tranquilizer from their doctor to take before the procedure. I've even had one patient refuse to go on with the scan."

That didn't help. Why hadn't my doctor offered a tranquilizer? I took a sip of water. "I didn't realize it was so closed in. Not open like a CAT scan."

"No, two different procedures. Some of the new MRI machines, they're more open, still noisy but not so closed in. Some even have headphones and a choice of music you can choose to help drown out the machine's noise. Ours is an older model. We're supposed to get a new one soon. They cost an arm and a leg as you can imagine." She took the cup from me, and I could tell she wanted to get on with the scan. She had more to do than baby me.

Not in any hurry, I kept feeling the need to explain. "It really felt as if I were in my coffin."

"Well, try to look at it as just a machine that wants to help keep you alive. It's a noisy old thing, but it won't hurt you. Maybe you could think of it as a cocoon. When you come out, you'll be a butterfly."

Cute, but it didn't help. I didn't want to be a butterfly.

The technician asked me if I was ready to try again. I told her I thought so. Hoped so. How was I to know?

"Good. I'll be right back and we'll have another go."

Her words stayed in my head, "...a machine that wants to help keep you alive."

The doughnut hole again began sucking me into its humming belly, preparing for its search mission. Me, thinking of Eliot's line, "like a patient etherized upon a table."

The results of those tests were not easy to bear either...

"Well, I have bad news and good news," the doctor had said.

"It's cancer." I tried to sound nonchalant, but inside I wasn't as prepared as I thought.

"Afraid so. Sorry. Of course, that's not what you wanted to hear. Look, let me show you." He fiddled with a small computer screen protruding from the wall and showed me a CT scan and some cystoscopy pictures. One of the photos of the insides of my bladder could have been a wild, red weave from a drunken spider.

"You have what's called a CIS, carcinoma in situ of the bladder." He showed a few more images, like a proud salesman proving he knew what he was talking about.

Too deadened to say anything, my head couldn't let go of the word "cancer."

I'd dealt with the Big C before. A malignant melanoma. Carved me up my side and removed all the lymph nodes under my left armpit. I told you that. Now this.

"But the good news is it's treatable," the doctor said.

A slight lifting of spirits.

The doctor explained that over a three-week period I would be given immunotherapy treatments where BCG, a bacterium similar to the bacteria that cause tuberculosis, is placed directly in the bladder through a catheter inserted in the penis. The BCG has to be held in the bladder for twenty or more minutes while it attaches to the inside lining of the bladder and triggers the immune system to destroy the cancer.

"Statistically, it has an eighty percent chance of working," he said.

During all three sessions, I couldn't hold the BCG in my bladder for longer than ten minutes. That put me in the twenty percent of those for whom it doesn't work.

I'd wanted to try again for another three sessions of immunotherapy, thinking maybe this time I could hold the drug in long enough to work. The doctor wasn't encouraging, but agreed and said that he would add Interferon, another drug, with the BCG.

Again, no good.

Time passed while I researched my condition, looking for any way I might avoid the inevitable, even offering to be a research guinea pig. I contacted the National Cancer Institute, the Mayo Clinic, MD Anderson, Johns Hopkins, even a clinic in Italy, looking for possible experimental trials dealing with bladder cancer. But after another biopsy and CT scan, the cancer had invaded the muscles of my bladder. Time got the better of me, the evidence was incontrovertible, leaving no choice but a radical cystectomy, removal of the entire bladder.

Demoralized, I listened to the doctor's operating alternatives. The surgeons could create a tube using a piece of my intestine that would run from my kidneys to the outside of my body where urine would drain into a pouch or urostomy bag worn on my stomach. Another choice was to use a piece of my intestine to create a small reservoir for urine inside my body that would be drained a few times a day through a hole in my stomach using a catheter. A third option was to use a piece of my intestine to make a neo-bladder inside my body and attach it to my urethra, allowing me to urinate normally. The only other option, he said, was to do nothing and keep my bladder and pain until death do us part.

None sounded appealing, but dealing with my problem became exigent. I went with the third option, the neo-bladder. It seemed manlier.

"Here's what we do," the doctor explained. "We make an incision in your lower abdomen and remove your bladder and anything else that looks cancerous. That we won't know until we get in there. Then we slice off a piece of your intestine and make a new bladder from it. It will look like a softball, sewing stitches and all. We'll stitch your intestine back together, and connect your new bladder to your urethra."

"And I'll pee normally after that?" (This was important to me! Why? Fear of being different?)

"Just like before, minus the burning pain you're feeling now."

The doctor warned me it would be a long and painful recovery, a loss of twenty pounds or more (that part wouldn't hurt me), the need to insert a catheter attached to a urine bag for at least a month (!), and a strict diet.

Eleven days in the hospital with an intense, unrelenting back pain. Slight pain came from where they cut me open, but why the back pain? The medical staff couldn't connect the back pain to the cystectomy. Worried more medication might be dangerous, they denied a larger dosage of morphine. No position gave comfort. None. Even in my on-and-off morphine dreams the pain insisted itself. I'd awake in a drugged state imagining hours had passed only to see a laughing clock on the wall show the minute hand barely moved. My mind at times took me to the edge of existence, a real nowhere man, but the severity of pain always drew me back to ponder the many types of possible deaths. Why had I submitted to this? Death equals no pain. Shame haunted me for not handling my dilemma better, and often drew thoughts of going gently into that goodnight.

When will it stop? When can I go home with my new softball bladder?

Not until I fart, they said.

Fart?

"You have to pass gas before we can consider letting you go."

What I hadn't been told until after the operation was that the muscles in the intestine were not like the muscles in the bladder. I would have to learn to overcome incontinence. Weeks (in my mind, much longer) after being home, the Foley catheter at last removed, I had to wear a pad while I trained my new bladder. To establish a urinary routine, I had to set my alarm clock for every two hours at night, wake up, go to the bathroom, unhook the catheter from the bag and pee, then hook it all back together once finished. After a few weeks, the alarm was set for three hours, then four, until a regular urinary bladder habit formed.

For five minutes, several times daily, I practiced doing Kegels to strengthen my pelvic muscles since I now had no strong sphincter muscle.

It took six months to gain back the weight and strength to feel normal, but a good year before I mentally adjusted to my new bladder and Kegel away the incontinence. But the cancer was gone. I'd lived through both the malignant melanoma and the bladder surgery. But I'd had help and support from Connie then. I don't know what I would have done without her.

Now I'm off for another MRI scan for something new...and I don't have Connie.

CHAPTER 26

"Get Outta My Way"

Those MRI tests revealed I had chronic myelogenous leukemia. At least it's treatable, and after experimenting with several wrenching, body-twitching, very expensive medicines, the doctors found one that helps keep my correct cell numbers in check. Cancer just can't leave me alone.

But I can live with it. What choice do I have, anyway. I'm not bed ridden, I can get around on my own, and I get my chemotherapy through pills instead of a drip. I have less energy and some days are worse than others, but I'm still above the grass, as they say.

You might not believe this. I'm still processing it...

I was heading for my parked car after a doctor visit at the Norris Cancer Center, checking something on my iPhone, when a man on a bike approached me from behind and tried to grab my phone. Straddling his bike, he managed to pull it from my hand, but the phone fell to the sidewalk. The guy pushed me off balance and I fell on my side. He got off his bike to retrieve my phone, then re-mounted his bike. But before he could get off to a good start, I stuck my cane into the spokes of his rear wheel. He tumbled over dropping my phone, his bike falling on him. While he was down and struggling, I managed to get up (a small adrenalin miracle) and whacked him a good one on his head with the metal end of my cane. I wanted him to feel some five-pointed stars. I picked up my phone, and while he held his head in his hands moaning, I pushed my cane several times as hard as I could into his ribs.

And these words (or the like) spewed out of me with fury: "Don't mess with dying old men. They've got nothing to lose!"

Then I stomped one foot on the spokes of one of the bike wheels and hurried to my car, looking back frequently, just in case.

Once in my car, I locked myself in and started shaking. While Lady, who'd been waiting in the car, licked the back of my ears, myriad thoughts stormed my brain. Someone tried to rob me and I stopped it. I didn't know if I was in physical pain from falling down and didn't feel it yet. I wondered if I injured my attacker. I think I saw blood on his hands. It must have hurt him. Maybe not his ribs. I'm not that strong. But my cane head is solid metal of some type. I could have caused him brain damage. Can a thief sue his victim? He doesn't know me. I could have let him have my phone. Is it that important to fight and maim over it? What's got in to me? Tyler. Remember Tyler from Boy Scout camp? I bloodied his nose. Am I feeling the same feelings? What kind of need is that? And the guy at the gas station who pushed me. I wanted to hit him back. Yes. I wanted to fight. (A story for another time.) It's still in me, even now, that feeling of hurting somebody who hurt you. Is there some reptilian part of my brain that hasn't developed? Turn the other cheek? Fuck that. I got my phone back. Yeah, but I could have been beaten or killed. Is this what being a man is? Was what I did worth it? Should I have called the police? Naw, they'd never would have shown up in time.

Am I proud or foolish?

I'll think on that.

My body shook as I drove home. Lady stayed still in the back seat, sensing I should be left alone for a while.

I couldn't stop thinking about the guy I'd left on the ground. Why did he want my phone? I must look like easy prey, some helpless old man. Scary thought. What would he have done with my phone if he had taken it? Sell it, maybe. Did he need money that badly? I wonder what I'd have done if he'd just asked me for money because he was hungry.

Would I have given it to him? Probably. But if I'd pulled out my wallet, he could have grabbed it, using hunger as a ploy. What must his life be like if he has to rob people? Maybe he's unemployed and has a family to feed. Should I feel sorry for him? Is he worth my sympathy? All that ruckus for a phone!

A phone that doesn't work now, I might add.

I'll get that taken care of later. Right now I'm a little shaky. Lady and I need a drink. A little Bailey's Irish Cream over rocks should do it. Then a soak in the hot tub.

What a world, huh?

CHAPTER 27

"Wintergreen for President"

I guess, since I'm searching for who I am, I should mention my politics or lack of.

Not much to say. I spent most of my young life accepting the political party of my parents. I think most people do. But I never examined what the party (not important which one) stood for, just went along with whoever ran on that ticket. Didn't have the time (Lie) or the inclination (Truth) to think through what both parties professed to believe, just accepted whatever my political party professed to be the right path forward.

After I was discharged from the navy, I went along with the party's nominee. During my college years, I was surrounded by students rallying in protests for and against what seemed like everything: corporate greed, racial discrimination, the Vietnam war, new Jim Crow attempts. Protests began to open my eyes to what I had been ignoring. The government lies when it's convenient. What I witnessed as a child in Mississippi hasn't changed much over the years. Racism hasn't gone away; I'd just not paid attention. I've seen different ways of "lynching" still going on. Politics doesn't seem to do much for that problem. But neither did I. I didn't get involved. Too busy living my sheltered life.

At one point, I did try to get involved. But it seems to me that one party sweeps in and makes changes; then the other party wins and reverses those changes, then loses again. Back and forth; back and forth. You know...Oh can you believe what's going on isn't it terrible oh unbelievable sad so sad what's the world coming to can you believe they said that what's to become of this country yes can things get worse we're all going to die where do you want to eat tonight…

Connie and I basically tuned out all that and fell into insouciance and continued with our lives, for which we luckily had no complaints, nor did we feel personally affected by politics. For me, my sardonic attitude toward politicians can be summed up in the musical "Of Thee I Sing," a musical that lampoons American politics.

You have a right to condemn me. I could study up on events, watch all the news channels, listen to the radio (I do, but to music) choose a side, protest, write letters, donate money to political causes (I do donate to what I feel are worthy "needy people causes"). I thought about not voting in the last elections out of disgust with all the rancor, confusion, frustration and lies, but I did vote, for whatever good it will do. And I pay my taxes along with complaint. For several years, I volunteered at Long Beach City College tutoring English to non-English speakers. And Connie did volunteer work for The Girls' Club and the Food Bank. We weren't totally out of touch with the world. I realize I'm blessed to be living in this country and state. I'm very aware of it. But I'm not a political animal. I'm not Bellow's Herzog, or Mr. Smith goes to Washington.

Even though at the time I didn't know where Korea was and what communism had to do with anything, I enlisted and took an oath to protect my country. Was I right? I wonder, with what I know now. By the way, that war still hasn't been declared over. Would I enlist again if I were younger and was called to war? I'd have to know the truth and reasons behind the call to give my life for some politician's ambitions. It seems to me once a politician gains power, she loses part or all of his soul trying to gain more power, even creating wars for the country's illegitimate gain over a poorer country. Our history reveals that's occurred frequently. I've discovered over time that I have no control over these things.

I sometimes wonder how long democracy can last. So many voters drink the kool aid of politicians who con them into believing falsehoods as truths. Democracy demands an educated populace and too many people seem to want to bow to an oligarch.

I've just tried to live my life without harming anyone. That's all I can do. Maybe my silence is to blame.

And so it goes...

CHAPTER 28

"Cheek to Cheek"

A strange thing happened on my last visit...

In a doctor's waiting room, like so many others I had endured over the years, I fidgeted on a hard-on-the back chair while six other restless patients, all ahead of me, waited for our names to be called. Like most of these offices, no window to the outside world, cream-colored walls, and white, square, perforated ceiling tiles with long tubed lighting. And don't forget the usual tall, phony, green, waxed-leaf plant in one corner. That faded, Van Gogh "Starry Night" print on the far wall needed straightening. I was tempted, but let it be. I wondered who, in their right mind, would select that particular art piece for a doctor's office? Nothing against Van Gogh, but come on.

No one now sat behind the small, cage-like glass window, where upon my arrival well over twenty minutes ago, I'd announced my name to a surly young woman who never looked up at me. Date of birth? Last name? (just told you) Which doctor are you seeing? She tapped it all into a computer and told me to take a seat. I guessed she'd gone into hiding from a mounting oppressive exasperation I sensed in the room. Lord knows how long the other restless patients had been waiting. Dr. Godot. Calling Dr. Godot. I couldn't contain the thought.

It hadn't taken me long to dismiss the dated, well-thumbed, tossed-about *Golfing*, *Yachting* and *Better Health* magazines spread about on a small table near the plant. I didn't play golf, nor did I own a boat anymore. And from the looks of most of the others filling the room, neither did they; well, maybe that one. Considering we were all waiting to see the doctor, the information in the health magazines no longer seemed relevant.

I'd forgotten to bring a book, so I had little to do but scan my forlorn confederates.

An elderly couple I assumed to be married sat so close together they could have been one. Small, frail, wrinkled, well-dressed, arms entwined, they appeared conspiratorial and deeply involved in a whispered conversation. Actually, the woman, irritation apparent, seemed to be doing most of the lip moving while the man nodded or shook his head. A conversation about what? Money? Family? Health? Did they still live in their own home, maybe with one of those reversed mortgage things? Or did the family send them to an assisted living facility? Can one of them still drive, or did one of those vans bring them? Which one had cancer? Both maybe. No, I'd bet the old man did. Too late for prostate. Probably bladder problems. Maybe colon cancer. Rough for an old man to deal....

What am I saying? We're probably both near ninety. Damn. I have a tendency to forget I'm not the young person I still think I am.

Drop that thought.

To the right of the old couple sat a fidgeting, middle-aged man I imagined to be wealthy. The man's strong, tanned face contained the look of success along with an irritation that he had more important things to do than sit in a doctor's waiting room, especially when his appointment time had passed. Tapping away on his iPhone, his brow furrowed, he was no doubt complaining to an associate that this waiting game was no way to run a business. Smartly dressed, dapper, (that's the word) I noticed his polished black Hubbard shoes, the black, sharp creased pants, and a turtle-neck sweater to match his pants, not an easy thing to do with the color black. He probably owns a yacht. I'll bet that if anyone ever showed up at that little glass window, this guy would beat out the rest of us to demand why he is being kept waiting. His cancer has him really pissed. I bet prostate, in this case, and the guy is worried about losing his sexual prowess. Well, can't blame him for that. I know that scare.

Next to the man in black sat a pleasant looking woman, fiftyish I'd guess, absorbed in her Kindle. She came prepared. Her short-cut brown hair held beginnings of grey. She dressed as if she were going to or coming from a yoga class or an athletic club workout: form-fitting, patterned-flower leggings, a tight blue top, probably a sports bra under whatever you call those tops. From what her clothes revealed, she kept herself in fine fit. From time to time, she consulted her Apple watch, looked around, then back to her Kindle. It appeared she had trouble concentrating. I wanted to ask her what she was reading, but thought she might think me weird or something. Besides, did I really want to know? To me, she looked too healthy to have cancer. But she was here. Maybe melanoma? Breast cancer?

Across from me sat a young woman I guessed to be about thirty. Maybe younger. I can't really guess people's ages anymore. The older I get, the younger everyone else looks. Still, the longer I stared at her face, the more I'd guess thirty. Beautiful? No, but not plain, either. Striking? Yes, that's the word. Demanding. A face that held your attention, interesting to look at, smooth, healthy skin. She wore all denim: jacket, shirt, jeans, with light blue Allbirds on her feet. Not staring at her became problematic. She looked healthy. Hard to say what she had. But cancer doesn't care how old you are.

One poor soul sitting hunched over like a squashed question mark appeared to be wearing layers of clothes. He wore a knitted navy cap with the sides rolled down over his ears. His worn, pulled-up khaki coat collar hid much of his drooping head. He looked to be sleeping and not at all like he belonged there. First thought – a homeless vet in from the cold. Except it wasn't cold inside or out. His tattered backpack covered with stickers tried to hide between his sandaled bare feet. A veteran myself, I couldn't help but be thankful I wasn't the one in those sandals. Then again, maybe the guy's not a vet, just stereotyping. The vacant chairs on both sides of maybe-a-vet-maybe-not worked as avoidance bookends. Whoever else came in would have to sit by him. Why hadn't I? Yeah, I know. Anyway, whatever cancer this guy has seems to have the better of him.

From all appearances, the Big C had us all playing the waiting game. So, here we are gathered together in commonality. Impatient patients. Waiting---in more ways than one.

Waiting I knew well. More than once, I'd waited for biopsy results. I'd waited for CT scan results. I'd waited for MRI results. I'd waited for blood test results. I'd waited for surgery results. I'd waited for medication results. I'd waited for the chemo to drip, drip, drip. I'd waited for pain and nausea to come and go away.

And now here I sat waiting to hear what was next. But no hurry, not really. I can wait. I am starting to feel a little dizzy, though. Those meds. It will it pass.

I smiled as I remembered a short story about an exasperated female hypnotist who was so fed up with waiting for the doctor that when she was finally admitted, she hypnotized the doctor into believing he was the patient. She had him undress and put on a backless examination gown and sit on the exam table. She told the doctor that she would be right back and left him sitting there. Then, as she left the office, she hypnotized the receptionist and told her the doctor would be busy for a while and was not to be disturbed. Maybe I didn't have the story exactly right, but I loved the concept.

What was keeping us waiting so long? Maybe I need some water. No water fountain I can see. Why isn't there someone at the window?

My eyes roamed, and I had difficulty stopping them from staring at the others, or from my hands in my lap, or from the phony plant in the corner. They need to dust the leaves. Was that a Sonos speaker attached to the ceiling just above the plant? Yes. And music. Yes. Strange, I hadn't heard any music before.

Wait. That tune. I know that tune. An old one. Wait. Louder now. Someone turned up the volume. Could it be? Yes. Yes. "On the Good Ship Lollipop." No way! God, what memories that conjures! Shirley Temple. 1930s. Her song, until Tiny Tim plunked it on his ukulele. My thoughts got caught up in the tune. Dah, dah, Dah, da, Dah, dah-dah --in the bed you hop-- dream away-- or something like that.

Shirley Temple. Back then, every mother knew her kid could be a child star like dimpled, curly-haired Shirley and become famous and rich and pull the family out of the Depression. Even my mother must have hoped that. How did she get me to take tap dancing lessons? At five! What was I promised? It couldn't possibly have been my idea. Somewhere there's a picture of me in my little tuxedo and patent leather tap shoes. I did recitals. Even sometimes had a girl partner. I must have been fairly competent. Yes. Remember that time an older boy in the class didn't remember how to shuffle off to Buffalo and the teacher had me show the boy how. How long did that last? Not too long. Someone called me a sissy, and I hung up my taps forever. Too bad. Maybe I could have been a contender. Move over Fred Astaire. Hah!

My mother loved to kick up her heels. She taught me the waltz (one-two-three; one-two-three), the Charleston (cross those arms, wobble those knees), all kinds of slick ballroom steps. The two of us would dance around the living room listening to that radio show, "Your Hit Parade." She never said it, and I never thought it until now, but she must have lived a vicarious dance life through me. My dad's dancing skills? Well, I never heard them talk about going out dancing. I became his wife's dance partner. Until it embarrassed me.

I miss dancing with Connie. I confess I considered myself a pretty good dancer back in the days, but she could match or beat anything I could do. Name the dance, we could do it. If we didn't know a particular step, we'd make it up as we went along. Play the music, we'd feel it and dance to it. Somewhere in the house were some trophies Connie and I won over the years. Those days!

Stuffy in here.

I looked across the waiting room and noticed the denim-dressed young lady's crossed leg moving in time with the music. "The Good Ship Lollipop" had sailed on, and now Sinatra taunted us to fly away with him. She noticed me looking at her and smiled. Caught, I snapped my head away toward the direction of the plant. Why had I looked away? What was I, twelve years old? Far from it. Would a smile back from an old man be politically incorrect?

That fuzzy plant. What was it doing?

Wait. Something's not right. Focus. Focus. That plant was...no...yes...I'm watching a hazy image emerge ...what is it...who is it...a young teenage girl...yes...I know her...what is she doing here...the older sister of my high school friend, Roger? My god, so long ago. What was her name? Virginia? Veronica? Something V. Valerie! Yes! She taught me the basic swing steps. That's right. To Glenn Miller's "In the Mood." Then we slow danced to that song that goes, "Dream when you're feeling blue; dream that's the thing to do." And a dream come true for me. I had such a crush on her, the first girl I'd ever danced with. She complimented me on how fast I picked up steps. Forgot how that even come about. She must have volunteered. I would have been too shy to ask. Roger must have had something to do with it. My first dance. I wanted to say something to her...

So many dances since then. So many. Tell her...

Then the plant was back.

I felt off center, a bit dizzy, and looked Denim's way again. She still looked at me, curiously, her head movements were...her leg...was keeping time to the music. I caught myself doing the same thing and stopped, embarrassed. I gave a shy smile back this time, holding her gaze for a moment, then looking down at the floor, unconscious of my leg again moving to the beat of the Bee Gee's "Stayin' Alive." Connie and I had danced to that one so many times.

When I looked up, Denim stood in front of me holding out her hands...beckoning?

With a jolt, I pressed back into my chair in disbelief and a touch of fright. What was she doing? What did she want?

What?

Preposterous!

Wait!

No!

Yes! Like a modern Circe, she summoned me to get up!

I closed my eyes, shook my head to rid myself of her image. It's the new medication. I'm hallucinating. Yes. All those meds. Of course. Didn't she see my cane?

Against my better judgment, I opened my eyes. She shouldn't be, but her sinewy form still stood there, nodding yes.

She reached for my hands. I looked into her cavernous, conquering eyes, hurling a hypnotic, mesmerizing draw—demanding! Come! Come! With no control, I succumbed, feeling a gentle invading tug at my heart as her smooth, soothing hands took my bent, arthritic fingers and drew me gently from my chair. My thin, trembling body fused into Denim's form as we glided, yes, glided to the center of the waiting room, my senses feeling overwhelmed by the brush of her soft, warm cheek against mine, her arms and mine now enveloping one body--and the one body began the sensation of rhythmic movement, leisurely at first, swaying, held together by the throaty, sexual call of Gato Barbieri's "Europa," proprioception taking control, as he/they hovered over the floor, nothing else existing now, only the one body experiencing the euphoria of Earth's cry, Heaven's smile.

Ebullient, I fathomed we weren't just dancing; no, we were the dance itself, the rhythm, the music, the movements; we had joined the iridescent Soul Gods of All Music as a long stream of familiar tunes merged into their rhythmic beats as we danced…danced…danced…nothing else existed…

I didn't want to, but I began to feel weak, warm… no, not now, I didn't want to stop…please don't make me stop…please…let the music stay…

But I felt forced, pressured to sit…my body…so heavy…yet so light, and my head so…muddled. Head in my hands, looking down at those feet, my feeble feet, that had just felt new life…how…what must the others be thinking…dancing in a doctor's office like that…

I looked up and around a room now void of music. The elderly woman continued to whisper in the old man's ear; the yacht guy still played with his iPhone; the yoga lady still read from her Kindle; the squashed question mark hadn't moved; and the Denim lady sat with her eyes closed, her ears held AirPods, her crossed leg keeping time with whatever music she was hearing.

CHAPTER 29

"Here's to Life"

Lady died today. By rights, I guess you could call it a form of murder. Well, maybe not strictly murder. That's too harsh a statement. Assisted suicide? Not really, she didn't personally request it. Not in so many words. Some form of euthanasia, I guess. Anyway, the vet said I should put her down. Now there's a phrase: "Put her down." What a wishy-washy phrase! Put her down...in the basement? On the floor? At my feet? The point is, she's dead, and I brought it about.

Lady, best I could figure, was a fifteen-year-old golden lab. I'm not sure how old that is in human years. I'd have to look it up. Probably older than me. She and I shared some symptoms: always tired, creaky bones, hard to get up, picky diet, loss of hearing, poor eyesight, flatulence, some incontinence. (Dare we eat a peach?) Well, her problems were a bit worse than mine. But it got to be difficult to watch her try to move. Sometimes her food bowl would stay full for a couple of days. Worst part, I had to clean up after her daily. So finally, I took Lady's head in my hands, looked deep into her foggy-grey eyes and asked her straight out if she would like to end it all. I have to believe she gave me a yes.

That's why I took her to the vet today. The vet was very nice, and I'm sure he has dealt with many pet owners dealing with death. He promised me Lady wouldn't feel a thing, that she'd be better off and out of pain, and that I could be with her until she "passed on." I don't like the phrase "passed on." Passed on to...what? Death, of course. Why not just say it? I think many people are afraid of saying the word "death" or "dead" or "die," like the words connote something offensive or cruel. Why not just say, "She died"? Why not say, "She's dead"? If you say "passed on," it implies the dead go somewhere. And where is that "somewhere"? You can't go anywhere if you're dead, so why say passed on? Technically, I guess you could say passed on to the crematorium or the burial ground. I know some people think there is another life waiting, or a heaven or a hell, and when you die you "pass on" to one place or the other and meet again. I'm not into that. I'm not going to see Lady again. She died, is dead, and now part of that realm called death.

Then there are those who just use the word "passed," like "Yesterday, my aunt passed." Or, "Didn't you hear? John passed." Such usage snarls with "past," as in past tense. If someone is dead, they are part of the past; in effect, no longer with us, meaning, dead. Like Connie; like my parents; like me soon. So let's honor the words "death," "dead," "die." Their meanings are quite clear and correct and we are all going to experience it.

Anyway, I sat on the floor of the vet's office and held Lady in my lap while he gave her the injection. She didn't feel a thing from what I could tell. But I did, and I swear there was a last dog smile and a wink. I think she was telling me I was next. Lady knew a thing or two.

I'm finished with dogs. Lady's dead, and that's the end of that. She had a better life than many dogs, as have I. And I have to believe I did her a favor by putting her out of her misery. I just hope when I've had enough of it all, and that could be fairly soon, that someone will look into my cataract eyes, see "yes," and do me the great favor.

CHAPTER 30

"The End of a Love Affair"

Well, that's it for me. It's a propitious time to stop. I'm pretty tired and beginning to wonder why I'm writing this. No more narratives or "window peeping." Not that there aren't more windows to look through after all these years, oh, my, yes, but they're becoming more and more smudged. As I said earlier, I find myself floating out of my body now and then. I've picked signature events in my past and hope my memory held up correctly. I might have slipped up here and there, memory being what it is. No intended offense to anyone.

I think I've taken care of what needs to be taken care of. My lawyer has my will. I'm to be cremated, ashes taken to sea, like Connie's. I'm leaving my house and possessions to various charities and neighbors since I have no kin. I'm leaving my records and CDs to the university. Some are quite rare. Who knows what will become of what you're reading. If someone like my cleaning lady finds me half-dead, leave me until I'm all dead, not saved. No home for the aged for me. Until then, I'll try to live the title from a Clark Terry documentary, "Keep On Keepin' On."

Not much choice anyway.

The point of all the window peeking started as an attempt to find out who I really am, if I lived my life well, some kind of an answer to the point of my life. And what have I learned from peering into all these shades of the past?

I chose to "do language," to put in words what I think I've discovered, but I'm not sure I've done that. I'll certainly not leave an important imprint on the world; no honors; I won't be remembered in the future, no memorials, no grave to be renowned. My life's been pretty self-centered and maybe lived selfishly. A lone wolf. Why is that? Did I ignore a role in life I should have lived? What would it have been? Should I be doing something I'm not doing now? Of course there is not much I can do at my age, but I'm not dead yet.

Why was I given so much time and others so little? I remember my friend Bard and I used to talk about life being controlled by the fickle finger of fate. I believe mine has been.

I regret Connie died before me. Not just because of my loss, but for her loss of time to live longer. I regret my mother died before I could tell her how much I loved and respected her. I regret I never had the talent to be a musician. For me, music is the ultimate art form. My biggest regret, at the moment anyway, is that I could never use words in my writing the way Miles could use notes to make us feel the depth of our emotions. Like the unsuccessful protagonist in my novel *No Way In*, I wasted a whale load of words trying. Still, lesser words I wrote fed me and took me places.

I regret not staying in touch with friends like Ted and Bard. So much of my younger life revolved around them and their influence. I wonder what their lives were like compared to mine. I should try to Google them. But I won't. I wonder if they ever think of me? If so, how? What was I to them? Have they, or for that matter, Grace or Suzanne or Diana or Bill ever read any of my writing? Do they remember what I remember? I seem to have more questions than answers.

I haven't given much to the world at large. I've pretty much stayed out of the world's way. I don't know if that's good or bad, but there is only so much a person can do, and unlike me, some are more capable and committed to making the world a better place. So often I read stories about homelessness, sexual abuse or abandonment, struggles for survival, or discrimination and hatred based on race and gender, or casualties from mental disorders, or gun violence. The sad, ugly side of life. My own pales in comparison. I think I've been given a good life.

So, has my life held any meaning?

For me it has.

I believe Mary Oliver's poem, "Wild Geese," sums it up for me. I'm an ordinary person given a life to live, and I've lived it best I could.

"So What?" I hear Miles challenge.

"Compared to What?" Eddie Harris demands.

"Is That All There Is?" Peggy Lee questions.

If you are expecting some grand climax and poignant denouement here, you've forgotten what you're reading.

I'm weary. Time to sit by the fire, re-read more from *The Odyssey* (yes, the copy Diana gave me) and sip some more Bailey's over ice. If I don't nod off, maybe I'll listen again to Nat King Cole's "Nature Boy," or maybe, depending on the effects of my drink, Nneena Freelon's rousing version. Because there is *one* thing I've come to understand...

And it's enough...

> *the greatest thing/ in all the world/ is just to...*

A Suggested Listening List:
As Time Goes By (Dooley Wilson)
Let's Face the music (Diana Krall)
Stardust (Willy Nelson)
Strange Fruit Hanging (Billy Holiday)
Slip Sliding Away (Paul Simon)
This Masquerade (George Benson)
You've Got a Friend (Carole King)
These Foolish Things (Bill Evans)
Hard to Say I'm Sorry (Chicago)
Cuts Like a Knife (Bryan Adams)
I'm Beginning to See the Light (Ella Fitzgerald)
Good Golly, Miss Molly (Little Richard)
Nice Work If You Can Get It (Frank Sinatra)
Unforgettable (Nat King Cole)
Teach Me Tonight (Diana Washington)
Falling in Love with Love (Bernadette Peters)
I Wish I Knew (Chet Baker)
Comin' Around Again (Carley Simon)
My Foolish Heart (Bill Evans)
Bewitched, Bothered and Bewildered (Doris Day)
This Can't Be Love (Sarah Vaughan)
Getting to Know You (James Taylor)
Smoke Gets in Your Eyes (Dinah Washington)
There Will Never Be Another You (John Coltrane)
All the Way (Frank Sinatra)
That's What Friends Are For (Elton John & Gladys Knight)
Down Here on the Ground (Wes Montgomery)
Stop the World I Want to Get Off (Sammy Davis Jr.)
Get Outta My Way (Kylie Minogue)
Wintergreen for President (Cast for *Of Thee I Sing*)
Here's to Life (Shirley Horn)
The End of a Love Affair (Wynton Marsalis)

W. Royce Adams' fictional works include The Rairarubia Series, *The Computer's Nerd, Me & Jay, Jay*, and *Against the Current*, a collection of short stories. He lives in Santa Barbara, California.

www.wroyceadams.com